The Puppy Who Found a Body

Aggie was sniffing around a tree stump. She was engrossed in sniffing and scratching and certainly wasn't paying any attention to me.

"Aggie, come," I said forcefully, like Dixie had instructed, but Aggie couldn't have cared less what I wanted and gave no indication she'd even heard me.

Dixie had warned me against repeating commands. Aggie needed to be trained to come the first time she was called. If she didn't, I was to pick her up.

I sighed as I walked over to pick her up. It was only then that I saw what she was digging at. She'd unearthed a man's shoe. Closer inspection showed the shoe was attached to a leg, a man's leg. I squealed and jumped back.

I have no idea how long I stood there, but eventually I pulled my cell phone out of my pocket and made several calls. The first was to Dixie, instructing her to get over here immediately. The second call was to my daughter, Stephanie. The message was roughly the same thing, except I ordered her to send Joe out here immediately.

The third call was to 9-1-1...

Books by V.M. Burns

Mystery Bookshop Series
The Plot Is Murder
Read Herring Hunt
The Novel Art of Murder

Dog Club Series
In the Dog House
The Puppy Who Knew Too Much

Published by Kensington Publishing Corporation

The Puppy Who Knew Too Much

V.M. Burns

LYRICAL UNDERGROUND
Kensington Publishing Corp.
www.kensingtonbooks.com

ACKNOWLEDGMENTS

Special thanks to Dawn Dowdle at Blue Ridge Literary. I don't know what I would do without all of the support you provide. Thank you to the wonderful people at Kensington Publishing for bringing my dreams to reality, especially my editor, John Scognamiglio.

Thank you to my fantastic Cleveland CXC family. Thanks to Anthony "Trooper Tony" Cameron for technical assistance. Thanks to the Barnyardians (Chuck, Jill, Lindsey and Tim) and to our fearless and courageous leader, Sandy Morrison for all of the support and encouragement. I'm grateful for my wonderful team (Jennifer, Eric, Amber, Robin, Derrick and Jonathan). Once a trainer, always a trainer and no matter what, you will always be my team (Tena, Grace, Jamie and Deborah), thank you all for always supporting me and especially for the plugs you've thrown my way. Special thanks to Monica Jill and Linda Kay for your great attitudes and willingness to allow me to borrow pieces of your personalities.

I will always be grateful to my Seton Hill University family and especially to my peeps. Love my Seton Hill Tribe: Patricia, Michelle, Jacki, Penny, Jessica, Anna, Matt, Jeff, Alex, Tyler, Kenya, Crystal, Dagmar, Lana and Gina.

I appreciate all of the enthusiastic supporters who have helped to promote, shared posts and left reviews. Thanks to Betty Tyler and all the fantastic writers at Cozy Mystery Crew. Thanks to Karen Owen and Colleen Finn for promotion help. Thanks to Linda Herold and Marie Roush for help naming Lucky and Denise Austin for recommending I feature a German Shepherd Dog in this book.

None of these books would be possible without the love and support of my family. Thank you, Benjamin Burns, Jackie, Jillian and Christopher Rucker. Last but not least, thanks to my good friends Sophia Muckerson and Shelitha Mckee. You guys are the absolute best.

Chapter 1

"I'm sorry I'm late." I flopped down in the seat across from Dixie. "*That* dog." I shook my head. "Remind me why I ever thought having a dog was a good idea?"

"Uh oh." Dixie chuckled. "What did Aggie do now?"

A waiter hovered near our table, and I shoved my coffee cup in his direction. He got the hint and filled the cup and discreetly backed away from the table.

"What did she do?" I took a sip of coffee and held up a hand and ticked off my grievances one at a time. "She chewed a hole in almost every pair of socks I own. Ripped her dog bed to shreds so there was nothing but foam all over the floor. She climbed up on the bed and left a deposit on my pillow, and I just spent fifteen minutes chasing her around the hotel room trying to get my underwear out of her mouth."

Dixie's eyes grew large, and the corners of her mouth twitched.

"Don't you dare laugh," I threatened, but it didn't do any good.

Dixie wasn't able to hold back the laughter. She guffawed and laughed so long and hard that people at nearby tables turned to stare and started to laugh too. After a few seconds, even I was laughing.

When I finally pulled myself together, I wiped tears out of my eyes. "This isn't funny. I can't believe I'm laughing."

"If you don't laugh, you'll cry." Dixie wiped her eyes with a napkin. "It's funny."

"No, it isn't." I leaned forward. "Seriously, I'm at my wits' end. She was such a good dog in Lighthouse Dunes. Now that we've moved to Chattanooga, she's become the devil's spawn and is intent on getting us tossed out of the hotel."

I'd recently relocated from Lighthouse Dunes, Indiana, to sunny Chattanooga, Tennessee, and was living in an extended-stay hotel that accepted pets.

"I told you, you're welcome to stay with us. Beau and I have plenty of room, and we'd love to have you."

Scarlett Jefferson—Dixie, to her friends—had been my best friend in college. She was a Southern belle who was close to six feet tall. She was thin, with big hair and a big heart to match. She and her husband, Beau, were willing to let us stay with them, but I'd been through a lot. Three months ago, I thought the fact that my husband was leaving me for a younger woman after twenty-five years of marriage was the worst thing that could happen to me. It probably was the worst thing until Albert was murdered and the police arrested me as the most likely suspect. Eventually I was cleared, but I was still working through my feelings and wasn't prepared to drag all of my emotional baggage into my friend's home.

I shook my head to clear the bad memories away. "I appreciate you both so much." I sighed. "But I don't want to be a bother." Dixie was about to interrupt, and I held up a hand to stop her. "I know what you're going to say, but I've still got a lot of things to work through, and I think it would be best if I don't drown your poor husband in all of my crazy drama at one time. Besides, I'm hoping we find a rental and can settle down." I sighed again. "Who knew it would take so long to find a reasonable rental in a good neighborhood that would allow pets?"

"Well, you know you always have a place with us," Dixie said.

I knew Dixie was sincere in her invitation, but I was still adjusting to life alone without Albert. In addition to moving six hundred miles from Indiana to Chattanooga, I had adopted a rescue, a toy poodle. I named her after my favorite mystery writer, Agatha Christie, Aggie, for short. I had had a lot of change in a relatively short period of time.

I nodded. "Thank you."

"Regardless of where you stay, you need to get Aggie trained. She's bored in that hotel room all day, which is why she's getting into trouble." She tilted her head to the side. "I thought you were going to crate her during the day."

I pulled out my cell phone and swiped until I came across a video and held it up. "I put her in the crate, but she's a little Houdini. Every day when I come home, she's out. At first, I thought the hotel staff were coming into the room and letting her out, but they swore they weren't. So I got one of those motion cameras and set it up." I leaned forward. "That little minx used her nose to slide the latch on the crate until she got it open and walked out like she was the queen of Sheba." I stared. "It didn't take her five minutes to get out of the crate."

Dixie laughed. "Well, that's the problem with smart dogs like poodles. They figure things out pretty quickly. You're going to need to get a different crate with a more challenging lock."

Aggie was a two-year-old toy poodle Dixie had rescued from a breeder. She was six pounds of adorableness, and I fell head over heels in love with her the first time she looked at me with those big brown eyes and laid her head on my shoulder. However, Dixie was right: she needed training.

"I signed up for your basic obedience class at the East Tennessee Dog Club. We'll be there with bells on Thursday night."

Dixie nodded. "Good. You'll need a six-foot leather leash, a plain, flat leather collar, and a pouch full of treats she'll sell her soul for."

"I have these dog biscuits that..."

Dixie was shaking her head before the words left my mouth, and she had that *You poor pitiful thing* look in her eyes that she always gave me before she said, "Bless your heart," which I'd learned was Southern speak for *You're an idiot*. "Dog biscuits are nice for everyday, but you want something that will drive her crazy so she'll want to do whatever you ask to get those treats."

"What do you have in mind?"

"Hot dogs or string cheese."

"You told me not to give her table food."

"True, but that was on a daily basis. Human food has preservatives, additives, tons of salt, and other things that aren't good for people or canines. But training is different. You can give her good dog treats too, but not the dog biscuits that she gets all of the time. This needs to be something special."

I pulled out my phone and added a reminder to myself. "Okay, I'll add soul-selling treats to the grocery list."

"Now, how is the house hunt going?" Dixie took a sip of her coffee and pointed to the newspaper I had placed on the table when I sat down.

"Not so good. I was supposed to look at a place this afternoon, but my realtor called and said I was too late. It's already rented."

"Maybe you should buy a house rather than renting," Dixie said. "There's a lovely home just down the street from me." She smiled enthusiastically.

I shook my head. "I can't afford your neighborhood; besides, I don't think I could drive there."

Dixie and Beau had a large, sprawling estate atop Lookout Mountain, overlooking the city. I never realized I had a problem with heights until I tried driving up Lookout Mountain. I'd lived most of my life in Indiana, which was flat and known for corn and wheat fields. I loved looking at the lush green mountains of Tennessee. However, driving them was a completely different matter. I couldn't believe how narrow the roads leading up the mountains were—only one lane in each direction. The roads had been carved out years ago and snaked up the steep, rocky terrain. On one side of the road, your car practically hugged the mountainside; then across the two lanes there was a steep drop-off with nothing to prevent cars from tumbling over the sides.

Dixie chuckled. "I remember the first time I took you to my house. Your eyes were as big as silver dollars." She laughed. "You kept saying, 'That aluminum foil rail isn't going to stop a car from falling off the side of the mountain.'"

"There need to be concrete barriers on that mountain."

"Concrete would ruin the views." Dixie shook her head.

"Falling off the side of the mountain will ruin it more."

Our waiter returned and took our orders. He was a friendly young man and smiled and called me *ma'am*. I'd only been here for two weeks and was still getting accustomed to the friendly moniker. However, I already knew I liked Chattanooga. The people were unbelievably friendly and the landscape picturesque. However, my favorite part of Chattanooga was the weather. We were sitting outside having brunch in December. The locals complained about the cold, but at sixty-seven degrees, I thought the temperature felt fantastic. I'd checked the weather in Lighthouse Dunes earlier. There was two feet of snow on the ground and more expected every day. I'd take sixty-seven over fifteen with highs expected in the upper twenties, when the wind chill would make it feel like only seven. The very thought caused me to shiver.

I looked up. Dixie was staring at me. She then glanced to the side, and I followed the direction of her gaze to the table next to us. A small lady was sitting there, staring and smiling at us. I glanced back at Dixie, who shrugged. I tried to ignore the woman, but, after a few moments, the woman leaned over.

"Excuse me. I'm sorry to interrupt, but did I overhear you say you were looking for a rental home in a good neighborhood that accepts pets?"

I always thought the Midwest was a relatively friendly area, but two weeks in Chattanooga showed me the South was on a totally different level of friendliness. Complete strangers talked to you. They walked up to you and held conversations, and as in this case, they joined in on your conversations. My initial instinct was to ignore her, but Dixie was a lot friendlier than me.

She turned to the lady and smiled. "Yes, my friend just moved here from Indiana, and she's been looking for a nice house in a decent neighborhood. Do you know of a place?"

The lady was older. She was small with dark hair and large glasses. "Actually, my son has a house in a great neighborhood. He's overseas at the moment, and he loves pets. In fact, he has a wonderful dog, Rusty. He's so smart and well trained. He adopted him from a colonel he knows." She smiled broadly and held her chest out proudly. "He's a military contractor stationed in the Cayman Islands."

I tilted my head and tried not to look puzzled. The Caymans weren't part of the United States. We had troops stationed all over the globe, but the Caymans? I looked from Dixie to the woman. "Is it listed with a realtor?"

She shook her head. "Not yet. You see, I live in Georgia, and I keep an eye on things for him when he's out of the country." She smiled again. "He had to leave the country very suddenly, and it'll be a long time before he returns, so I thought there's no sense in that house sitting empty. He might as well let someone live in it and let the house make money for him. I have to do some shopping, so I thought I'd come check on it." Her eyes got large. "It's a good thing I did. He left in such a hurry, the front door was open." She shook her head in dismay.

"Well, maybe you could give me your son's telephone number or e-mail address, and I can talk to him and arrange to see the house." I pulled a pen out of my purse and picked up a paper napkin so I could write down the information.

"Well, I was thinking that since I'm here and you're here, maybe I could show you the house now. That way I won't have to drive back from Georgia." She looked eagerly from Dixie to me. "My eyesight isn't what it used to be, and I hate driving in traffic if I can avoid it."

I looked at Dixie and tried to use telepathy to ask, *Is this woman crazy?* However, either my mental telepathy wasn't working or Dixie decided to ignore me.

"Why, that sounds like a great idea. My name is Dixie, and this is my friend Lilly." She pointed to me.

"Oh, excuse my manners. I'm Jo Ellen Hansen." She shook hands with Dixie and then me. "It's a lovely house, and I was thinking that if I rented it right away, then my son would be so pleased when he came back." She smiled.

The waiter brought our food, and Mrs. Hansen stepped out of the way. When the waiter left, she said, "Why don't I let you ladies finish eating and I'll go run a few errands. Then we could meet at the house in an hour. Would that work for you?" She looked eagerly from Dixie to me.

Dixie stared at me, and I nodded. "That would be fine, but we'll need the address."

She giggled and told me the address. I wrote it on my napkin. She gave directions to Dixie that didn't mean anything to me. However, Dixie must have known the area.

When Mrs. Hansen left, I looked at Dixie expectantly. "So?"

She shoveled a forkful of hash browns into her mouth and washed it down with coffee. "It's a nice area. I guess we should have asked how much she wants for rent and a pet deposit, but it's not very far from here."

We finished eating, and I followed Dixie to the house, which was less than five minutes away from where we were eating near the mall. The subdivision was small, with only one way in or out. It was tucked away but close to two elementary schools.

The houses were newer, probably built in the last ten years. When we pulled in front of the address Mrs. Hansen had given us, there was already a car in the driveway, and the lady in question hopped out as soon as she saw us and waved. We parked and followed her inside.

The house was a Craftsman-style home with thick wooden beams atop stone columns supporting a wood-covered overhang. Inside, we were greeted with dark hardwood floors, high ceilings, and a massive stone fireplace. The kitchen was huge, with tons of cabinets. The house was very open and had a contemporary feel, despite the Craftsman architecture. There were three bedrooms on the first floor and a large finished bonus room upstairs with a bathroom. My only complaint was that the bedrooms and the master bath were small. In fact, one of the bedrooms was barely bigger than a closet. However, I reminded myself that I was now single with an empty nest. My two children, Stephanie and David, were grown and had moved away; they had lives of their own and would only visit on occasion. Stephanie was a successful attorney in Chicago, and David was a successful actor who was currently touring Europe with a repertoire company. So the house would be more than an adequate size for me and a six-pound poodle.

Mrs. Hansen pointed out every feature with pride. When the tour was over, we stood in the empty great-room area. "What do you think? I can give you the keys, and you can move in immediately. I can have all of his furniture and belongings moved to storage since he'll be gone for an extended period."

"We can take care of getting the furniture put in storage," Dixie said.

"Thank you." Mrs. Hansen breathed a sigh of relief and then smiled at me.

"It's a lovely house," I said hesitantly. "Don't you need to talk to your son? Run my credit report? Have me fill out an application or sign a lease?" I wanted the house, but I'd never experienced anything like this before. "I mean, I don't even have a job yet."

She smiled. "What do you do?"

"I'm a certified public accountant."

Her eyes widened, and she clapped her hands. "This must be destiny. I just so happen to know someone looking for an accountant."

This seemed too good to be true. "Really?"

"My son, Robert, used to work with one of the Hopewells." She smiled and waited expectantly.

I merely stared back.

"You know, *the* Hopewells."

I shook my head. "Sorry, I'm not from here."

"Of course, that explains it." For the second time today, I got the *You poor pitiful thing* look. "I'm sure if I make a call, they'll hire you." She smiled. "Our meeting today was blessed by providence. I don't see why we need to go through any formalities. My son gave me power of attorney since he's overseas," she said proudly. "Plus, I consider myself a good judge of character. You both look like nice people." She turned to Dixie. "Plus, you drive a Lexus."

It took about thirty seconds before I realized my mouth was open and closed it. I struggled to understand how the type of car Dixie drove mattered the least bit in terms of me renting this house. "You know I'm the one who'll be renting the property, right?"

"Oh yes, but you look like an honest person." She smiled.

I was dumbstruck.

"Well, I can tell you my friend is definitely honest and trustworthy." Dixie turned away from the woman and winked at me. "How much is the rent?"

She gave me a price, and I nearly choked. However, I needn't have worried. Dixie turned on her Southern charm and negotiated the rent down a couple of hundred dollars to a number that was still higher than I would have liked but was within a comfortable range. She also arranged for a refundable pet deposit that was half what I'd been quoted by other landlords.

I was adamant about a lease and called my daughter, Stephanie, and explained the situation. She quickly sent an electronic copy of a standard tenant/lease agreement with all of the particulars. We were able to sign electronically. I handed over a check for the security deposit, pet fee, and first month's rent, and Mrs. Hansen handed over the keys and promised to get in touch with her friend about the job.

"My son's girlfriend, Lynn, lives near here, and I'm sure if you need anything, she'll be more than willing to help you. Plus, you can always give me a call." She handed me a card with her telephone number. She seemed thrilled and smiled broadly before she hurried out to get on the interstate before the traffic got too bad, and left Dixie and me standing alone in my new rental.

"What just happened?"

Dixie shook her head. "You just rented a decent house in a decent neighborhood. So, you and Aggie can get out of that hotel room, and you might have also landed a new job. Let's go and pack up your stuff and get the utilities set up so you can move in as soon as possible."

Three phone calls had the electric, water, and trash switched to my name. The owner had left so quickly the cable and Internet hadn't been disconnected, so I was able to get that transferred into my name too. My furniture, clothes, and belongings were in storage, so packing up the hotel room only took a couple of hours. By the end of the day, with Dixie's help, Aggie and I were in our new home. Since the landlord had left in such a hurry and his furniture was still there, Aggie and I had a place to sleep that was better than the hotel.

Dixie was a master at arranging things. I was able to check out of my extended-stay hotel without a penalty. She even arranged for the movers to pack the landlord's furniture into a storage pod, as Mrs. Hansen requested, and to bring my belongings the next day, which was a feat I hadn't thought possible. Apparently, a Southern accent, used properly, could unlock quite a few doors. When I asked Dixie how she managed, she merely laughed and tossed her head back. "It's a gift, honey."

I was grateful she was using her gift on my behalf and accepted the statement as truth.

The next day, I made an early-morning trip to the airport and picked up my daughter, Stephanie. She had planned to come for a week to help me get settled. When the house hunt took so long, we decided to set up the visit whether I was in a place or not. I was grateful she wasn't going to have to stay in a hotel. The airport was very close to the rental.

Stephanie was tall, thin, and beautiful, with dark brown hair and eyes. She hurried to the car, shedding her coat as she walked. I hopped out of the car and opened the back hatch so she could put in her luggage.

We hugged and she smiled. "I can't believe this weather. It was freezing in Chicago."

We hurried into the car before we got in trouble for parking in front of the terminal entrance. It was so good to see her.

"Are you hungry?"

She shook her head. "Not yet. I ate before I got on the plane."

I followed my car's GPS back to the house. I was able to make the trip there and back in less than thirty minutes.

The movers arrived on schedule and set up my furniture and left me a path that wound around a mountain of boxes. I'd gotten rid of a ton of things when I sold my house in Indiana; however, you wouldn't know it by looking at the boxes I had left. Admittedly, most of them were books. I loved books and couldn't part with them when it came time to move. Dixie wasn't only great at arranging; she was also a hard worker and soon had all of the kitchen equipment unboxed, linens put away, and clothes in the closet. Tonight, I would be able to take a shower, sleep in my own bed, and cook. I had an entire year to unpack my books. So I moved the boxes of books into the closet and promptly closed the door. Out of sight, out of mind. However, Stephanie had other ideas. She immediately started putting the books on the shelves. I wasn't sure if this was out of a desire to help or because she wanted to make sure she had plenty of reading material while she was here. Regardless, she shelved all of the books and helped set up one of the guest rooms as an office.

While the movers unloaded my things, the neighbors from across the street came over to introduce themselves. Michael and Charity Cunningham were a smart, bubbly young couple. Both had the lean bodies of runners and nearly perfect teeth, which they displayed a lot while their eyes darted around the room taking in each and every detail.

"Is it just you?" Charity flashed her perfect teeth.

I tried not to grind my teeth, but my jaw clenched. I had grown to hate the word *just* since my husband's death. Waiters used it when I went to restaurants alone. *Will there be just one for dinner?* Some days I wanted to scream. I'm not *just* anything. However, screaming at a complete stranger wasn't a great way to make friends in my new city. So I plastered on my fake smile. "No. It's not *just* me. I have Aggie." I held up my black toy poodle and waved her paw.

"Oh, isn't she cute." Charity reached out and scratched Aggie behind her ear.

Aggie wiggled and fanned her tail like the blades of a fan.

"Thank you!"

Michael displayed his perfect teeth. "I think Charity meant are you married? Is there a Mr. Echosby?"

I ground my teeth further. "No, my husband—"

"Died suddenly a few months ago," Dixie said in the soft, quiet voice people reserved for funerals and talking about the dead.

Michael and Charity immediately retracted their perfect teeth, tilted their heads to the side, and offered their solemn condolences.

"Please don't hesitate to stop by if you need anything once you're settled. We're just across the street," Charity said as she and Michael backed out of the door and made a hasty retreat.

When they were gone, I turned to Dixie. I knew my face wore the question I hadn't spoken aloud.

She merely shrugged. "No need going into all of the ugly details about how Albert was a low-down, dirty snake in the grass who was in the process of divorcing you so he could run off with his pole-dancing tart when he was murdered. Besides, nothing clears a room faster than grief on display."

"But I'm not grieving. I'm at peace with myself. I've embraced being single and my new life."

"I know that, and you know that, but Mr. and Mrs. Super Shiny Veneers don't need to know."

"You think those were veneers?"

Dixie nodded. "Of course. I almost put on my sunglasses."

We laughed but quickly got back to the business of unpacking and arranging furniture. After a day of unpacking, Dixie went home to check on her dogs and her husband. Dixie had two standard poodles that were former show dogs. She'd traveled all over the country competing in conformation dog shows. However, Champion Galactic Imperial Resistance Leader—Leia, for short—and Champion Chyna, the Ninth Wonder of the World—also known as Chyna—were retired from competitions now and living the life of the pampered in Dixie's sprawling estate atop Lookout Mountain.

Aggie spent most of her time sniffing every crack, corner, and crevice. I spent my time, between unpacking and tearing down boxes, following her around to make sure she didn't squat and pee. The last thing I wanted to deal with was losing my security deposit. When we'd unpacked what felt like the millionth box, I decided to explore the neighborhood. Stephanie begged off, saying she was tired and wanted a shower and an early night. So it was just me and Aggie.

One unfortunate thing about the house was that it lacked a fence. I had hoped for a level, fenced-in backyard where I could let Aggie outside to play. I could have gotten an invisible fence, but I wasn't crazy about the idea of shocking my poor little dog. However, once again, Dixie had come to the rescue with a brilliant solution. She had brought over a metal dog pen that I set up at the bottom of the deck stairs. It wasn't a big pen, but it provided ample space for Aggie to take care of her business without me having to run outside to make sure she didn't run away. It wasn't an ideal situation, and a big dog would have easily knocked over the pen, but Aggie wasn't a big dog. The pen had a small door with a sliding latch that made it easy to get the dogs out. She warned me that since Aggie was able to use her nose to get out of her crate whenever she wanted, she would be able to get out of the pen too, so I needed to pick up some zip ties to prevent her from escaping.

I made a mental note to add zip ties to my shopping list. I put Aggie on a retractable leash and grabbed some plastic bags for waste, and we headed out to explore our environs.

The subdivision wasn't large. There were probably fifty houses. There was a community building with a sign outside, near the entrance, that gave updates on events and a gazebo near the center of the subdivision that looked like a nice place to sit and relax, so we headed toward it.

It was a nice day, and we encountered quite a few people out enjoying the weather. The adults smiled or waved. Southerners were definitely a friendly bunch. The children went on about their play. There was an intense basketball game going on at the house down the street from ours. Aggie and I sat on the bench in the gazebo and watched for a while until she got bored with the game and pulled on her leash to keep moving. I turned away from the game and rose to continue my walk and collided with a surly, sour-faced older man.

"I'm so sorry. I didn't see you—"

"Then you must be blind."

His hateful attitude took me by surprise; however, I took a deep breath and reminded myself I was in the wrong. I had bumped into him, and I didn't want to get off to a bad start with my neighbors. "I'm very sorry. It was an accident. I was watching the game and not paying attention."

"Obviously you weren't paying attention to me or your dog." He glowered at Aggie.

"Excuse me?"

"I nearly stepped in a pile of crap." He pointed down to a large pile of dog poop that was outside of the gazebo. "I'm tired of you people parading your pets all over the neighborhood and not picking up after them. This is the third time this month, and I'm going to report you to the neighborhood association at the meeting tomorrow night."

"You can report whatever you want. I just moved into this neighborhood today, so my dog isn't responsible for any of that." I held up the plastic bags in my hand. "Besides, I'm a responsible pet owner, and I always clean up after my pet."

He literally growled. "Well, you may not be responsible for the other times, but you can't deny the evidence." He pointed again toward the large pile of dog poop. "Or are you stupid as well as blind? Anyone with an ounce of the sense the universe bestowed upon a grasshopper could see that a dog"—he pointed to Aggie—"is at fault."

That did it. I'd had enough of this cantankerous blowhard. "I'm neither stupid nor blind, but anyone with a shred of the sense God gave a grasshopper could see that my six-pound dog would be physically incapable of leaving a pile of dog crap that size." I pointed to the dog poop. "Little dogs leave little logs."

Our screaming had caused a stir, and several people had gathered to watch.

"However, even though my dog *obviously* isn't responsible for this, I'm going to do the *neighborly* thing and clean it up." I marched down the stairs of the gazebo and used my bag to pick up the offending pile. Once I had it bagged and closed, I deposited it into a nearby receptacle designated for the purpose. When I was done, I turned, bowed, and marched away with Aggie.

"You haven't heard the last of me."

I fought down an overwhelming desire to flip him the bird and, instead, satisfied my flesh by using an arm gesture I'd seen truckers use that was extremely unladylike. It was a childish gesture but surprisingly satisfying.

I stomped away. My phone vibrated in my pocket, and I whipped it out. I didn't recognize the number but swiped it. "What?"

There was a pause at the other end before a hesitant voice asked, "I'm sorry, is this Lilly Echosby?"

I took a deep breath. "Yes, I'm sorry. This is Lilly Echosby speaking."

The voice was still tentative but continued. "This is Laura Tatum from Tatum Temp Services. Your name was given to us by Jo Ellen Hansen for an accounting job listed with one of our companies."

"Yes. I'm so sorry. I just had...well, I'm sorry for the way I answered the phone."

"Can you provide me some information about yourself?"

I filled her in on my background and essentials, and promised to send a resume.

"We'll need to run a background check, and the position is only temporary, but they're desperate and you came very highly recommended. If you can start immediately, I'll get busy with the legalities."

"I'm very interested in the job. Where do you want me and when?"

She laughed. "I need someone to start tomorrow, if you're available, at the Chattanooga Museum of Art at nine."

"Great. I'll be there."

"Don't you want to know how much the position pays?"

"It doesn't really matter. I need the work."

She laughed but quickly filled me in on the pay and the other particulars. The pay wasn't anything to write home about, but it was a job. My late husband, Albert, hadn't wanted me to work, despite the fact that I was a certified public accountant. So, apart from helping him get his car dealership established and doing his books during the early years of the business, I hadn't worked outside of the home in over twenty years. As a widow, I had what was left of the life insurance and the proceeds from the sale of our home to live on. While I wasn't hurting for cash, I also needed to secure my future, which would start with establishing a work history without a twenty-year gap.

When I hung up, I was still miffed about the disagreement with the sour-faced grouch. In fact, whenever I thought about the altercation, it made my heart race and my muscles tense. It took several minutes, quite a number of deep breaths, and a spirited internal conversation that included quite a few witty responses I wished I'd had the quick wit to have delivered at the time, but eventually, I calmed down. When I finally looked up, I had walked quite a distance. I took a deep breath and shook myself like an Etch A Sketch to erase the bad memories of the altercation from my mind. It was a lovely evening, and I wanted to focus on enjoying it. I slowed down my gait and forced myself to concentrate on the beauty around me.

There was a path that provided a number of great spots for Aggie to sniff and leave her scent. Ultimately, the path led to a small wooded area that was yet to be developed. Aggie tugged at her leash, anxious to explore, but I wasn't as keen on leaving the beaten path as she was. Even though she was only six pounds, she could be a determined force when she chose, and today was one of those days. She tugged and pulled, but I held firm. Initially, I tried to coax her by making the kissing sound Dixie suggested. When that didn't work, I tried my forceful mommy voice. It had always worked with my children, David and Stephanie, but Aggie didn't budge. In fact, she planted her feet, and I had to drag her. Eventually, I scooped her up and carried her home.

Once we were inside, I let her go and glowered at her. Aggie's response was to walk to the wool rug in the living room, squat, and pee.

I stared openmouthed for several seconds. "Kennel!" I said through gritted teeth.

She stared at me for ten seconds, but when I took a step toward her, she ran into her crate.

I closed the door, none too gently, and locked it. I then proceeded to clean the rug and make sure nothing had leaked underneath to damage the floors. The good thing about wool was that it was super absorbent. The bad thing about wool was that it was super absorbent and expensive to clean. However, I located the handheld spot lifter Dixie had encouraged me to buy. It worked like a small carpet cleaner and sucked up the liquid and steam-cleaned the small area of the rug. By the time I'd finished, I looked over at Aggie as she lay in her crate with her head resting on her paws, and my anger subsided. She was so cute it was hard for me to stay angry at her for long. I suspected, as Dixie told me, that she was playing me like a fiddle, but then it wasn't the first time I'd been played. In fact, my husband had been a fiddle master when it came to playing people, especially me. I sighed and let her out of the crate. She snuggled up next to me, laid her head on my leg, and then looked at me with big brown sad eyes.

I looked at her and sighed. "You are going to obedience class, and you're going to learn to be a good girl. Aren't you?"

Aggie released a sigh.

"I'll take that as a *yes*." I scratched her ear.

I don't know how long I slept, but I was awakened when Aggie used my body as a walkway, traveled from my leg to my chest, and then used my chest as a diving board. She stood at the door growling.

"What's going—"

There was a loud crash, and the motion detector lights went on. Aggie used her tough-dog bark and lunged at the door. The light went on in the living room, and I knew Stephanie was up. I rushed out of bed and hurried to the living room. As soon as the door opened, Aggie shot through and charged for the back door.

"What do you think it is?" Stephanie was dressed in yoga pants and a T-shirt.

I shrugged. "No idea. It could be a skunk or opossum," I said hopefully. "Dixie warned me there are a lot of them down here."

We heard a bark and then a loud yelp. Stephanie and I looked at each other. There was an animal in trouble. Stephanie headed for the back door.

"Wait." I stopped long enough to grab a weapon, just in case the animal wasn't the friendly sort. Unfortunately, the first thing at hand was a large spatula. I grabbed it and hurried outside.

Stephanie and Aggie were at the bottom of the deck. "Mom, can you get Aggie?"

I hurried down the stairs. "What is it?"

"It's a dog."

I picked up Aggie, whose bark had gone from Defcon 1, *There's a stranger, and I'm going to rip his face off*, to Defcon 4, *There's another dog on my turf*. She might be only six pounds, but she could intimidate when she wanted to, and apparently, this was one of those times.

Stephanie lay down on her belly and reached under the deck, all the time talking quietly.

"Be careful."

There was a yelp.

"Mom, he's hurt. Get a blanket."

I hurried upstairs with Aggie in tow and found a blanket in the linen closet. I left Aggie in her crate and hurried back downstairs. The dog might be injured, but I knew that might make him even more dangerous. However, when I got back, Stephanie had coaxed the dog out and had him cradled in her arms.

We wrapped him in the blanket and hurried inside.

Inside, we could see it was a bedraggled golden retriever. I held Aggie's water dish to his mouth, and he drank as if he'd just spent the last week in the desert.

"We've got to get him to the vet." Stephanie headed for the garage.

I grabbed my car keys and followed her out, stopping to put on shoes and grab jackets for both of us.

One of the selling points of this area was that there were a lot of businesses nearby. Dixie had pointed out an emergency vet near the mall, and I headed in that direction.

The emergency vet was indeed open, and Stephanie carried the dog in while I parked the car. Once inside, Stephanie was immediately directed to an examination room. Memories of a similar incident when Aggie was hurt flooded my mind, but I pushed those thoughts aside and focused on the task at hand and the millions of questions the staff were throwing at us.

"We don't know anything about him. We just found him hiding under our deck," I said. "He's limping and holding his paw, and we thought maybe he was hit by a car."

The dog looked frightened, but Stephanie stroked him and whispered soft words of comforting nonsense, which he seemed to appreciate.

The vet was a large, burly man with kind eyes and a deep voice. He was gentle but thorough. There were two assistants, one with curly brown hair, named Dale, and a slightly older woman, named Tonya. Both were friendly and efficient.

They took our new friend to the back for X-rays while Stephanie and I waited in the exam room. Stephanie paced.

"What a way to welcome you to Chattanooga," I said.

Stephanie shook her head. "This isn't your fault."

"No, but I won't be able to stay. I've got to go to work tomorrow."

"No worries. Just leave me here. I'll call Aunt Dixie to pick me up when they finish, or I'll call a taxi."

"I hate to leave you here alone, in a strange city in the middle of the night."

She stared at me. "Mom, I'm twenty-five, not seven." She smiled. "Plus, you live in the suburbs, which is nothing compared to Chicago." She hugged me. "Besides, Joe has taught me so many self-defense moves that I'd actually like a chance to try them out."

The look on my face must have been hilarious based on the way she laughed. When she pulled herself together, she said, "Trust me. I'll be fine."

"I wanted to spend time with you. I shouldn't have taken this job. Maybe I should call and—"

"Oh no you don't. You've been talking about finding a job and starting over and finding your happy place for months. Go! I'll be fine."

"Are you sure?" I stared at my daughter.

She had always been a defender of the poor and downtrodden. She had a compassionate heart, but she seemed to have bonded with this dog, and I was afraid of what the X-rays would show. If he had been hit by a car, he might have internal bleeding, which wouldn't bode well.

"Mom, I held him in my arms, and he looked at me with those big trusting brown eyes and...something inside of me melted." She stopped pacing and looked at me. Tears streamed down her face. "I can't let him down."

I stood and hugged her, and we cried together until we were interrupted by the assistant, Tonya, and the vet.

"Well, it isn't as bad as we thought." Our burly vet marched into the room with X-rays; he pushed them into a square device on the wall and flipped a switch, which illuminated the box.

Stephanie and I crowded closer and Tonya gave Stephanie's hand a reassuring squeeze.

"Thankfully, it doesn't look like there's any internal hemorrhaging. He has a badly sprained front right leg, but here's the curious thing." He quickly whipped out the X-ray and inserted another one in its place. "It looks like he's swallowed something." He pointed to an oddly shaped item on the X-ray. "That needs to come out. We'll need to operate." He turned and looked at Stephanie and then to me. "I know he's not your dog, and there's no microchip or tattoo, so we don't know who he belongs to. The cost of the surgery will be—"

"I don't care what it costs. I'll pay." Stephanie walked over to the chair where I'd left her jacket and pulled a credit card from her pocket and handed it to Tonya.

The vet smiled. "I better get scrubbed, and we'll take care of him." He patted Stephanie on the shoulder. "Don't worry."

The surgery was brief, and just as I was preparing to leave, the veterinarian returned.

He smiled. "Everything went well, and he's recovering nicely. You'll be able to take him home in a few hours."

Stephanie released a heavy sigh, which had apparently held back a flood of tears. She was so emotional she was shaking. She stood and hugged the doctor and then excused herself as she hurried to the restroom.

Dr. Hamilton smiled. "I usually don't have that effect on women." He held up a small plastic bag.

Puzzled, I took the bag and held it up to the light. It contained a few small items not bigger than a quarter and a large piece of cloth. I stared for several minutes. "Is that a sock?"

He nodded. "You're going to need to watch him. He apparently likes to eat fabric. We call it pica behavior. It's a compulsive disorder that affects a lot of canines, some felines, and is also found in humans."

Dr. Hamilton went on to explain pica behavior and its causes, but I wasn't particularly interested and zoned out for most of it. Although he had attempted to clean the objects, there was a film and red stains, which I didn't particularly want to think about. In fact, looking at the objects in that bag turned my stomach and made me feel queasy. I glanced at my watch and realized I needed to hustle to be able to make it to work on time in the morning. So I shoved the bag into my purse. Maybe I'd take a closer look inside the bag later, or maybe I'd just chuck it into the trash. After all, nothing in the bag belonged to me, and I doubted if anyone would want those things back, especially the sock.

"Thank you so much." I shook hands with the vet and hurried back home to get whatever sleep I could before starting my new job in the morning.

Chapter 2

Between the anxious excitement associated with finding the dog and the nervous excitement of the new job, I couldn't sleep. At five, I gave up trying. I got dressed and made sure everything was ready, or as ready as a woman who hadn't worked outside the home in well over twenty years could be. I tried not to dwell on my age. Instead, I focused on making sure the address was programmed correctly in my cell phone and on the GPS in my car as well as the map on my laptop. All devices aligned. I didn't want to get delayed by the notorious traffic on the interstate, so I gave myself close to two hours lead time. Aggie wasn't crazy about being left behind. She really wasn't happy about having to stay in the crate while I was gone. However, I wasn't ready to take chances in the new rental. Stephanie would let her out and make sure she didn't starve. In the meantime, it was the crate. I hardened my heart to her sad eyes and turned and marched out. Stephanie's friend/boyfriend Joe Harrison was coming in later today. Before Dixie had left the previous day, we arranged that Dixie would pick up Stephanie and drop her at the airport to meet Joe. He was going to rent a car so he and Stephanie would be able to get around and sightsee without Dixie or me as chauffeur.

On my way out of the subdivision, I noted that the sign outside the community building included a notice of an association meeting that night. I made a mental note to attend as I headed my vehicle toward the downtown area. The morning traffic was light, and I made the trip to the museum with over an hour to spare. The museum was located on a bluff that overlooked the Tennessee River in downtown Chattanooga near the Walnut Street Bridge. I parked in the lot adjacent to the museum. The area was known as the Bluff View Art District. In addition to the Chattanooga Museum of Art, there were several smaller museums inside converted houses. There was a small coffee shop a half block away. I decided I would look less pathetic if I hung out there rather than standing in front of the museum, waiting for it to open. Besides, Da Vinci's was a European-style café, with a wide assortment of coffees, artisan breads, and handmade pastries.

Dixie had taken me here during one of our sightseeing trips around town, and the café had been packed. Today it was busy too, but I managed to snag a small bistro table near the window and enjoyed a rich coffee with a buttery, flaky croissant. I savored the moment and enjoyed watching the variety of people who patronized the bakery. Men and women, young and old, all seemed to find something to like at Da Vinci's.

At twenty minutes to nine, I headed to the museum. The time at the café had settled my nerves enough that, by the time I walked into the front of the museum and asked to see the executive director, as instructed, I was fairly calm, and my voice barely shook.

"May I help you?"

I turned around. "Are you the executive director?" I tried to adjust my face not to register surprise at the boy who stared back at me.

"Good Lord, no." He rolled his eyes and smiled big. "I'm Jacob Flemings." He extended a hand. "Linda Kay Weyman is the executive director. She runs this ship. I'm first mate." He saluted and smiled.

He said Linda Kay as though it was one word. I wondered if her name was really Linda Kay or if her first name was Linda and her middle name Kay. Quite a few people in the South used both their first and middle names, far more than I'd encountered living in Indiana. Another common practice seemed to be people going by their middle name more than their first name. I decided to call her Mrs. Weyman to be safe. I smiled and shook the hand he extended. "I'm Lilly Echosby. Tatum Temp Services sent me. I'm the CPA."

"Linda Kay told me you were coming. She's running late this morning. Her kickboxing class went over. She'll be here shortly, but she asked me to show you around and help you get settled, and then she should be in."

"Great." I smiled and followed him beyond a door marked EMPLOYEES ONLY. There was an area with mauve panels and cubicles. We passed by and headed to the back to an elevator.

Jacob pushed the button, and the doors immediately opened. He stepped aside for me to precede him and then got in. He punched the button for the top floor, and we waited while the elevator ascended.

I took a moment to assess my young guide. Jacob looked to be in his early twenties. He was thin but fastidiously dressed in skinny jeans, a crisp white shirt, and a sweater you could tell was cashmere, even if you didn't see the designer emblem. He had long, dark curly hair pulled back into a ponytail and dark eyes. He wore bright red rectangular glasses that made him look cultured and artistic.

On the top floor, the doors opened. Again, he waited while I exited before leaving and then directed me toward a wall with offices.

"This is my desk." He pointed toward a large desk positioned outside a door with a plate indicating the executive director's office lay behind. We stopped at the next office. Jacob took out a key ring and unlocked the door. He waited until I entered and then followed me inside and handed me a ring with three keys.

"This is my office?" I looked around at the massive room.

Jacob nodded. "It is for the time being, anyway, until we hire a permanent accountant." He looked around. "There's a coatrack behind the door." He closed the door so I could see. "One of those keys unlocks your office door. The other unlocks your desk, and the third is for the file room down the hall."

"File room?"

He looked puzzled. "Yes, it's where we keep the files." He had a frightened expression, as though to say, *What planet did you come from?*

I hurried to explain. "I'm sorry. I know I must sound like a complete idiot parroting everything you say. It's just a bit surprising to find that companies still have file rooms in this day and age."

He nodded. "I understand completely. Unfortunately, the objets d'art aren't the only relics in the museum. While most of the modern world is careening into the digital age of the twenty-first century, the Museum of Art is crawling into the twentieth century."

I smiled.

"Why don't you take a few minutes to get familiar with your office, and then whenever you're ready, just step outside, and I'll give you the grand tour."

I thanked him and stood staring at the massive office for close to a minute after Jacob left.

The office was larger than the hotel room I had just moved out of. It had a wall of windows that overlooked the Tennessee River and let a lot of light into the room. I flopped down in the chair and swiveled around so I could stare out at the magnificent view. "I don't see how you can ever get tired of that," I said aloud and enjoyed it for a few additional minutes. "But I'm here to do a job, and I'd better get to it." I put my purse in the desk drawer. I decided it might be a good idea to get my bearings before the executive director arrived, so I went outside and got Jacob, and we started our tour.

Jacob showed me the file room, which, if the labels on the drawers were accurate, held years of information.

I sighed. "You really shouldn't keep financial information this long."

He shrugged. "Freemont had it brought out of storage."

"Freemont?"

"Freemont Hopewell, our previous financial manager." He took a finger and wrote his name in the dust that covered the file cabinet. "Freemont was a family legacy."

"What's a family legacy?"

He smiled. "That means he is a relative from the family that founded the museum and was therefore guaranteed a job whenever needed."

I waited for more, but nothing more came. Instead, he continued on and showed me the restrooms, employee lounge, and vending area. He was just about to take me downstairs to the snack bar when his cell phone rang. He glanced at the number. "That's the boss."

He engaged in a brief conversation and then disconnected. "Linda Kay's back and is anxious to get acquainted."

We hurried back down to the office, where the door behind Jacob's desk was open. Still, he knocked and then stepped aside for me to enter. "Linda Kay, this is Lilly Echosby." He turned to me. "Linda Kay Weyman."

I entered, and then he backed out and closed the door behind him.

If I thought my office was impressive, it was nothing compared to the executive director's office. The space had probably at one time been two offices that had been combined to form one massive space. The walls were painted a rich eggplant and there was a thick, sumptuous pewter carpet. One side of the room held a huge desk, while a large conference table with eight chairs took up the other side of the room. The view out of the window was spectacular, and there were lots of homey touches around the room, including vases and paintings I felt confident were worth a small fortune.

Behind the desk sat a middle-aged woman with thick red hair, bright eyes, and a big smile that made me feel warm and welcomed. "Come in." She extended a hand from behind her desk but didn't stand.

I walked up to the desk and shook.

"Please sit down." She gestured to a large leather wingback chair in front of the desk.

"Thank you, Mrs. Weyman, I'm very pleased to meet you. I—"

"Call me Linda Kay. Everyone does."

I sat. "Please call me Lilly."

She smiled. "I'm very sorry I wasn't here to greet you, but you were in good hands with Jacob."

I nodded. "He was wonderful. He was just taking me on a tour of the building."

"How far did you get?"

I told her the areas I'd seen. "We were just about to go downstairs."

"Wonderful." She clapped her hands. "Then I'll continue where Jacob left off." She turned and swiveled around, and I noticed the electric scooter positioned behind her chair for the first time. Linda Kay slid from her chair onto the scooter and then backed out from behind the desk. It was only then I noticed she was missing a leg.

I tried not to stare and quickly moved to open the door so she could precede me out of the room.

Linda Kay motored past Jacob but stopped long enough to tell him where we were going and to give him instructions.

I followed her to the elevator and then got in. We went back to the first floor but took a different path than the one I had taken earlier with Jacob. We went down a ramp and turned a corner. The hall was too narrow for us to walk side by side, so I followed close behind Linda Kay. At the end of the hall, there was a large square on the wall that allowed her to open the door with a push. Once inside, we were in a small café where museum patrons could purchase coffee, tea, and sandwiches.

"I didn't know about this place. I went to Da Vinci's."

"Coffee is free for employees." Linda Kay leaned close and whispered, "But they get the pastries from Da Vinci's and tack on an extra charge. You're better off to just walk a block and save the money." She smiled.

She pulled up to the coffee counter and poured herself a cup. "Would you care for anything? It's one of the perks of working here. You get free coffee—or tea, if you prefer."

I was pretty well caffeinated from my stop at Da Vinci's, but it looked as though Linda Kay planned a rest stop, so I poured a half cup of coffee and followed her to a seat near the window.

Once we were settled in, she smiled at me. "I thought I'd start by giving you a little background and explaining why you're here."

I wished I'd thought to bring along a pen and notepad but took my phone out of my pocket and placed it on the table. If worse came to worse, I could always type notes on my phone.

She took a deep drink of her coffee. "You're not from here, are you?"

I shook my head. "No. I recently moved to Chattanooga from Indiana."

She nodded. "I could tell by your accent you weren't from around here."

I smiled at the thought that, here in the South, I was the one with the accent. "My husband died about three months ago, and I needed a change.

My best friend from college lives in Chattanooga, and I decided it would be a good place to start over." This was a temporary position, and I didn't feel it necessary to go into a lot of detail about Albert.

She took a drink of coffee before she started. "The Chattanooga Museum of Art started out as a legacy from the Hopewell family. Ulysses Hopewell was a tycoon who made a ton of money and built a big mansion on the bluffs. His wife, Sarah Jane, was a socialite who loved art. She wanted to be an artist herself, but her family didn't feel that was an acceptable career for a well-bred woman back then. However, she never gave up her passion for art. When her husband died, she threw herself into the arts. She bought a lot of paintings and sponsored promising artists from all over the world. Before she died, she established the Hopewell Art Museum and Trust and endowed the organization with ten million dollars."

"That's impressive."

She nodded. "Especially in nineteen-twenties dollars."

"Did she have children?"

"Oh yes. She had a large family. Unfortunately, most of them have died except for a great-great grandson, Freemont, and a few others."

"Freemont whose job I'm taking over?"

She smiled. "I see Jacob has already filled you in."

"No, he didn't." I didn't want her to think Jacob had been gossiping and hurried to explain. "He only mentioned that Freemont kept a lot of records when he showed me the file room."

She waved away my protest. "It's okay. Jacob and Freemont never got on. Freemont was far too smooth for Jacob's liking. He said Freemont still had delusions of grandeur." She sat up straight and pushed her nose in the air. "Too much to the manor born, if you know what I mean." She laughed.

"Jacob did mention he was a Hopewell legacy, but he didn't completely explain what that meant."

"It means that because he is a Hopewell, he gets preferential treatment. His family founded the museum, so whenever a Hopewell needs a job, the museum hires them." She shook her head. "Which is really odd now that I think about it. Freemont certainly acts as though he has plenty of money. He drives around in fancy cars and wears designer clothes. He owns an antiques shop or something. I thought that was doing well." She shook her head again. "No matter how incompetent they are, we find positions for Hopewells. Unfortunately, the only job that needed to be filled was financial manager, so I was pressured by the board of directors to hire him." She sipped her coffee and stared out the window. After a few seconds, she must have made up her mind. "I might as well prepare you. Freemont didn't have a clue what he was doing, and the books are a mess. In fact, the financial position of the museum is a mess." She sighed.

"Do you think he was embezzling money?"

She shrugged. "I doubt it. I think it was just pure incompetence. But since he didn't know what he was doing, he didn't file the right papers with the IRS, and our tax-exempt status is in jeopardy. It's a hornet's nest, and we have an auditor arriving in a few months. The problem is that when I confronted Freemont, he quit. So now it will be my butt in a sling if I can't figure out what he's done and straighten it out."

I sighed. "Why didn't you hire a firm to help? This might be too much for one person."

"The board won't approve the money for that." She sat up tall and puffed out her chest and her cheeks. In a blustery voice, she said, "We can't do anything that would in any way diminish the good name of Hopewell or tarnish one of the foremost families of Chattanooga society." She shrugged and resumed her normal posture. "The only thing I can do is hire a replacement for Freemont. So"—she spread her hands out—"here you are."

Here I was. What had I gotten myself into now?

Chapter 3

I spent the rest of the day looking through files. Apparently, Freemont didn't use any financial software, so everything he did was handwritten. Prior to Freemont joining the museum staff, the financial information was managed by a very competent woman named Alice Foxworth. Alice was a paragon of detail, and her books were a thing of beauty. Apparently, she retired and went to stay with her daughter in Florida, as I learned from Linda Kay. Alice's records could have been framed and held up as a model of accounting excellence. Unfortunately, Freemont's weren't. His ledgers were messy, and there were stains and a lot of erasures that blotted out numbers and made the recordkeeping even more challenging to follow. I buried myself in ledgers from the last few years, the period when Freemont had been in charge. I was pretty certain Alice's figures were perfectly aligned down to the last penny. It might have been a stereotype, but I didn't care. I'd stake my reputation that Alice's figures were right.

I lifted my head from the ledgers three times. Once when Jacob brought me a tuna fish sandwich from the café, once to answer the call of nature, and once when Stephanie phoned to let me know the golden retriever was awake and well. Dixie was taking her to the airport to pick up her boyfriend, Joe, and they would then go back to the emergency clinic in their rental to get our new houseguest.

Later, Linda Kay rolled into the office and said my name. "Lilly!"

I looked up dazed. "I'm sorry. I was engrossed." I rubbed my eyes.

"I can tell." She came into the room. "It's time to go home."

I looked at my watch. "I didn't realize how late it is."

"Well, you've had your head buried in those books long enough. Go home!" She smiled. "There'll be plenty of time to look through those tomorrow." She turned the scooter around to face the door. She stopped before she left and looked at me over her shoulder. "You are coming back tomorrow, aren't you?"

"Of course." I stood up to stretch.

She nodded. "Good. Then I'll see you then." She waved over her shoulder and motored out of the room and down the hall.

I tidied my desk and gathered my things. It was later than I realized, and I needed to hurry home to attend the neighborhood association meeting tonight.

Traffic on the way home wasn't nearly as obliging as it was in the morning, but I made the drive in a little over thirty minutes. Tomorrow I'd explore alternative routes that would allow me to bypass the interstate.

Aggie was barking when I pulled into the garage. By the time I made it to her crate in the bedroom, she was spinning in circles. One of the things I liked about this house was the master bedroom had a door that allowed me to quickly let her out onto the deck. I flung the crate door open and ran out the door and onto the deck as Dixie had told me. Sure enough, Aggie followed at a quick pace and once outside, she wasted no time taking care of business.

I put Aggie's food out, but she was more interested in watching me change out of my work clothes into jeans and a light sweater. No matter how much I encouraged her, she refused to eat and instead followed me through the house as I prepared to go to the meeting. I waited as long as I dared, but still she didn't eat.

"I'm sorry, but you're going to have to go back in the crate." I looked at Aggie as she stared up at me. I walked to the crate and held the door. "Kennel."

Unfortunately, Aggie must have had enough of the crate for one day because she took off running, and a chase ensued. Eventually, I cornered her and scooped her up and carried her to the crate. However, by the time our little game of tag was over, I was frustrated and in a foul temper.

I tossed a couple of dog biscuits inside the crate, turned the television back to the home decorating channel, turned off the lights, and left.

The neighborhood association meetings were held in the community building in the center of the subdivision. I walked quickly, which meant I was hot and sweaty by the time I got there. When I entered, the meeting had already started, and I quickly found a seat at the back of the room and tried to collect my breath. Unfortunately, I didn't have much time. Just as I sat down, a man I assumed was the association president asked if there was any new business. He was one of four people seated at a table at the front of the room.

The grumpy old man who yelled at me stood.

Several of the people at the head table rolled their eyes, and there was a general groan from the audience.

The president sighed. "The floor recognizes Theodore Livingston."

"I have several complaints to bring to the board."

"Of course you do," said a large man with a pointy head and a grisly beard that extended almost to his navel.

The crowd laughed, and the president took a small gavel and pounded it a couple of times to regain order.

None of the comments seemed to bother Mr. Grumpy. Theodore Livingston walked to the front of the room. "First, the bylaws for the association clearly state that the grass must be mowed and kept to not more than two inches in height." He held up a ruler. "I measured the grass at lot fourteen, and the grass was over three inches tall."

More groans from the audience.

A thin-faced woman stood. "Why, you mean old coot, that's my yard. I should have known you were up to no good when I saw you nosing around my block at five in the morning."

Theodore Livingston smiled. "I always get up early. The early bird gets the worm."

The president pounded his gavel, but the thin-faced woman wasn't about to be deterred.

"I keep my grass cut." She looked around at her fellow neighbors, who all nodded. "But I can't do it right now on account of my broken foot." She pointed to her leg, which was in a cast.

Grumpy Mr. Livingston refused to make eye contact. "I can't help that. The rules is the rules."

The president pounded his gavel. "Order."

"I'll take care of Mrs. Herrington's yard, first thing Saturday," a man yelled from one side of the room.

"Thank you, Mr. Leonard," the president acknowledged.

Mrs. Herrington thanked Mr. Leonard, scowled at Mr. Livingston, and sat down.

"If that's all—" the president started.

"No. That's not all," Mr. Livingston continued. "I have another complaint. We have rules in the covenant about animals leaving waste throughout the subdivision and the owners cleaning up after them."

Here it comes. I knew this one was directed at me, even though I had only been in the neighborhood two days and I cleaned up after my dog. I sat up straight and leaned forward to make sure I heard every word.

"There are some folks that let their dogs go piddling and pooping all over the neighborhood and don't clean up. Plus, noise restrictions. There are noise restrictions that are being violated. Today, the person who recently moved into lot seven left her dog inside all day, and it barked, which is a violation of the restrictive covenant."

I had no idea what lot number I was on, but I knew, in my bones, that Mr. Grumpy was talking about me. Before I thought about it, I was on my feet. "Are you referring to me?"

Grumpy face turned and glared at me. "If the shoe fits..."

"I've got a shoe for you," I mumbled loud enough for him to hear me.

His face was beet red, and he sputtered, "You people move into a neighborhood and think you own the place. I had to put up with that trained demon of Hansen's because he owned the place, but I don't have to put up with some yippity-yappity ankle-biting rodent masquerading as a dog leaving piles of dog crap all over the neighborhood and disturbing the peace so I can't enjoy my garden. If I had my way, that little runt dog would have been drowned at birth."

I didn't know if it was the "you people" or the "ankle-biting rodent" or a combination of everything, but something snapped. I marched up to the grumpy-faced man. I stood toe to toe and practically nose to nose. "I don't know what barnyard you were raised in, but I don't appreciate being spoken about like that. What exactly do you mean by 'you people'?"

He scowled. "Yankees." He hacked a large brown wad of spittle onto the floor.

I didn't even try to hide the disgust on my face. "Well, this Yankee isn't afraid of a grumpy old troll who doesn't have anything better to do than to go around complaining about his neighbors and threatening poor, defenseless dogs."

"If I see that little runt in my yard, I'll squash it like a bug." He stomped his foot on the floor and twisted it. Then he looked at me with a snide smile. "No one around here will be able to stop me because I know all the dirty secrets."

I wasn't sure what he meant, but I didn't really care. At that point, something rose up inside of me, and I saw red. I clenched and unclenched my fists. I ached to wipe that unpleasant, smug expression off of his face. Before I knew it, I had provided a sharp uppercut, which caused his neck to snap back. Before he could fully recover, I followed that with a knee to the groin.

He dropped like a rock.

Arms came around me, pulling me away.

Though the blood was pounding in my ears, I heard him wheezing. "I'll file charges. I'll see you in jail."

I spun away from the flood of hands propelling me away and marched back and leaned down to stare him in the face. "If you lay one finger on my dog, so help me God, I'll strangle you."

I turned and walked away. The sea of bodies parted, and I threw open the door and allowed it to slam as I left the building. My anger propelled me home so quickly I didn't even recall the walk. Once inside, I paced for a quarter of an hour before I was calm enough to sit down.

Aggie watched in silence as I paced around boxes and slammed cabinet doors. The front doorbell rang. I assumed he'd made good on his threats and called the police, so I grabbed my cell phone and dialed my daughter, Stephanie.

"Hello, Mom, I—"

"Sorry, but I don't have time for pleasantries. I just struck one of my neighbors at the neighborhood association meeting and threatened him in front of a room full of people. I think he's called the police. I wanted to have the phone where you can hear what happens." I walked to the door and swung it open.

To my surprise, it wasn't the police but the president of the association, along with the woman I'd seen earlier at the association meeting. "I was expecting the police."

"May we come in?" he asked.

I stepped aside. "Of course. I'm sorry. Despite my behavior earlier, I do have manners."

Once they were inside, I closed the door and remembered I still had Stephanie on the phone. "I'm sorry, dear, but I'm going to need to call you back."

"Mom, don't you dare hang up that phone. What on earth is going on? You can't just call and tell me you hit someone and are expecting the police and then hang up. What has happened to you?"

"I can't talk right now, but I promise I'll call you back shortly." I hung up.

"Please sit down." I extended a hand toward the sofa, but both of them declined.

"We won't be here long. My name's Jackson Phillips, and this is Carol Lynn Hargrove. I'm the association president, and Carol Lynn is the treasurer. We wanted to apologize and make sure you're okay."

"Apologize? I'm sure I'm the one who needs to apologize. I just moved into the neighborhood, and I hit someone." I shook my head. "I can't believe I did that." I paced. "I was just so angry."

He held up his hands. "Understandable. You're not the first person to strike Theodore Livingston. In fact, when Mrs. Hansen called and told me a nice accountant had rented the house, I meant to come over and warn you about our neighborhood crackpot."

"Wait...someone else hit him?" I stared from the president to Carol Lynn. They both nodded.

"Practically everyone in the subdivision has had an altercation with him at one time or another. Unfortunately, several have led to blows." His lips twitched, and he struggled to keep from laughing. "Although most women don't pack quite the same wallop. You have quite a right hook."

I stared openmouthed. "You must be joking."

They shook their heads.

"The man's a menace. He needs to be locked up. I thought you were the police coming to arrest me."

Carol Lynn placed a hand on my arm. "Honey, Theodore Livingston has called the police so many times they've threatened to arrest him if he calls for a nonemergency again."

My face must have reflected the disbelief racing through my mind because both of them nodded to reassure me of their truthfulness.

"But...that isn't right. I mean, I was angry, and I shouldn't have hit him, but..."

Carol Lynn shrugged. "Theodore Livingston is a cantankerous old fool. He's a mean, vicious, troublemaker who would find fault with God Himself."

Jackson rubbed the back of his neck. "I'm afraid Carol Lynn's right. I'm sorry your first introduction to the neighborhood involved dealing with Theodore Livingston."

"What's wrong with him?" I asked.

"Touched in the head." Carol Lynn swirled her fingers in the universal sign for crazy.

"We've even tried to buy him out," Jackson said. "Robert Hansen tried several times to buy his house, but he won't sell. The entire subdivision voted to buy his house at market rate, but he refuses to move." He shook his head again. He reached out a hand to me. "Are you okay?"

I nodded. "I'll be fine. I can't remember when I've been that angry." I hid my face with my hands. "I feel so ashamed."

They both tried to soothe my feelings, but once the anger died, there was nothing left but shame.

I stared through my fingers. "I need to apologize to him. I raised my children to believe there's no right way to do a wrong thing." I sighed. "Just because someone's rude and nasty to me doesn't mean I should sink to their level. I should've taken the high ground. I should've walked away."

Jackson and Carol Lynn spent a few minutes trying to convince me I was wrong, but my conscience wasn't having any of it.

After a while, Jackson looked at his watch. "I need to get home. I've got a lot of papers to grade before school tomorrow." He looked at me carefully. "Are you sure you're okay?"

I nodded. "I'll have a talk with Theodore tomorrow. It'll be fine."

I held the door open as he and Carol Lynn headed out. "Thank you both for coming over. I appreciate your concern for my feelings. Tomorrow, I'll apologize to Mr. Livingston. I used to get along beautifully with my neighbors in Lighthouse Dunes. They were older, and one of them had dementia."

I smiled at the thought of my neighbor, Bradley Hurston, a retired cop. He had once been a vibrant, caring man who was struck down with mental illness that left him crippled and locked in a mental fog of confusion and paranoia. He was killed, and I mourned for the man he used to be.

I sighed. "Unfortunately, he was killed. There are so many angry people around. I'm afraid if Theodore Livingston isn't careful, he's going to go too far and someone won't stop at merely punching him."

A strong wind blew through the house and sent a chill up my spine. Aggie did something I've never heard her do before. She howled.

Chapter 4

Stephanie and Joe rushed home, and I filled them in on the events from the association meeting. Joe was a Lighthouse Dunes policeman who had helped us figure out who killed Albert. He was a part of the K-9 division and had brought along his almost constant companion, Turbo, a Plott hound who thought Aggie was the bees' knees. Clearly, one of the stops Stephanie had made was to a pet store because she came home with a large dog bed, which she placed near the fireplace. Joe carried the golden retriever and placed him in the dog bed. He looked woozy, but that was probably due to the anesthesia. Once in the bed, he curled up into a large ball and slept. Aggie and Turbo played tug-of-war and keep-away with a stuffed bear. I was surprised at how gentle the larger dog was with her. I suspected the Plott hound got quite a bit of pleasure watching her prance around the house with the toy in her mouth, as though she really was tough enough to have won the battle fair and square. The two friends played together until they were both tired and then curled up together on the rug. We stayed up late, talking, but I was both physically and emotionally drained and left the younger crowd and went to bed.

I had a difficult time sleeping. I couldn't get what I'd done out of my mind. I'd actually struck another human being. Shame and guilt tortured my thoughts. I tossed and turned for most of the night. For the second night in a row, I gave up on the idea of sleep and got up and baked shortbread cookies. They were quick and easy and required very little mental acuity, which was good, given the fact I hadn't slept well for the past two nights. I even went so far as to dip some of the cookies into melted chocolate. They were a thing of beauty and left my house smelling wonderful.

While the cookies cooled, I took a long, hot shower. I heard my cell phone ring while I was in the bathroom, toweling off. "Stephanie, can you get that?" I yelled. I waited and the phone stopped, so I assumed she'd taken care of it.

By the time I got out and dressed, I heard the shower in the guest bedroom. I hoped the hot water heater was sufficient to provide two long, relaxing showers.

I looked down as Aggie scavenged the kitchen floor for crumbs and realized I'd neglected her. I glanced at my watch and saw I had time to take her for a quick walk before I needed to head out to work. So I packed the cookies into a tin and grabbed my cell phone from the counter, along with Aggie's leash. I tossed my phone into my pocket and hurried out the door. It was early, but I remembered Theodore Livingston say at the association meeting that he got up early. While I still had the nerve, I dashed next door and quickly rang the bell. I waited and practiced deep-breathing exercises, which were supposed to calm and relax. After close to a minute, I rang the bell again and also pounded on the door. When no one answered, I wondered if Mr. Livingston truly wasn't home or if he was still angry and avoiding me. I shook myself. "He's probably still asleep or in the bathroom," I told Aggie. "Let's take our walk and try again when we get back."

Aggie must have thought that was the best idea because she wagged her tail and anxiously pulled on her leash.

We walked the same path we'd taken two days ago, past the gazebo and toward the wooded area. Aggie stopped a couple of times along the way and took care of business. I was careful to clean up and properly dispose of the waste. As we walked, I thought through what I'd say if I found myself face-to-face with Theodore Livingston again. A sincere apology was the first course of action. I would own my behavior and assure him it would never happen again. My mind wandered, and my stomach clenched at the thought of how he would respond. I thought through various scenarios, including doors slammed in my face. Honestly, I couldn't blame him. He was rude, but there was never an excuse for violence. However, the more I thought about it, the worse the scenarios became. Eventually, I decided to stop thinking about it and just get it over with.

I stopped walking and turned. "Come on, Aggie. Let's get this over with and go home." I tugged on her leash.

Aggie was sniffing around a tree stump. She was engrossed in sniffing and scratching and certainly wasn't paying any attention to me.

"Aggie, come," I said forcefully, like Dixie had instructed, but Aggie couldn't have cared less what I wanted and gave no indication she'd even heard me.

Dixie had warned me against repeating commands. Aggie needed to be trained to come the first time she was called. If she didn't, I was to pick her up.

I sighed as I walked over to pick her up. It was only then that I saw what she was digging at. She'd unearthed a man's shoe. Closer inspection showed the shoe was attached to a leg, a man's leg. I squealed and jumped back. "OHMYGOD! OHMYGOD! OHMYGOD!"

I had no idea how long I stood there, but eventually I pulled my cell phone out of my pocket and made several calls. The first was to Dixie, instructing her to get over here immediately. The second call was to my daughter, Stephanie. The message was roughly the same thing, except I ordered her to send Joe out here immediately.

The third call was to 9-1-1.

Chapter 5

Joe and Turbo arrived first. Turbo was wearing his police K-9 unit vest and harness, and although Joe was wearing jeans and a T-shirt, there was something about both of their attitudes and demeanors that indicated vacation was over. They were working. Joe had a gun strapped around his waist. I'd never thought about it, but it made sense he would travel with it. I was a bit squeamish about guns. I never really liked them, although my husband had had one. If Dixie was to be believed, practically everyone in the South had a gun.

I released a breath and tried to steady my hands, which were shaking.

"You okay?" He stared at me with his steely-blue eyes.

I nodded. "I'm fine." I took a couple of deep breaths.

There was a park bench nearby, and he escorted me to it and helped me sit. "Wait here."

Whether it was concern for my well-being or a desire to make sure I didn't interfere, I didn't know, nor did I care. I flopped down on the seat and clutched Aggie to my chest.

He and Turbo went into the wooded area. I tried not to watch, but, as with a train wreck, I couldn't seem to stop glancing over.

Not long afterward, I heard sirens as the first patrol car careened into the subdivision. Joe and Turbo emerged from the woods and flagged it down.

An officer got out of the car, and Joe and Turbo approached. Joe flashed his shield, and they shook hands. They stood talking for what felt like an eternity, but they were outside of hearing distance, so I could only speculate about the conversation. Joe gestured in my direction but otherwise ignored me.

"Mom, are you okay?"

I turned. Stephanie hurried to my bench. The policeman looked as though he was going to stop her, but Joe held up a hand, I assumed to indicate that Stephanie was neither the homicidal maniac who had just killed someone or a nosy neighbor intent on contaminating his crime scene.

Two more police cars pulled up behind the first one.

Stephanie threw her arms around me and hugged Aggie and me. "Are you okay?"

"I'm fine," I lied.

Joe and the first patrolman walked over to the bench. The officer was shorter than Joe, who I knew was over six feet. He was a fair-skinned African American with light gray eyes.

"Mrs. Echosby, my name is Officer Lewis. You found the body?"

I nodded. "Yes." My voice cracked, so I cleared it and tried again. "Yes. My dog found it...ah, I mean him...the body." I held up Aggie.

He nodded. "If you'll wait here, I'm going to take a look. Then I'll be back to take your statement."

I nodded, and he headed to the woods.

Joe hung back and looked at Stephanie. "I thought we agreed you'd wait at the house."

She tossed her head. "No, you agreed."

He shook his head and tried to hide a smile. Then he and Turbo followed Officer Lewis into the woods.

There were quite a few police officers walking around the area, and many of my neighbors were now awake and curious about the sirens. I recognized Carol Lynn Hargrove and a few others from the association meeting, but they maintained their distance.

Stephanie and I sat quietly on the bench and waited. Eventually, Joe and the policeman returned.

Officer Lewis took out a notepad. "First, let me get your name and address. Do you have any identification on you?"

I shook my head.

"Oh." Stephanie rummaged in her pocket and pulled out my wallet. "I grabbed this on my way out of the house." She handed it to me and shot Joe a smug look that said, *I was right to ignore you.*

I pulled my driver's license out and handed it over.

He stared hard at my picture and then looked at me. "This says you live in Lighthouse Dunes, Indiana."

"I moved here a few weeks ago. Actually, I just moved into this neighborhood this week, and I haven't had time to get my Tennessee driver's license yet. I actually just got a permanent address. Well, not really permanent. I'm only renting at the moment." I was rambling but couldn't stop myself.

Officer Lewis nodded and made notes. He asked for my current address, and I gave it to him.

He paused and stared at me. "Did you know the deceased?"

I shook my head. "Actually, I didn't really look at him."

"Would you mind taking a look now?"

I didn't want to look at his shoes, let alone his face.

"You don't have to do this." Stephanie tightened her arm around my shoulders.

"Who are you again?" Officer Lewis looked at Stephanie, and I could feel her back straighten.

"I'm her lawyer." She looked him straight in the eyes and glared.

Officer Lewis turned to Joe. "I thought you said she was the daughter?"

Joe shook his head.

"She is my daughter and my lawyer." I took a deep breath. "Look, I—"

"Lilly!"

I turned at the sound of my name. Dixie was at the edge of the police barricade.

"Dixie."

I turned to Officer Lewis.

"Let me guess, another attorney?"

"No, but she is my friend."

Officer Lewis reluctantly lifted his hand and beckoned for Dixie to enter.

She ran to me and gave me a big hug. Her mental state was reflected by the fact that my fastidious friend still had one large curler hanging from the back of her head and wasn't wearing makeup.

"Anyone else coming?" Office Lewis asked.

"No, that's it." I pulled away from Dixie and stood. "However, I think I'm ready to take a look now."

"Are you sure?" Stephanie rose. "You don't have to do this."

I sighed. "I know, but...well, it's the right thing to do, right?" I looked from Stephanie to Dixie.

Dixie folded her arms. "Well, that depends. How bad is it?" She looked from Officer Lewis to Joe.

Joe shrugged. "He hasn't been dead long." He stared at me. "Stephanie's right. You don't have to do this, especially if you're going to puke." He turned to Officer Lewis. "She could stop by the coroner's office later, couldn't she?"

Officer Lewis wasn't pleased with that suggestion, but he shrugged.

I thought about it. "I'd rather get it over with now." I looked at the policeman. "Can Dixie come with me?"

He nodded.

I handed Aggie to Stephanie and clutched Dixie's hand. Together, we walked to the wooded area. By now, a host of policemen were taking pictures, videotaping, and leaving yellow markers beside anything that looked like it didn't belong, including gum wrappers and cigarette butts. At the edge of the scene, I craned my neck and looked at the body lying on the ground. "I've never seen him before."

"Are you sure?" Officer Lewis asked. "Maybe you should take a closer look."

I backed out. "I'm sure. I don't know him, but then I just moved here this week, so I've only met a handful of people. Maybe some of the residents who've lived here longer may know who he is." Something about the way Officer Lewis stared at me made me ask, "Why do you think I know who he is?"

He stared at me. "Because, unless you're lying to me, you both live at the same address."

Chapter 6

It took all four of us and quite a bit of time to convince Officer Lewis I wasn't lying. We went back to the house and showed him the lease agreement, but it wasn't until he called the landlord's mother, Jo Ellen Hansen, that he believed me. He learned Robert Hansen wasn't expected back from the Caymans until Christmas, but she hadn't actually talked to her son, other than to tell him she'd rented the house to me. Officer Lewis didn't tell her why he was asking questions about her son. Thankfully, Mrs. Hansen wasn't overly curious and accepted Officer Lewis's questions with as much trust as she'd exhibited while renting a house to a complete stranger without a background check, credit check, or references. When he hung up, he told us he'd have uniformed police notify her about her son's death.

I called Linda Kay to let her know I was going to be late and why, and she sympathized and told me to take the day off. I had no intention of taking her up on that offer, especially since this was only my second day on the job. However, by the time Officer Lewis left, it was noon. I was hungry, tired, and frustrated. My landlord was dead. I'd fought with my neighbor and actually struck him in a public meeting. I had to question if Chattanooga was going to be the happy place I'd left Lighthouse Dunes in search of. Officer Lewis had looked at me like a homicidal maniac who traveled the country looking for men to murder.

We sat in an exhausted silence for several moments after Officer Lewis left. My stomach growled.

Dixie grabbed her purse. "Let's go get something to eat."

Stephanie checked on the golden retriever. He looked up but curled back into a ball and continued to sleep.

I left Turbo and Aggie in my bedroom with the television on for company. We loaded into Dixie's SUV. She didn't ask what we wanted to eat. Instead, she headed to a nearby restaurant very close to the mall and parked. Inside, I was thankful there wasn't a line. We walked up to the hostess station and indicated a table for four. The young girl, who looked about twelve but was probably close to twenty, walked us past a large well-stocked bar to a booth.

Our waiter was a young man with a long red beard and a bald head. He smiled as he approached the table. Before he could speak, Dixie held up a hand.

"Look, we've had a rough morning, and I for one need a drink." She looked around.

We all nodded.

The waiter took out a pen, quickly jotted down our drink orders, and then hurried away.

We sat quietly for several minutes. The waiter must have sensed our desperation because he returned in record time with our drinks. Before he left, Dixie indicated he should bring another round.

He nodded and hurried away.

We sat in peace and drank our liquid courage.

Dixie tossed back her martini like someone taking shots.

I looked at Joe's shocked expression and burst out laughing. After a few seconds, we were all laughing.

I wiped tears from my eyes. "This is not funny, but I definitely needed a laugh." I reached over and removed the curler from Dixie's hair, and she put it in her purse.

The waiter looked even more frightened by our laughter than he had earlier. He quickly brought our second round of drinks, removed the empty glasses, and then backed away from the table.

"That poor kid will never be the same," Joe said.

I sipped a fruity sangria and looked over the menu. Dixie recommended the Kobe beef meat loaf, which came with mashed potatoes and gravy and green beans with almonds. Meat loaf was comfort food, and I needed comfort at the moment.

The waiter returned, took our orders, and left two loaves of bread on the table. We buttered our bread and ate for several seconds.

Dixie looked around the table. "Are we going to talk about the two-ton elephant in the room, or are we going to pretend it never happened?"

"I'm all for pretending it never happened." I raised a hand and looked around. "Who's with me?"

Stephanie raised her hand.

"We can't pretend it didn't happen." Joe sighed. "Although I'd like nothing better."

"Surely they can't blame Mom for this one." Stephanie's eyes pleaded. "She's never even met the man."

Joe shrugged. "Officer Lewis only has your mom's word for that and... and if I were investigating this murder, I don't know if I'd believe her." He looked at me. "Sorry."

"Well, I don't know that man. I've never even spoken to him. So it shouldn't take them long to find that out, and then, hopefully, all of this will be behind me."

Stephanie looked down but then quickly took a breath. "Mom, there's something I think you should know."

"What's that, dear?"

She sighed. "Robert Hansen called. He called your cell phone this morning when you were in the shower."

I shrugged. "I remember now. The phone rang when I was in the shower. I asked you to get it for me." I looked at my daughter, who was looking like she wanted to crawl under the table. "Did something happen?"

She released a heavy sigh. "I missed the phone call, but he sent a long text message about how he hadn't authorized his mother to rent the house. He didn't authorize pets, and he wanted you out as soon as possible."

I stared with my mouth open. "You're joking."

She shook her head. "I told him that his mother had power of attorney, and she had signed the lease, which was legally binding under the law." Her eyes pleaded. "I'm so sorry, Mom, but if the police see that text message, they'll think you sent it and were lying about knowing him."

"Ugh." I drained my sangria.

"I'm so sorry."

I reached across and patted Stephanie's hand. "It's okay. It's not your fault. We'll just have to call Officer Lewis and tell him what happened. Honesty is the best policy."

Stephanie and Joe exchanged a look that indicated they weren't quite as confident in this case.

"It's going to look pretty bad for you, Lilly." Dixie leaned forward. "Are they sure it was murder? I mean, how was he killed?"

Unfortunately, the waiter took that moment to show up with our food. The shocked expression on his face, followed by a flush that started at his neck and crept above his beard, told us he'd overheard at least the tail end of our conversation. Although he didn't say anything, his hands shook slightly as he placed our plates on the table. "Can I get you folks anything else?" He barely waited for a response before he scurried away.

We watched him look over his shoulder as he left and burst out laughing.

Joe wiped his eyes with a napkin, repeating, "That poor man will never be the same."

The food was delicious and plentiful. The Kobe beef meat loaf was everything Dixie said it was and more. I stuffed myself.

We ate in silence for several minutes until we'd knocked the edge off of our hunger. When everyone started to slow down, the conversation started again.

"You can't honestly believe they think my mom had anything to do with that man's death." Stephanie stared at Joe.

He took a deep breath. "I don't know, but the address thing looks bad." He squeezed her hand. "The text messages will look even worse."

I pulled my phone out. "I should at least read them." Dixie glanced over my shoulder while I swiped up and read the text messages. Stephanie looked pale. The messages were worse than I thought. Apparently, Robert Hansen's vocabulary was limited to four-letter words I'd often seen spray-painted on the side of buildings or scratched onto bathroom walls in public toilets. Stephanie's responses, which all appeared to have come from me, were terse and strongly worded. When I was done, I handed the phone across to Joe for him to read.

He scrolled through the messages and silently returned my phone.

"Well?" I asked.

"At least there was no threat of bodily harm, only legal action." He rubbed the back of his neck.

"But I can explain that Stephanie sent the messages."

Joe looked skeptical. "He won't believe she sent the messages. He'll think she's lying to protect you."

"Okay, so what do I do?"

He shrugged. "I'd recommend you stay out of it. Leave the investigation to the professionals, and trust the system to find the killer, but..."

"But?" I asked.

He sighed. "But I doubt very seriously that you're going to follow my advice. You didn't listen to me when it came to your husband's murder, and I doubt very seriously that you're going to listen to me now."

Again, our waiter showed impeccable timing and came to check on us at the absolute wrong moment. His eyes got large, and he tried to hide that he'd overheard our conversation, but he was too young and innocent to have developed a mask. "Did you save room for dessert?"

We declined dessert, and Dixie asked for the check. We protested, but she was quicker on the draw with her credit card.

By the time we got home, it was much too late for me to consider driving to work. I changed into jeans and a sweat shirt while Joe and Stephanie took the dogs outside. Turbo and Aggie hurried down the stairs from the deck. The golden retriever moved at a slower pace, but if the speed of his tail wag was any indication, he was doing much better.

Dixie fired up the coffee maker and was sipping a cup at the breakfast bar when I returned.

"That smells delicious." I sniffed. I walked to the coffee maker and noticed she had already made a cup for me. I picked it up and inhaled deeply before I took a sip. "Hmmm. That's good stuff." I grabbed the canister containing the shortbread cookies I'd made in the early morning and brought them to the breakfast bar. I unscrewed the lid.

Dixie looked inside the canister and grabbed one of the cookies dipped in chocolate and took a bite. "Hmmm."

I leaned against the bar and allowed the steam from my cup and the delicious aroma to waft up into my face.

"So what are you going to do?" Dixie asked.

I took a deep breath. I wanted to pretend I had no idea what she was talking about. However, I knew she was referring to my dead landlord's body. I grabbed a cookie from the canister. "I'm going to eat a cookie, drink coffee, and spend time with my daughter and her boyfriend."

"You know what I mean."

"I don't know what to do. I mean, figuring out who killed Albert was easier because I knew the people." I shook my head. "This is different. I don't know any of the people here. I have no idea who killed Robert Hansen or why." I ate another of the chocolate-dipped shortbread cookies and suddenly remembered why I'd baked them in the first place. The sudden shock of remembering sent the delicious morsel down the wrong pipe. I coughed.

Dixie looked stricken and patted me on the back. "You okay?"

"I forgot all about Mr. Livingston."

"Who's Mr. Livingston?"

"My neighbor." I gulped my coffee and coughed again. "I need to apologize for hitting him."

"You hit someone?" Dixie stared. "He must have done something pretty horrific for you to resort to violence."

I quickly told her about the association meeting as I donned my coat and grabbed the cookies I'd made earlier from the counter, where I'd tossed them when we returned with Officer Lewis.

Dixie grabbed her coat. "I'll go with you. You need an escort."

I looked at her puzzled.

"You've only been in this house a couple of days and you've gotten into a verbal argument with your neighbor, found a dead body, been accused of murder, and struck someone." She glanced at me. "I'm thinking Chattanooga may have unleashed something primal inside of you."

Chapter 7

I opened the front door. A man stood on the porch, hand raised, prepared to knock.

"I'm sorry. Can I help you?" I asked.

"I heard you found a dog, my dog." He looked around. "Were you going somewhere?"

"It's Michael Cunningham, right?"

He nodded.

"I was just going next door." I stepped aside. "But, please, come in."

He came in and looked around. "I heard you found my dog."

"Really? I didn't know you had a dog."

"Yes, my wife and I love dogs." He looked around again. "Is he here?"

"Not at the moment. My daughter took him for a walk." I motioned toward the sofa. "Perhaps you'd like to have a seat. I'm sure she'll be back soon."

His gaze darted around the room. He forced a smile. "If it's no bother." He walked to the sofa and perched on the edge.

Stephanie had gotten very fond of the dog and would be disappointed to find its owner.

Dixie sat on the armrest and stared. "My friend found the dog in her backyard, hiding under the deck."

Michael Cunningham tsked and shook his head.

Dixie was relentless. "How did he get away?"

For a split second, a look of shock flashed across his eyes but was quickly replaced. Michael Cunningham chuckled. "Well, normally we keep him tied up, but someone must have left the gate open." He shook his head. "I'm always telling my wife she needs to make sure the gate is secure." He shrugged jovially. "She must have forgotten."

Dixie's face didn't crack. "He looked thin, like he hasn't been eating. He also didn't have any tags or a microchip."

"I've been meaning to get around to having that done, but the time just flew by." He chuckled.

"What's the dog's name?" she asked.

He hesitated too long. "Buddy."

The door opened, and Stephanie, Joe, and the three dogs entered.

I rose and walked over to Stephanie. I was just about to break the news to Stephanie that someone had come to claim the dog when I caught a look from Dixie.

She looked at the golden retriever and said, "Buddy, come."

The dog sat down by Stephanie's side and looked at her.

Stephanie looked from Dixie to me. "What's going on?"

"This is my neighbor, Michael Cunningham," I said.

"Mr. Cunningham claims this is his dog, Buddy," Dixie said.

Michael Cunningham rose. "He never was very bright." He laughed and walked forward with his hand outstretched to take the leash from Stephanie. "I'll just take him home."

Stephanie looked on the verge of tears. Turbo, on the other hand, stood very stiff and growled at Mr. Cunningham's outstretched hand.

"That dog seems vicious. Is he dangerous?" He stared at Turbo.

"He can be if needed. He's a police dog," Joe said in the cold, steely voice he used when he was working. "Turbo, platz." He gave the German command for down used in Schutzhund dog training.

Turbo immediately lay by his side. Surprisingly, the golden also lay down by Stephanie's side.

We all stared at the dog in shocked silence. After a brief second, Dixie walked about six feet from the golden. She established eye contact. "Sitz." Which sounded like *fits*. The golden immediately rose and sat. Next, Dixie raised her right arm above her head. With her hand in a flat position, she slowly brought it down so that her arm was by her side with her hand remaining in a flat, open position.

The golden immediately lay back down.

She raised her right arm again, this time bending it at the elbow and stopping when the palm was facing up and her elbow and arm were at ninety degrees.

The dog returned to a sitting position.

Finally, she outstretched her right arm to the side so that it was parallel with the floor with her palm facing out. She then slowly swept her arm to her chest so that her palm touched her chest.

The dog rose and slowly walked toward Dixie, stopping only when he was squarely sitting between her feet. He looked at her.

This time she took her left hand and made a circular motion. The dog immediately stood up and scooted his butt around so he was sitting perfectly by her left side.

We watched in dazed silence.

Dixie looked at the dog and then relaxed her body. "Free."

Only then did the dog relax. He rose and wagged his tail as she praised and petted him and reached into her pocket and pulled out a treat, which she gave him. "Good boy." She turned to Michael Cunningham. "Doesn't look like a dumb dog to me. In fact, this is a well-trained dog." She looked at the dog. "However, I doubt very seriously that his name is Buddy."

We all stared at Michael Cunningham. A flush of color came up his neck. His ears were red. "Well, he's my dog, and I'm taking him." He reached for the leash and once again Turbo growled.

Joe stepped forward. "I don't think so." He pulled out his shield and flashed it at Michael Cunningham. "We're not turning over the dog until you provide proof of ownership."

Michael Cunningham looked shocked.

"I'm sure the local police will also want to question you for animal abuse and cruelty," Stephanie said.

Michael Cunningham replaced his facial expression with one of outrage and indignation. "You'll be hearing from my lawyer."

Stephanie reached into her pocket and pulled out one of her business cards and handed it to him. "Good. Have him call me."

Michael Cunningham marched to the door and let himself out.

I stared at Dixie. "Wow, how did you know he could do all of that?"

Dixie shook her head. "I didn't, but when he went down when Joe gave the German command, I thought it was worth a shot." She looked at Stephanie, who was on her knees hugging and petting the golden retriever. "Someone has spent a lot of time training this dog. I don't know how much he knows, but he isn't just a pet."

Stephanie buried her face in the golden's coat. "I don't care. I love him."

Joe, Dixie, and I exchanged looks that said, *This isn't going to be good.* Stephanie was obviously attached to the dog. When the owner was found, she was going to have to relinquish him, and that would be hard.

Turbo whined, and Joe released him from his forced position and removed his harness, which told Turbo he was no longer working and could return to play, which suited Aggie just fine.

Turbo stretched, with his front paws down and his rear in the air, indicating he wanted to play. Aggie returned the pose, and a chase ensued. Initially, I had been concerned about my six-pound poodle playing with a male police dog who was ten times her size. However, Turbo surprised me by the gentle way he played with her. He literally treated her as gently as a puppy should be treated. When Dixie's two standard poodles were around, the play was a lot rougher, but still, all the dogs demonstrated tremendous restraint with Aggie. Nevertheless, Dixie, Joe, and I always kept a close eye whenever Aggie played with them to make sure she didn't get injured accidentally.

A loud whine from the golden indicated he wanted to join in on the play. Stephanie unhooked his leash, and he quickly joined in the chase. Aggie grabbed a stuffed toy and zipped around the room. The larger dogs gave chase. Aggie was fast and could turn on a dime, something that was a lot harder for the bigger dogs, who often slid for a few feet when they tried to turn, carried away by their momentum. The golden was still slower from his surgery but he was smart and managed to play without exerting himself too much.

We stood and watched the dogs play for several seconds.

"Were you going someplace?" Stephanie asked.

I remembered the cookies and once again started out to apologize to Mr. Livingston. Dixie and I hurried outside and quickly made our way across the lawn. Just as we reached the front door of Mr. Livingston's house, one of the curtains moved. Before we could ring the bell, the door flew open.

"How dare you traipse across my lawn," Livingston bellowed. "You're trespassing."

I swallowed the lump in my throat and held up my tin of cookies. "I'm very sorry. I—"

"Come to do me in like you did that other fellow?"

Heat rose up my neck. "I didn't kill anyone." I took a deep breath. "Actually, I wanted to apologize." I held out my tin of cookies.

He sneered. "Is that how you did it? Poison?"

"Good grief." Dixie reached over and pulled the lid off the tin. She took a cookie out and shoved it into her mouth. "There's nothing wrong with these cookies, you crazy old coot!"

Theodore Livingston flushed. "Get off my property." He snatched the tin out of my hands. "And stay off my grass." He slammed the door in our faces.

Dixie and I stared at the solid door for nearly a minute before we turned around and walked away. This time we were careful to walk on the sidewalk.

We ran into Carol Lynn Hargrove and Jackson Phillips at the end of the walk. I was curious if something romantic was going on between the two, but I didn't notice any particular demonstrations of affection. Besides, it was none of my business.

"Visiting our local crackpot?" he asked.

"Actually, I went over to apologize. I took a peace offering."

Carol Lynn chuckled. "I'll bet the cheap geezer took your offering, but not your apology."

"How did you know?" I asked.

"I know Theodore Livingston. Now you see why no one was shocked when you hit him. He's an odious old fart."

Dixie snorted. "It's a wonder all you did was strike the old fool. I would have strangled the mean old snake."

Chapter 8

It took two more shortbread cookies and a cup of hot chocolate before I calmed down. Dixie required something stronger. Having already consumed two martinis, her limit, she went home so she could indulge without the worry of having to wend her way up the mountain.

When I sat down, I sensed the atmosphere was different. On the surface, Joe and Stephanie looked much the same. However, there was a static current floating between the two of them, and the room was charged.

Turbo napped on the floor next to Joe, with his head on Joe's foot. Across the room, Stephanie sat on the floor and stroked the golden's head, which was resting in her lap. Periodically, his tail wagged, and he looked into her eyes adoringly. Aggie lay perched around my shoulder like a fur stole.

"What's going on?" I asked when the tension got to be too much.

"Nothing!" They both snapped so quickly it was obviously a lie.

Nevertheless, I waited.

Stephanie cracked first. "He thinks I should turn the golden over to that odious man without a fight."

"That's not true."

She turned to glare at him. "Did you or did you not tell me I should surrender the dog?"

"I did, but—"

"I rest my case!"

"I hate when you talk to me like I'm some criminal in the witness box."

"I hate when you act like a cop and use words like 'surrender the dog.'"

His eyes flashed. "I am a cop, and you know as well as I do you have no legal right to that dog."

"That's not true. He escaped from an abusive owner and came here seeking sanctuary."

"You don't know that."

"I know he was cold and hungry and in need of medical attention."

"He could have gotten spooked and run into traffic. You don't know how he injured his leg." He spoke softly, "Somewhere out there is a person or family who spent a lot of time and money training him."

The eyes were a mirror into the soul, and Stephanie's eyes looked stricken. "How would you feel if someone tried to take Turbo?"

He hesitated. "I'd probably want to break their neck." He paused and looked at Turbo and then across at Stephanie. "But there's a difference," he said softly. "Turbo is my dog. Unfortunately, this dog doesn't belong to you."

Tears streamed down her face, and she buried her head in the golden's coat. "That's where you're wrong. He absolutely belongs to me."

Joe looked across at me.

I shook my head. Stephanie knew right from wrong, and if there's one thing I knew about my daughter, it was that she would always do the right thing.

The rest of the evening was thankfully uneventful. I was exhausted and made an early night of it.

I lay down, unsure whether I'd sleep or if visions of my landlord's face would be etched into my brain. I contemplated taking a melatonin, but before I could make my way to the bathroom to get the pill, I was asleep. My next conscious thought was trying to figure out what the weight I felt on my chest was. When I opened my eyes, it was Aggie. Six pounds could feel like a ton when it was pressed on your chest.

In the morning, I moved Aggie into her crate while I showered and got ready for work. She wasn't happy about the move, but it was easier than worrying about what she might do to the landlord's floors. Although I wasn't quite sure what to expect now that the landlord was dead. Would my lease still be honored, or would I have to find yet another place to live? I made a mental note to ask Stephanie later.

Once I was dressed, I got Aggie and put her outside to take care of her business. When I went into the living room, I saw Stephanie and Joe asleep on the sofa. She had her head on his shoulder, and he had his arm wrapped around her. Apparently, they had resolved their differences. The golden and Turbo were also curled up on the floor beside the fireplace.

I tried not to make any noise, but these wood floors squeaked more than I remembered.

"Mom?"

I turned and whispered, "I'm so sorry, honey. I didn't mean to wake you."

"No need to whisper. I'm up." Joe stretched.

"I'm just leaving for work. Go back to sleep."

Stephanie stood up and stretched. "What time is it?"

"Early." I looked at the clock on the microwave. "Seven."

Joe got up and opened the door to the deck, where Aggie was scratching to come in. Turbo and the golden got up and walked out. "I'll just let the dogs out." He walked outside and closed the door behind him.

"Did you two make up?" I asked casually.

Stephanie shrugged. "Let's just say we reached an agreement."

"Okay." I waited for her to elaborate.

She walked to the cabinet and got two mugs and two single-serve pods and pressed BREW. "I agreed to make a good-faith effort to find the owner. I will contact the shelters, post flyers, and notify the local police. Last night, we posted on some online bulletin boards and social media sites. We agreed that if the owner doesn't come forward with valid proof of ownership within a reasonable amount of time, then I'm keeping him."

"What's the reasonable amount of time?"

She smiled. "We're still negotiating."

"Good luck!"

I left Stephanie and Joe to take care of Aggie and hurried off to work. I felt horrible for missing work after only having been on the job for one day. So I stopped at Da Vinci's and picked up an assortment of pastries, donuts, and tarts as an apology-please-forgive-me peace offering. I parked where Jacob had told me to park and juggled my box of pastries, my purse, my keys, and the employee card key that unlocked the door. I managed to get the door unlocked, but pulling it open proved to be too much. My bundle shifted, and I nearly dropped everything. In the split second before catastrophe hit, I made a decision. I dropped everything else and clutched my box of pastries like a life preserver.

"Here, let me help you with that."

A tall, handsome, well-groomed man came up behind me and picked up my scattered belongings. He then took the card key from my mouth and waved it in front of the card reader. I heard the click, and he opened the door.

"Thank you."

"You're very welcome." He spoke with a slow Southern drawl. "It's not every day I get to come to the aid of a beautiful woman." He smiled.

Heat rose up my neck, and I knew I was blushing like a silly schoolgirl, but it had been a long time since anyone had flirted with me. I was out of practice. Then I did something I hadn't done in over thirty years. I giggled.

"Perhaps you'd allow me to carry these items for you."

"Really, that won't be necessary. I don't want to impose."

"Impose? Why, it would be my pleasure."

Another giggle escaped, and I quickly turned and entered the building. This wasn't the same door I'd entered the day before yesterday, and I was slightly turned around, but I stopped and got my bearings. I turned left and walked a short distance to the elevator. I faced my rescuer. "If you'll just press the button, I can take it from here."

He pressed the button, and the doors quickly opened.

Once inside, I turned and smiled. "I can take it from here."

"Are you sure? I don't mind." He held up my purse and keys.

"No, really. Thank you. I've got it."

Jacob walked into the elevator and took the pastry box, so my hands were free.

I took my purse and keys. Jacob glanced at the stranger and did a double take. "Hello, Freemont." Before the stranger could respond, he used his elbow to press the button for the top floor, and the doors closed right in the stranger's face.

"Freemont?" I turned to look at Jacob.

He nodded. "Freemont Hopewell."

The heat rose again. "I had no idea. I was struggling with the door, and he just came up and helped me."

"You really had no idea who he was?"

I shook my head. "I hope I didn't do anything wrong."

He smiled. "Well, that depends. Are those pastries from Da Vinci's?"

"Yes."

He nodded. "All is forgiven."

The elevator doors opened, and Jacob stood in the doorway so I could precede him before following along behind me.

I went to my office and unlocked the door. By the time I hung up my coat and put my purse and keys away, I could smell the glorious aroma of coffee. I followed my nose to Linda Kay's office and stood outside the door and inhaled the wonderful fragrance. On the conference table, the pastries were displayed on a beautiful silver tray. Even from a distance, I could tell the tray was real silver and worth a small fortune. Next to the tray was a French press.

"Come in." Linda Kay smiled and motioned for me to enter.

I looked over the spread. "Wow. You really know how to entertain."

She motored from behind her desk to the conference table.

Jacob placed cloth napkins on the table next to silver tongs and bone china cups and saucers.

"Well, if you're going to eat, you might as well do it in style." Jacob smiled.

"Access to beautiful things is one of the perks of working in a museum. However, I don't believe in putting your best items away on a shelf and only using them once or twice a year." She put a napkin on her lap. "The antiques in our possession weren't just for holidays and special occasions. They were used on a daily basis." She took a sip of the coffee that Jacob had poured for her. "Some of these were gifted by the family, and some are items I've collected over the years. Unless the pieces are delicate or fragile, we use them."

"Well, this is amazing. Everything looks so nice and inviting." I smiled.

"Good. Then, let's eat." Linda Kay picked up a silver fork and cut into a strawberry tart. "I just love Da Vinci's strawberry tarts." Gooey filling oozed out of the sides of her mouth.

Jacob poured coffee into one of the cups and handed it to me, and then sat down and tucked into a cheese Danish.

Settled at the conference table with pastries and coffee, we ate in a companionable silence for several moments, savoring each delicious morsel. The only noise was the clink of our silverware or the clank of the china cups as they hit the china saucers. From time to time, an occasional and unconscious moan of delight escaped one of our lips.

After two cups of coffee and more pastries than I wanted to admit to eating, I leaned back and sighed. I then told Linda Kay and Jacob about the horror of finding a dead body. They were shocked and naturally curious. When we'd exhausted the topic, Jacob left to get back to work.

I started to rise but sat at Linda Kay's request.

I experienced a moment of panic that the pastries weren't sufficient to make up for missing work yesterday.

However, Linda Kay's smile put my fears at ease. "So I heard you met Freemont Hopewell today." She looked stern, but a twitch at the corners of her mouth told me she was joking.

"I'm so sorry. I didn't know who he was. He just came up behind me and offered to help, and I was juggling the pastries and my purse and my card key and—"

Linda Kay held up a hand to stem my flood of words. "It's okay. You don't have to apologize."

"But he doesn't work here anymore, and I shouldn't have let him in the building, even if he was helping—"

"It's okay. Freemont is a Hopewell. He doesn't work here anymore, but he isn't banned from the building." She chuckled. "I was just curious what you thought about him." She grinned. "If that color in your cheeks is any indication, I'd say he made quite the impression."

I stared at her for a few seconds and then burst out laughing.

"Now why don't you sit back and tell me all about it."

"Well, I think he's very handsome and charming."

She waited.

"I only spent a few minutes with him, so I didn't get to form an opinion about him, other than the fact he's very good-looking."

She smiled. "Yes, he is."

I glanced at my cup and tried to form a question. "Is he...married?"

"No. He's single."

I took a sip of my coffee to hide the smile I wasn't able to stop from forming.

"Freemont is one of the most eligible bachelors in Chattanooga. He's been photographed with various widows and divorcees, but no one has managed to wrangle him."

"Why not?" I hurriedly continued, "Not that I'm looking for a husband or anything."

Linda Kay shrugged. "No idea. My husband thinks he hasn't found anyone wealthy enough to keep him in the lifestyle he thinks he deserves." She shrugged again.

"So it sounds like you don't like him."

"Actually, I do like him. It's hard not to. Like you said, he's very charming. He's good-looking and always a perfect gentleman..."

"But?"

She sighed. "But he can be a bit of a snob at times, and he certainly doesn't know anything about bookkeeping, but then, I don't know if that's his fault. I was ordered to hire him."

"Well, I'm not looking for romance. I'm still adjusting to being single and coping with the emotions from my husband's death."

"That's a lot to work through."

"Besides, all he did was help me open a couple of doors. It's not likely that I'll see him again."

She smiled and took a sip of coffee. Something about her smile made me ask.

"What?"

"Nothing. It's just that there is a museum gala next month—to raise money for charity, of course. You don't *have* to attend, but it's expected that the senior staff support the events. Technically, you're a contractor, not officially on staff, but...it might help me to convince the board to hire you full-time if you make a good impression." She sipped her coffee.

"No pressure. Just show up at the gala and impress the board of directors?"

Jacob sailed into the room and refilled the water. He grinned as he cleared away the dirty dishes and then turned and walked out.

I worked the rest of the day in my office and tried not to think of Freemont Hopewell, which was more challenging than I would have thought. The fact that my work involved trying to make sense of his bookkeeping and accounting left me puzzled and frustrated. Thankfully, Freemont hadn't worked here long. The previous accountant had used the standard accrual accounting method. Everything was neat and orderly. All of the amounts balanced. It was a thing of beauty. I had yet to divine exactly what method Freemont had used. Frequently, columns didn't balance, and when they did, there was usually a miscellaneous entry added in the exact amount needed for the balance to zero out; however, there was never any notation that justified the entry.

"This doesn't make any sense," I muttered.

"Anything I can do to help?"

I jumped. I hadn't heard Jacob enter.

"No, I'm sorry. I was just talking to myself." I smiled. "I didn't hear you come in."

He smiled. "I knocked, but you were so engrossed in those books, you must not have heard." He walked to my desk with a tray. "Linda Kay says you have to keep your strength up." He placed the tray with steaming-hot broccoli cheddar soup and a chicken salad sandwich on my desk.

"Hmmm." I sniffed. "That smells amazing." I looked at the clock on the wall. "It can't be that late."

Jacob nodded. "Yes, it's almost three, and you haven't budged from your desk."

I opened my desk drawer and pulled out my purse. "How much do I owe you?"

He shook his head. "Nothing. Courtesy of Linda Kay."

I pulled out a twenty. "Then please let me pay her back."

He stood at the door with one hand on his hip and another on the knob. "That's between you and Linda Kay, but since I've known her a lot longer than you, let me tell you she will be insulted if you try to repay her kindness."

"Really?"

He nodded. "It's a Southern thing. We're always trying to feed people and get them married off." He winked. "Now eat up." He walked out and closed the door behind him. After a brief pause, he reopened the door and stuck his head in. "By the way, you can place orders online from the café and have lunch delivered. They will even run a tab." He smiled. "One of the perks of working here." He ducked back out and closed the door.

The soup smelled wonderful and tasted even better. Once I got a good whiff, my stomach growled. I devoured the soup and sandwich in record time. While I ate the sandwich, I quickly went online to the café's website and set up a tab. I ordered lunch for the rest of the week and gave them my credit card number.

Something told me Linda Kay wouldn't accept my money, so I wracked my brain, thinking of a way to pay her back for her kindness. She was a very nice person. I swiveled around in my chair and stared out the window at the view. I would thoroughly enjoy working here full-time. I liked Linda Kay and Jacob.

There was a tap on the door.

"Come in." I swiveled around.

Jacob entered with a beautiful bouquet of flowers. They were a lovely mixture of bright orange Asiatic lilies, pink carnations, red asters, and lavender button poms. They were in a glass vase.

"Wow. Is that for me?"

Jacob smiled and lifted an eyebrow as he handed me the card. He quickly left the room.

I took a whiff of the flowers and then opened the card.

Something to brighten your day the way your smile brightened mine.
—Freemont

Jacob re-entered the room carrying two vases; one was a beautiful crystal, while the other was Asian. "The flowers are lovely, but that cheap vase will have to go." He held up the two options. "Which do you prefer?"

I stared. "They're both beautiful, but the Asian one seems a bit busy, don't you think?"

He stared at the vases. "You're right. We'll definitely go with the Tiffany."

I nearly choked. "Tiffany? You don't mean *Tiffany*, like real *the Tiffany*, as in *Breakfast at Tiffany's*?"

He smiled. "Yes, darling, I mean Louis Comfort Tiffany, son of Charles Lewis Tiffany. *The Tiffany*." He placed the flowers into the vase. "This is a peacock blue favrile glass vase designed by Louis Comfort Tiffany circa nineteen hundred." He recited as if conducting a tour as he arranged the flowers.

I nearly collapsed when he poured water into the vase. "I can't believe you're putting water in that vase."

He turned to look at me as he placed the vase on my desk. "Well, we wouldn't want your flowers to die, would we?" He smiled.

"But that vase is a *Tiffany*. We can't actually use it. I mean, aren't there rules about using the museum's possessions. Besides, it must have cost a small fortune."

"It did cost a fortune, but it doesn't belong to the museum." He grinned. "That's Linda Kay's vase, and she believes in using objects, not just putting them on a pedestal and admiring them."

"But I would be terrified someone would break it or"—I whispered— "steal it."

He waved a hand. "It's insured." He turned and walked out. At the door, he turned around and came back. He picked up the Asian vase. "Mustn't forget this. Perhaps we'll use the Ming another time." He grinned and pranced out of the room.

I stared at the door for several seconds and then tentatively leaned toward the flowers and smiled as I took a big whiff.

"They are beautiful." Linda Kay motored into the room. "And that vase is perfect."

"I can't believe you have a real Tiffany vase and that you're letting me use it." I rushed over and hugged her. After a few seconds, I quickly stood up. "I'm so sorry, I'm sure that's not allowed, I didn't mean to...I mean, I haven't worked in a long time, and I know there are all kinds of rules about harassment, and I'm sorry."

Linda Kay smiled. "Honey, you're in the South. We believe in hugs." She grinned. "Well, I believe in them anyway."

I reached down and hugged her again. "I've never been this close to an actual Tiffany vase." I stood up and stared at the vase of flowers on the desk.

"Well, you just need to get used to it." She smiled and leaned forward. "Touch it. You know you want to."

I tentatively reached out a finger and touched the vase. "I just touched a real Tiffany vase."

"Oh my God. Are we still talking about the vase?" Jacob waltzed into the room. He turned to Linda Kay. "Your husband, Edward, is waiting for you." He turned to me. "Didn't you mention something about obedience class?"

I glanced at my watch. "I completely forgot."

"That's what I'm here for." He smiled. "Now get out of here, and I'll lock up. You can admire the flowers and the Tiffany vase tomorrow."

I grabbed my coat and purse, took one last glance at the flowers and the beautiful vase, and headed out.

Chapter 9

I made it home with just enough time to change into comfortable clothes and shoes. I changed Aggie's collar to the flat leather one Dixie recommended and grabbed the six-foot matching leather leash. I had convinced Stephanie and Joe to come along by bribing them with the promise of dinner at Dixie's mountaintop home. I grabbed the string cheese from the fridge, and three adults and three dogs piled into my SUV and headed to the East Tennessee Dog Club, which was located at the base of the mountain we'd need to scale to reach Dixie's house.

The building wasn't fancy. It was long and flat, with a metal roof and a gravel parking lot. However, according to Dixie, the selling point for the dog club purchasing the building was the fact that there were over three acres of land behind the building, most of which was fenced and provided plenty of space for parking.

We pulled into the parking lot. I recognized Dixie's RV and pulled in beside her.

"That's one nice RV." Joe admired the luxury vehicle Dixie used to travel around the country with her standard poodles.

"It's nicer than most houses inside too," I said as we disembarked with our dogs. "She used to drive her standard poodles, Chyna and Leia, around in style when she was competing in conformation."

"What exactly is conformation?" Stephanie asked.

"Have you ever seen the *Westminster Dog Show* on television?" I asked. Stephanie and Joe both nodded.

"Well, that's conformation."

"Actually, conformation is where dogs compete against the breed standard." Dixie came outside and opened the door to her RV. Two of the most regal black standard poodles on the planet pranced out of the RV. They stretched several times and then walked over to a grassy area near the side of the building, squatted, and took care of their business. When they were done, they walked over to Dixie and sat by her side.

At the sight of her friends Leia and Chyna, Aggie had gotten excited and was barking and running, trying to get them to play. I was struggling to keep her quiet and had managed to get her leash wrapped around my legs. Eventually, I gave up and bent down and picked her up. "When can I learn to train my dog to behave like that?" I pointed at the standards.

Dixie grinned. "Aggie is a good dog. She's a quick learner. All poodles are. Once she understands what you want from her, she'll be able to do it. However," she turned to face me, "the training is more for you than it is for her."

"Great." I followed Dixie and her beautifully behaved dogs into the building and hoped I would learn as quickly as the poodles.

Joe and Turbo and Stephanie and the golden retriever came behind.

Inside, the building was crude. It had a concrete floor with metal walls that weren't insulated. There were rustic shelves that weren't fancy but serviceable. In the main section of the building, there were various pieces of equipment affixed to the wall by chains. There were two large inverted Vs, one on each side of the room. In addition, there was what appeared to be a ramp and a balance beam. The floor in the main section had a large rubber mat.

Dixie stood in the middle of the floor and welcomed everyone. Leia and Chyna lay in their queenly fashion on either side of her.

Stephanie and Joe found two folding chairs and sat.

Dixie took attendance and then welcomed all of us. "Welcome to East Tennessee Dog Club—or ETDC, as we call it. My name is Dixie Jefferson." She started by introducing her dogs. She walked about six feet away from them while she talked. Her dogs didn't budge from their positions. She then turned to face her dogs. "Chyna, come."

One of the standards stood and walked to Dixie. She didn't stop until her nose was at Dixie's belly button. Then she stopped and sat. Dixie made a move with her left hand and the dog stood and scooted its butt around so she was sitting perfectly straight at Dixie's left side.

We all applauded.

After a brief moment, she said, "Okay."

Only then did Chyna move. Dixie rewarded her with a treat, which she pulled from a small pouch she wore around her waist. She bent down and gave the dog a pet. "This is Champion Chyna, Ninth Wonder of the

World. She's a champion show dog in both AKC and UKC, and she has obedience and agility titles." She then used a hand signal, and Leia moved from her prostrate position into a sit. Then Dixie made an elaborate arm motion, and Leia moved in front of her and sat. With a hand signal, Leia then moved to sit beside Chyna. "And this is Grand Champion Galactic Imperial Resistance Leader, or Leia."

A short man with a bald, egg-shaped head and a large mustache, who had a choke collar on a large German shepherd, raised his hand. "What does that mean?" He looked around the crowd for support but didn't get much.

"The titles champion and grand champion mean both of these dogs have competed in and won titles in what is known as conformation, which is where each breed of dog recognized by the American Kennel Club is judged against the breed standard. If you've seen the *Westminster Dog Show* on television, that's conformation."

The bald egghead snorted. "A beauty contest for dogs."

"Actually, it's not a beauty contest." Dixie crossed her arms but maintained a smile. "You have a German shepherd dog, sometimes called an Alsatian. There is basically no real difference between Alsatians and German shepherds. Alsatians were from the Alsace region of France, and German shepherds were from Germany. Between the wars, the British didn't want to call their dogs German and changed the name to Alsatians. Later, the name was changed back to German shepherd dog. It's one of the few breeds that includes dog in the name, at least in English." She walked over to the dog. "This is a breed that is a good working dog." She held out her hand. "May I?"

Egghead handed her the leash. "He's a big dog, not like those princesses." He chuckled. "Sure you can handle him?"

Dixie grinned. "I'm sure." Once she had the leash, she removed the choke collar. She took a flat collar and simple leather leash from a back pocket and put it around the dog's neck. She then took a treat from her pocket and showed it to the dog. Initially, he got on his hind legs and attempted to take the treat. Dixie made a quick leash correction. "Off." He tried once more. She repeated the movement and the command. The dog stopped jumping and sat. When his butt was down on the floor, she smiled, gave him the treat, and petted him. "German shepherds are smart and eager to please. They're energetic." She ran her hands over the dog while she spoke. "They should have a deep chest and be solid." She picked up the leash and walked. The dog pranced beside her. Eventually, she broke into a run around the inside of the building. The dog adjusted his gait to match hers. When she stopped, the dog stopped and looked at her. She adjusted the dog's legs and then moved out to the end of the six-foot leash and stood. The dog stood without moving. "They should be alert, and they require a good amount of physical and mental exercise." She released the dog and gave him a treat. The dog wagged his tail and stared lovingly at her. She petted him affectionately and then walked him back to Egghead and handed him the leash. "This is a very fine example of the breed. During conformation, the judge compares each dog against the breed standard. Is the dog the proper weight, is it alert, and is it ready to work? What does the dog's gait look like?"

Egghead took the leash and looked sheepish.

The other people in the room all applauded.

"But we aren't here to learn conformation," Dixie said. "We're here to learn basic obedience." She walked back to the center of the room. "What I showed you with my dogs was what we teach in competition obedience. This is to show you what is possible if you want to keep working with your dogs."

Egghead raised his hand again. "That's all great, but when would we ever need all of that hand-signal stuff?" He chuckled.

I noticed a few of the people roll their eyes.

"For normal everyday life, you may never need hand signals."

"I think it's great, and I'd love to be able to do that." A large African American woman with a white dog I recognized as a West Highland terrier stared at Egghead. "So I'd appreciate it if you would shut up and let her continue with the class."

There were lots of grunts of approval, and a couple of people applauded.

"Thank you, but it's okay." Dixie looked at Egghead. "I don't mind skeptics. All I ask is that you keep an open mind."

Everyone nodded.

"Good. Now, we have a couple of guests with us tonight." She pointed to Stephanie and Joe. "Stephanie has found this beautiful dog." She petted the golden retriever, who stood and wagged his tail enthusiastically. "We don't know much about him, but someone has spent quite a bit of time training him." She quickly demonstrated the hand signals she'd used previously when my neighbor had tried to claim him. Once again, the dog followed the signals and was rewarded with a treat and lavish praise. "Joe is a police officer with the Lighthouse Dunes, Indiana, K-9 Unit, and this is his partner, Turbo."

The crowd applauded.

"If we have time, perhaps Joe and Turbo will do a demonstration for us at the end of class?"

Joe shrugged and nodded.

"Great. Now, let's get down to work."

Dixie was an excellent instructor. She stayed in the middle of the room with her two dogs and positioned each of us around the outside like the numbers of a clock. She demonstrated each command with one of her two dogs and then walked around from person to person and watched as we emulated what she had shown us. The first lesson was about teaching your dog to come when called and teaching the dog to sit on command.

"One thing I want to stress is the importance of only giving a command once. You need to give each command one time and one time only. If your dog does not obey, then you must either go and get him or physically place him in position."

Dixie split the class into two groups, small dogs and large dogs. She then had us take the small dogs off leash and allowed the dogs to play. Aggie and the West Highland Terrier were roughly the same size and quickly engaged in a game of chase. After a few moments, the Westie's owner and I were instructed to call our dogs. Needless to say, neither of the dogs wanted to leave their play, and both ignored us; we were instructed to approach the dogs, attach their leashes, and pull them away. She then did the same thing with the big dog group and got the same result. Unfortunately, attaching the leashes to the big dogs proved a lot more challenging than it had for the small dogs. Max, the German shepherd, used his fast gait to play keep away from Egghead, who got more and more frustrated. Eventually, he managed to corner Max and attached the leash. Frustrated, he lifted his hand to strike the dog but was stopped when Dixie grabbed his hand.

"We *never* hit our dogs."

From the way Max cowered, it wasn't the first time he'd felt Egghead's wrath.

"Don't tell me you're one of those bleeding-heart liberals who don't believe in spanking your kids either?"

Dixie maintained her composure, but her voice left no uncertainty as to her meaning. "Actually, I was never blessed with children, so I don't really have a position on whether or not a parent should spank their children. However, the difference is that this dog doesn't speak the same language as you and me. He doesn't know what you want him to do. Beating a dog who doesn't obey your command is like beating someone from another country who doesn't speak English. Besides, you never want your dog to fear you. Your dog should respect you but never be afraid of you, because then he will never want to come to you." She released Egghead's arm.

She turned back to face the entire class. "I'm sure some of you were wondering about my request that you bring treats that your dog will sell his soul for." She looked at the nods around the room. "Here's why. Our dogs don't speak the same language that you and I do. However, they want to learn. So, if we give them an extra-special treat that they love, then regardless of how excited they are to play, they will eagerly come running to you to get that treat." She turned back to Egghead. "Let's try again." She asked a tall thin woman with long brown hair and a rambunctious black dog with a white spot on his chest, to release the dog, who was named Jac. Max and Jac immediately began to play. After a few minutes, she took a treat out of her pouch and put it in front of Max's nose. "Max, come." Max immediately turned away from his playmate. Dixie took several steps backward to Egghead. When he was there, she instructed Egghead to attach the leash. Once the leash was attached, she gave the dog the treat and tons of praise.

"We want Max to associate you with good things, like hot dogs and cheese. So when you call, regardless of what he's doing, he will gladly give that up to be with you. He needs to always want to come to you, the first time you call."

Egghead looked at his dog as he sat by his side.

"Now, pet him and tell him what a good boy he is."

Egghead petted and scratched behind the German shepherd's ear.

Max leaned into his hand and eventually turned and gave it a lick. Egghead cracked the first real smile I'd seen from him.

The African American woman raised her hand. "Why is it so important that they come the very first time you call?" She looked at her dog. "Snowball is pretty good about coming when I call her most times, but sometimes I have to repeat myself."

"If your dog is about to run into the street in front of traffic, you don't have time to repeat yourself multiple times. Or, let's say your dog is about to eat something you know is poisonous like antifreeze. You need your dog to obey your commands the first time. It can save his life."

"Lord have mercy. I never thought about that," she said.

Egghead mumbled, "I live on the corner of a busy street. Cars plow through there all the time." He stared at Max.

Dixie saved the last ten minutes of class for Joe and Turbo's presentation, while she went toward the office area.

Joe did a lot of presentations for schools and was good at talking in front of groups. He explained how acute a dog's sense of smell was. He talked about the various scents Turbo had been trained to detect, then said, "I asked Dixie to hide." He took Dixie's jacket and put it to the dog's nose. Then he released Turbo and gave him the command to find. Turbo sniffed around the room and followed the path Dixie had taken. Eventually, he moved near the bleachers and sat.

"Sitting is how he indicates he's got something." He secured the dog's harness and lifted the bottom of the bleachers.

Dixie rolled out from her hiding place.

The group applauded, and Turbo was rewarded with his treat.

Dixie stood and dusted herself off. "Well, that's enough for tonight. I want all of you to practice getting your dogs to come when called and to sit. Next week, we'll work on down and heel." Before we left, she passed out flyers about the East Tennessee Dog Club and the upcoming events. The club had an obedience show coming up, and she encouraged everyone to stop by and observe. Aggie and I were already planning to join the dog club, but it would be nice to have other novices join who were as green as we were.

Egghead spent ten minutes in conversation with Dixie after class. Eventually, he left, and Dixie locked up. I still wasn't prepared to drive up Lookout Mountain, so we agreed to go in the RV. However, Joe felt he wanted to give it a try. So Aggie and I rode in the RV, and Joe and Stephanie followed us with their two dogs. Dixie took the twists and turns a lot slower since she knew she was being followed; however, I made the mistake of looking out at the view, which was a complete drop-off, and nearly lost my lunch. I rode the rest of the way with my head back, eyes closed, and hands clutching the door's armrest. I think Dixie talked, but I wasn't paying attention.

When she pulled into the driveway, she turned off the engine. "It's okay. You can open your eyes now."

"Praise God almighty!"

She laughed. "It wasn't that bad." She turned to look as Joe pulled up behind her. "See, Joe made it just fine."

It took several deep breaths before I was able to release the seat belt and get out of the car. My legs felt wobbly. I looked at Stephanie and felt comforted by seeing I wasn't the only one who looked a little green.

She stumbled out of the car. "Now I understand what you were talking about."

Joe shook his head. "That was definitely an experience." He wiped the sweat off his head. "I can understand why you didn't want to make the drive."

Dixie's husband, Beau, walked up and smacked Joe on the back. "Welcome." He held out a bottle of beer. "You look like you could use this." He laughed and smacked Joe again.

"Thank you." Joe took the bottle but didn't drink it.

Beau stepped up to Stephanie and gave her a friendly bear hug before moving on. He was a large man, well over six feet. He wore his hair short and always seemed to have a smile. He had been the star quarterback on his high school and college football teams. An injury in college left him with a large scar over his knee and a limp when the weather was damp. After college, he started a tech company and made tons of money.

He moved to help Dixie remove some equipment from the back of the RV.

I moved closer to Joe. "Do you think you can drive down? If not, we can get Dixie to drive us. Beau will follow and bring her back."

He shook his head. "No. I can do it." He handed Stephanie his beer. "However, I think I'll skip the alcohol. I need to keep my wits about me."

"Good idea." Stephanie took a swig.

Joe smiled. "I didn't think you liked beer."

She took another drink. "I hate beer, but I need something to steady my nerves."

Once you got to the top of Lookout Mountain, the views were spectacular. The surrounding landscape was relatively flat, and you didn't feel as though you were perched atop a peak. Beau and Dixie lived in a three-bedroom, four-bath Frank Lloyd Wright–inspired home that was over three thousand square feet. It had a brick and stone exterior. From the road, the house looked modest and unassuming. However, when you entered, the spectacular views and luxurious design really hit you. Stephanie and I followed Dixie inside, while Beau and Joe lingered outside.

Stephanie gasped. In addition to the mahogany and travertine floors and the granite counters, the back of the house was a wall of windows that overlooked the city of Chattanooga, the Tennessee River, and the surrounding mountain ranges. There were two levels, and each had a stone deck with breathtaking views. The lower level had a heated dipping pool, and the home was impeccably designed to maximize the space, light, and million-dollar views.

On my first visit, I had been conscious of each move Aggie made. However, Beau and Dixie quickly put me at ease. Even though they lived in a lovely home, which I was sure would sell for millions, they were relaxed and comfortable.

"WOW!" Stephanie said in a reverential whisper, like most people used at church. "That's the most amazing view."

Dixie took her on a tour and explained that the house was a dump when they purchased it twenty years ago. "There was actually a tree that had grown inside the brick and through the roof."

The home had been owned by an elderly couple. "There was hideous green shag carpet and velvet wallpaper in practically every room." Dixie laughed. "Beau thought I'd lost my mind when I told him we could make it into our dream house." She smiled.

"I love that you have two laundry rooms," I said as Dixie took us to the lower level of the home.

"It's very convenient. Initially, I thought two laundry rooms was a waste of money for two people. However, it's really convenient with the dogs."

Dixie had turned the second laundry area into a dog-grooming area. She had a large walk-in tub where she could bathe the dogs and a ramp that led up to her grooming table so she could easily prepare her dogs for shows without injuring her back lifting them onto grooming tables. The lower-level deck curved around and provided easy access to the side of the house, where she parked the RV. We found the men outside on the deck. Beau had an outdoor kitchen that was twice the size of the one in my home in Lighthouse Dunes. There were four large televisions on the wall, which he had on and turned to a football game. He was tending to a grill, where several whole chickens were impaled on a long spit. Joe lounged in a chair on the deck while three poodles, a golden, and a Plott hound lay on the floor chewing on all-natural, gourmet dog treats designed to look like marrow-filled bones—large bones for the bigger dogs and a small, toy poodle–sized bone for Aggie, which demonstrated Dixie's thoughtfulness to think of Aggie.

The aroma from the grill made my mouth water.

"That smells incredible." Stephanie's stomach growled.

"It'll be done in a few." Beau laughed. "Grab some of those snacks and a glass of wine or another beer."

By "snacks," Beau meant a huge spread of fresh fruit salad, Caesar salad, iceberg salad, at least five different types of cheese on crackers, marinated vegetables, baked potatoes with toppings, and grilled bread. On another counter, there were cookies, pies, and cakes.

The weather was cool, but they had heat lamps and a firepit, which made the area warm and toasty.

We loaded our plates and sat to enjoy an evening of conversation and delicious food. I talked about my new job. Dixie and Beau were patrons of the museum and were acquainted with Linda Kay. As Chattanooga natives, they were, of course, familiar with the Hopewells.

"Everything was delicious. So what do you know about Freemont Hopewell?" I took a sip of wine and was thankful it was too dark for them to notice the heat rising to my cheeks.

"He's a Hopewell." Dixie sipped her wine and shrugged. "Thinks quite a bit of himself."

"Rumored to be a bit of a playboy. Always shows up at local benefits and fund-raisers with some beautiful woman on his arm," Beau said. "Last year, he was seen running around with that supermodel Linda Herold."

"I thought she was dating that famous NFL quarterback," Joe said.

"Yeah, Hopewell was last season." Beau chuckled. "Ouch."

Dixie smiled sweetly at her husband. "Oh dear, was that your knee?"

"Anybody recently?" I asked casually, but not casually enough to escape Dixie or Stephanie's notice.

Beau stood up. "I think Joe and I need to make our exit before this conversation turns into one of those women's flowery romance shows Dixie likes to watch. Or before I have to get a knee replacement." Joe quickly gathered his drink, and they hightailed it inside and headed to the area Dixie described as Beau's man cave, which included one of the largest televisions I'd ever seen inside a house, as well as a pool table, a bar, and a game table for poker.

"Mom, is there something you want to tell us?" Stephanie stared with one raised eyebrow.

"I don't know what you mean?" I hedged.

"I think you know exactly what she means." Dixie turned her seat so she was facing me directly.

"Now, what's going on with Freemont Hopewell?"

Dixie and Stephanie leaned their faces on their hands and stared at me.

I hesitated but eventually caved in under their intense stares and giggled. "Well, I ran into him today on my way into work." I quickly told them of the encounter, short as it was, and the flowers that had arrived.

"Flowers? You must have made quite an impression on Mr. Hopewell." Dixie grinned.

I shrugged. "Maybe. He's very handsome." I hesitated. "I'm not sure if I'm ready for any type of relationship. Not that this is going to turn into anything. I mean, he may just be really nice and thought I seemed pathetic, and so he sent me flowers."

"Mom, men don't send flowers unless they like you." Stephanie smiled. "So he at least likes you. I think it's great. You should date. Have fun. Enjoy yourself."

I laughed. "It's been so long since I've dated, I don't even remember how."

"It's like riding a bike." Stephanie hugged me.

"I was never very good at that either."

"I have to go downtown tomorrow for lunch with the Chattanooga Historic Society. Maybe I'll swing by and see those flowers."

We talked a little longer. I admired the city lights below until I remembered we still had to head back down the mountain. I was very concerned about Joe driving down the mountain, especially in the dark. However, I needn't have bothered. Joe was a good driver and took his time. There were no streetlights and only light from the moon and the city lights from the valley to illuminate the way, but once he made it down the mountain, he was easily able to make the short distance to the main roads and then took the interstate home.

Joe pulled the car in front of the house and stopped.

I keep the button for the garage door on the visor. When he didn't immediately push the button to open the garage door, I reached from the back between the seats and pointed toward the button.

Joe held up a hand. Something in his demeanor and the overall climate within the vehicle, which had moments earlier been friendly and warm as we talked about our evening, was now cold and foreboding.

All conversation stopped. Joe reached into a duffel bag under the seat and pulled out a gun.

"Stay here. Lock the doors," he said in a steely voice that froze the words in my throat. He fixed his blue, laser-sharp gaze on Stephanie and then me. "Do not follow me. If I'm not out in five minutes, call nine-one-one." He got out of the car and went to the back and opened the door for Turbo. In a flash, he put on the vest that instantly transformed Turbo from a house pet to a highly trained police dog.

Aggie growled and lunged at the door. She wanted to get out, but I clutched her to my chest. Surprisingly, the golden retriever seemed excited rather than anxious and looked on, tail wagging with an occasional whimper. Nevertheless, I held fast to his collar.

Gun raised, Joe and Turbo approached the front door, which I now noticed was open.

Chapter 10

I held my cell phone. At some point, I had grabbed Stephanie's hand, which I noticed trembled slightly. I gave it a squeeze and tried not to notice how cold her hand felt. We sat in cold silence. Both Aggie and the golden sat at attention. All eyes were fixed on the front door. I glanced at my phone, noting the time. It felt like an hour, but only four minutes had passed. Then Turbo and Joe came out; Joe's gun was lowered, and his shoulders were relaxed. Stephanie and I exhaled.

He opened the door. "The house was ransacked, but whoever did it is gone."

"Do you want me to call the police?" I held out my phone.

"I already did."

That was when we heard the sirens.

Officer Lewis was the first police officer to arrive.

Whoever broke in had apparently been looking for something. They had rummaged and ransacked the house. Drawers had been opened and dumped out.

I nearly collapsed when I saw the extent of the damage. Flour and sugar were dumped out. Dog-food bags were cut open and left all over the kitchen floor. Every drawer was opened, and my clothes were strewn all over. After all the work of getting moved in, someone had undone it in a matter of hours. I walked around, speechless, staring openmouthed at the damage. It was overwhelming, and I felt paralyzed, thinking about where to start. The dogs must have thought it was Christmas because Aggie, the golden, and Turbo, who was no longer wearing his vest and had returned to pet status, were gulping down dog food and sugar at record speed.

Joe and Stephanie put the dogs outside to prevent further binging. I flopped down on the sofa and stared.

Stephanie leaned against the counter and pulled out her phone. She sent several text messages and eventually put her phone away and walked to the sofa. "Mom, are you okay?" She sat beside me.

"Why would anyone do this?"

Officer Lewis walked over. "Can you tell if anything's been stolen?"

I stared at him as though he were speaking a foreign language. "Stolen? You must be kidding." I spread my hands. "I have no idea in all of this mess."

He must have sensed I was on edge because he didn't press the point. "Mrs. Echosby, do you have any idea what the perpetrator could have been looking for?"

Again, I stared and shook my head. "I've only been here a few days. I don't know what they think I could have of value in the flour or sugar canisters." I stared at Joe. "Is there some drug that kids make from flour and dog food?"

He shook his head.

"Then why?" I spread my arms wide to encompass the totality of the devastation.

"Mrs. Echosby, do you have any enemies?"

"What about that crazy neighbor you hit?" Stephanie asked.

I shook my head but then stopped.

"What?" Lewis asked. "You hit someone?"

"No." I shook my head. "Well, yes, I did hit him, but I don't think he would..."

"Maybe you should tell me about this man." He stood, pen and notepad poised to write down everything.

I hesitated.

"If you know of anyone who has anything against you, we need to know."

I told Officer Lewis about the altercations I'd had with Theodore Livingston. The moment I mentioned his name, a look of recognition and something else crossed his face. When I was done, Officer Lewis rubbed the back of his neck.

"Theodore Livingston is a crackpot, but I've never known him to do anything like this." He paced in front of the sofa, carefully avoiding the debris. "However, maybe getting beat up by a woman in front of the entire neighborhood sent him over the top." His lips twitched, and there was a gleam in his eyes.

"I baked him cookies as a peace offering, and he took them. So you'd think if he ate my cookies, he wouldn't have felt the need for revenge."

"Maybe he didn't like the cookies," Officer Lewis said.

I stared.

"Just kidding." He held up his hands. "I'll have a talk with Mr. Livingston." He looked around. "In the meantime, are you okay?"

I assured him I was.

Joe let him out and then walked over to the sofa, where Stephanie and I were sitting in stunned silence. "Stephanie and I are scheduled to leave tomorrow. I wish I could stay longer, but I have to get back to work."

I shook my head. "I can't let myself give in to fear." I could feel the argument coming and held up my hand to stave it off. "Aggie and I will be fine. The house has an alarm system. I didn't think I would need it, but I will use it." I patted Stephanie's hand. "I know you two have to get back to work. Please don't worry. I'll be fine." I smiled.

"I don't think you should stay here alone. I know you don't like the drive down the mountain, but maybe you should pack a bag and stay with Dixie," Joe said.

"She won't be alone." Stephanie looked up. "I'm staying." Her eyes were steel, and her jaw was set.

"Don't you have a court case or something?" I asked.

"I sent a text to my boss letting him know I was staying an extra week." She clasped my hand and gave it a squeeze.

"Are you sure?" I asked.

She nodded.

Joe rubbed the back of his neck. I felt sorry for him. Instead of just worrying about me, he now had Stephanie to worry about. However, he merely took a few deep breaths and nodded. "Okay, I have a friend who works with the TBI, the Tennessee Bureau of Investigation; his name is Dennis Olson." He pulled out his phone. "I'm going to give him a call and ask him to come by and check on you both." He sensed the objection that was rising in both Stephanie and me, but he held up one finger and gave us his steely I-Mean-Business-and-Don't-Even-Try-Me policeman stare, which stopped us both cold. "This is not negotiable. I care about both of you, and if I can't be here, then at least I can have some peace knowing Red is keeping an eye out."

"Red?" Stephanie asked.

"His name is Dennis, but everyone calls him Red." He called. After a few moments of small talk, he quickly brought his friend up to speed on what had happened and got a promise from him to come by to keep an eye on us. Conversation over, he hung up. He must have expected more arguing because he planted his feet and crossed his arms.

"Thank you." I stood and went over and gave him a hug.

Stephanie followed and gave him a hug and a passionate kiss. After a few seconds, she pulled away.

"Now I'm tired. I'm going to bed." I walked to the back door. There were three dogs sitting with noses pressed against the glass. I let them in, picked Aggie up before she could make a dash for the kitchen, and headed to the bedroom. "I'll clean that up tomorrow."

I found it hard to believe I slept, but, sure enough, I woke up with Aggie lying on my head. When I opened my eyes, there were two brown ones staring back at me. I must have been more tired than I'd realized, because I hadn't bothered to pick up any of the clothes, shoes, or clutter the intruder had left for me. Maybe it was knowing there was an armed policeman asleep in the house along with a highly trained police K-9 dog that I had no doubt would rip an intruder apart if ordered. Or maybe it was the hope that after searching the house and finding nothing, because there was nothing to find, the intruder would move on.

Regardless, I stretched and got out of bed. I put Aggie outside and returned as many things to their rightful place as possible before hopping into the shower. While the hot water pelted my skin, I made a mental checklist. I was confident Dixie would be able to help me find a cleaning company to get the house back in order. The intruder had kicked in the front door, breaking the lock and splitting the wood around the hinges. Thankfully, Joe had noticed another door in the garage, which he and Officer Lewis had used to replace the front door. However, I needed to phone Mrs. Hansen and notify her of the break-in, a task I wasn't looking forward to. Apart from the fact she was most certainly mourning the loss of her son, the last thing she needed to think about was a tenant. Nevertheless, it needed to be done. I needed to get the security system transferred over into my name in order to activate it, plus I needed groceries and dog food. There was a lot to be done, but I needed to get to work. I couldn't possibly ask Linda Kay for two days off during my first week on a new job. She was understanding, but that was a lot to expect of any employer.

By the time I was dressed, I had a good idea of what needed to be done. I opened the bedroom door and stopped in amazement. I'd mentally prepared myself for the mess. However, seeing the living room and kitchen completely cleaned was a bigger shock. "What the—"

Stephanie and Joe were sitting at the breakfast bar drinking coffee from Styrofoam cups embossed with the logo of a well-known donut shop. When I walked over, she held up a steaming cup of coffee.

"Are there donuts?"

She smiled and slid a plate with a chocolate glazed donut on it.

I took a bite and moaned. "Bless you."

She laughed. "We decided we deserved to treat ourselves."

I looked around. "I can't believe you guys cleaned this. I was going to call a cleaning company to take care of the mess." I took a long sip of coffee. "This must have taken you all night."

"Most of the night, but we were up talking." She snuck a glance at Joe and then hurried on. "Might as well talk and work at the same time."

"I'm sorry." I stared at Joe. "I should have helped. I'm sure that's not how you wanted to spend your last night here."

"It's okay. We had a lot to talk over, so it worked out," Stephanie said.

I looked from Stephanie to Joe. There was an undercurrent that was charged. Neither one volunteered information, but I noticed a few glances. Well, they were adults, and whatever happened was their business, for now, anyway. I looked around. "Where are the dogs?"

Joe took a sip of coffee and nodded toward the back deck.

I turned and again saw three noses pressed against the glass. "I was thinking about taking Aggie to a doggie day care."

"There's one next to the emergency vet where we took the golden. Maybe I can swing by there today and get some information." Stephanie glanced at Joe. "I know *some people* don't think I should get attached, but I need to come up with a name for him."

I glanced at my watch. "I've got to get to work." I turned to Joe. "What time does your flight leave?"

"Late, eight. I'm not able to stay, but by flying into Chicago, I could move to a later departure time. It's a longer drive, but that's okay." He glanced at Stephanie, who blushed. "Also, I want to be here to introduce you both to my friend Dennis Olson."

"Great, then I'll save my good-byes until later."

I grabbed my coffee and an old-fashioned donut for the road and hurried away.

My morning commute was uneventful. Thanks to Bluetooth technology, I was able to take care of business without losing focus on the traffic, which was a plus. I called Dixie and updated her on recent events.

I got to work and looked around my surroundings a great deal more than normal. I told myself I was just being cautious; however, there was a part of me that felt disappointed when I entered the building and went up in the elevator, although I refused to acknowledge why.

When I got upstairs, the lights were on. Jacob's jacket was hung up, and his computer was on, although he wasn't at his desk. He had, however, unlocked my office. When I went in, he was there with the fancy Chinese vase. He was arranging yellow roses.

"Those are beautiful." I walked up behind him and took a big whiff. "Who sent them?" My nose was buried in the roses.

"I think you know. Someone must have made quite the impression with Mr. Hopewell." He adjusted the flowers and then took a step back and admired his handiwork. Pleased, he swept the leaves and cast-off stems into my wastebasket and tossed the empty box into the trash. He slid the card toward me and smiled. He picked up a pair of scissors and then turned and walked out.

I sniffed the flowers and then sat down and opened the envelope. As Jacob suspected, the flowers were from Freemont Hopewell. The card had very few words.

Lunch? F.H.

I took that to indicate Freemont Hopewell was inviting me to lunch. I refused to call it a lunch date. I hadn't dated in over twenty-five years. The very idea of a date made my hands sweaty. I sat in my chair with a silly grin on my face for several minutes. Eventually, I sat up and got to work. At first, I caught myself glancing at the clock every fifteen minutes. Before long, I was engrossed in figures. Freemont was handsome, but he had no clue what he was doing when it came to accounting. Honestly, the mess he had created was tedious and time-consuming to figure out but seemed harmless enough. I decided to prioritize. I focused on the taxes and spent a couple of hours on the phone with an extremely chatty IRS agent named Denise Austin. Denise sounded young and perky, or maybe I was having a flashback to an aerobics instructor of the same name. Usually, IRS agents didn't give their full names, but Denise was so friendly, I felt like we were long-lost friends. Obviously, she had yet to get beaten down by the day-to-day monotony of working for one of the most hated organizations in the United States. At the end of that conversation, I was tired but had completed the paperwork the IRS needed to insure the museum kept their nonprofit status, and I felt good. As I hung up the phone, there was a knock on my door, and in walked Freemont with a small bouquet.

"I tried to call, but I was told you were on the phone, so I took a chance and came in person."

"I'm sorry. I've been on the phone for a while."

Jacob walked in with a small cobalt blue vase. "Told you." He rolled his eyes.

"Hello, Jacob. Always a pleasure."

I looked at my phone. "What time is it?"

"Noon," Freemont said. "Are you available for lunch?"

I looked at my desk, which was covered in papers.

"Come on, you have to eat," Freemont pleaded.

"You go to lunch, and I'll take care of things here." Jacob extended a hand toward Freemont, who passed the flowers to him.

"They're beautiful, aren't they?" I glanced at Jacob, who was removing the dead leaves and rearranging the flowers so they looked their best.

"Hmmm." Jacob sniffed. "Running low on vases. Maybe you should get creative and try something unique."

I scowled at Jacob for his rude behavior. "I love flowers."

Jacob sniffed and continued arranging the flowers in the new vase.

Freemont shrugged and smiled. "I'll take that as a challenge."

I got up and took my purse out of the drawer. Freemont helped me on with my coat and then held the door for me, something my late husband rarely did, even when we were dating.

We took the elevator downstairs. Once outside, Freemont led me to a small red BMW convertible. He held the door, and I lifted my leg to get inside. Unfortunately, the suit I'd worn that day had a pencil skirt that prevented me from separating my legs more than a few inches, which wasn't enough to allow me to get into the car gracefully. After a couple of failed attempts, I tossed grace to the curb, hiked my skirt up over my knees, and folded myself down into the car.

To his credit, Freemont didn't say a word, although the corners of his mouth twitched. He quickly closed the door and walked around to the driver's side.

"I made reservations at my favorite restaurant." He backed out of the parking lot and whizzed through the narrow streets of the historic district at a speed that made me clutch the door handle.

"Are we late?" I asked after he nearly collided with a bus that had stopped to let passengers off.

He laughed. "What's the fun of having a finely tuned German vehicle if you're going to drive it like a minivan?"

My foot automatically pressed the floor as though there were a brake I could apply, and Freemont raced around a corner, causing another car to screech to a halt. The driver leaned on the horn. Based on the arm gestures, pointed fingers, and body language, the driver had a few ideas about what he'd like to do to that finely tuned German vehicle. Yet Freemont merely waved and sped off.

He pulled into a parking lot, hopped out of the car, and headed around to open the passenger door for me.

I took a few deep breaths to steady my nerves and then again pulled my dress up so I could get out without falling on my face. Freemont held out a hand and helped to pull me up. Unfortunately, my foot got caught on the door, and I lurched forward. I would have fallen if Freemont hadn't been standing there. I put out my arms to brace myself and fell into his arms.

I looked into his face and got a whiff of his cologne, which smelled citrusy with a touch of spice. His gaze looked intense.

"You smell good."

He smiled. "Clive Christian," he said with a husky voice.

"Excuse me?"

"My cologne. It's Clive Christian eighteen seventy-two. It's over three hundred dollars a bottle. I have to order it from Britain."

I pushed myself away. "It smells good."

He nodded and closed the car door. He held out an arm, and we walked into the restaurant.

Inside, the restaurant was dimly lit for the middle of the day. The young hostess greeted Freemont with a smile. "Mr. Hopewell, we have your table ready."

He nodded. Obviously, he was well-known here.

The girl led us to a booth near the window. Freemont helped me off with my coat and then held out my chair. He handed the hostess both of our coats before sitting down.

Once seated, there was an awkward moment when we sat staring at each other. Thankfully, the waiter came and filled our glasses with water, which gave me something else to stare at other than Freemont Hopewell.

The waiter gave us a rundown on the daily specials.

"Actually, if you will allow me, I can order for both of us." Freemont smiled at me.

I closed my menu and forced a smile. It was one meal. In old-fashioned romance novels, his gesture might have been perceived as romantic. However, in the twenty-first century, it annoyed me. I was perfectly capable of ordering for myself. However, I took a deep breath. I repeated the phrase over in my mind. *It is only one meal.* I forced a smile, which felt like a grimace, and waited.

Freemont turned to the waiter and rattled off the order. Considering how long he talked, it sounded like he was ordering for an army. Eventually, the waiter nodded, took our menus, and walked away.

"Wow. That sounded like a lot of food. Are you expecting someone else to join us for lunch?" I joked.

He smiled, and I noticed how white and perfectly straight his teeth were. I wondered if he had worn braces as a child. My musings had obviously distracted me from whatever he was talking about because his mouth was no longer moving, and he was looking as though he were waiting for me to say something.

I took a sip of water. "I'm sorry. I was distracted." I didn't say "by the brilliance of your teeth," but the phrase floated in my head.

"I was just explaining that food is a passion of mine. This is one of the best, and most expensive, restaurants in Chattanooga. The chef is a personal friend of mine." He grinned. "He's French, of course."

"Of course."

He leaned across the table. "I wanted you to experience the best cuisine, and there's an order that should be observed."

The waiter returned with a bottle of wine, which he showed to Freemont.

Freemont glanced at the label and nodded. The waiter decorked the bottle and handed him the cork, which he sniffed. Then the waiter poured a small amount into a glass, which he handed to Freemont. Freemont held the glass up to the light, then swished it around and looked intently at it. After a few seconds, he brought the glass to his nose and sniffed. Then he tasted it. He smacked his lips for a few seconds and then nodded. Only then did the waiter acknowledge my existence as he filled our glasses.

Freemont held up his glass and smiled broadly. "This is an excellent rosé. It's from Provence, Commanderie de la Bargemone, and will pair wonderfully with meaty fish dishes like the grilled swordfish I ordered."

I sipped the wine and nodded. I wasn't a big fan of swordfish, but maybe this would change my mind. I reminded myself to have an open mind.

The waiter brought a plate of steamed oysters. He smiled and then hurried away.

I stared at the plate. I prided myself on being open-minded, but oysters were one of the few foods about which my mind remained closed.

Freemont had slurped three oysters out of the shell before he noticed I hadn't indulged. "What's wrong? Don't tell me you don't like oysters?"

"Okay." I sat and stared. "I won't."

The silence grew. Eventually, he said, "Seriously, you don't like oysters?"

I shook my head.

"You must not have ever tried these. They steam them with lemon and garlic." He looked like a sad puppy. "At least give it a try?"

I glanced at Freemont and saw a look of disappointment. He had tried to provide a unique experience, and I was being difficult. Relationships were about give and take. Compromise, right? Yet, here I was, refusing to share something that was obviously important to him.

I stared at the cyclops on my plate, picked up my fork, and stabbed it. Without thinking, I shoved it into my mouth. The moment it touched my tongue, I knew oysters weren't going to be something I indulged in. I looked up and noticed him staring. I tried to smile and pretend as though I was chewing. Thankfully, the waiter showed up with our main course. I picked up my glass and gulped down a large amount of wine, which allowed me to swallow the crustacean whole. Unfortunately, the oyster didn't want to go down without a fight and lodged in my throat. I broke into a coughing fit in an attempt to dislodge it.

"Are you okay?"

I shook my head, but he stared and then looked around. "People are staring."

At that moment, I could have cared less who stared. I felt as though I couldn't breathe. I tried to cough and flopped around, knocking silverware and other items to the floor. Imagine my surprise when the eggheaded man from the obedience class the previous night approached the table. He was dressed in a suit. He looked into my eyes. "Are you choking?"

I nodded.

He reached around and grabbed me by the waist; then, with his fist in my abdomen, he squeezed. All of the air stopped, and I felt lightheaded, but immediately, I felt pressure and then the oyster flew out of my mouth and landed on the floor. Afterward, he helped me return to my seat.

"Breathe." He took my pulse. Satisfied, he then handed me a glass of water.

I took several breaths. My hands were shaking as I drank.

"Just take deep breaths, hold them, and then release." He squatted next to me. After several seconds, I felt calm.

"Thank you," I croaked. My throat felt raw.

"Glad I was able to help." He smiled. "Your throat will be sore for a bit." He stared at the swordfish the waiter had placed on the table. "You may want to stick to soft foods for a bit."

I was so thankful I could have kissed Egghead for not only saving my life but for helping me avoid further sea battles.

He patted me on the knee and then rose to his feet. "I'll see you at class."

People at nearby tables burst into spontaneous applause.

I glanced across at Freemont, who looked as though he wanted to crawl under the table.

"I'm sorry," I said, although I had no idea why I was apologizing.

He flushed. "I'm sure you couldn't help it, but, well, you'll have to admit it has rather ruined the mood."

"Sorry my nearly choking to death ruined your mood." I stood up and tossed my napkin on the table.

He glanced around. "Sit down."

"Lilly?" Dixie hurried to the table and threw her arms around my neck. "Oh God! I'm so glad you're okay." She hugged me again. "I'm so glad Dr. Morgan was here."

"Dr. Morgan?" I stared. "Oh, Egghead from the obedience class?"

She smiled. "He's a coroner, but they're still doctors." She shot Freemont a glance that would have curdled milk. "At least he did more than just sit there and stare." She turned back to me. "Can I give you a ride?"

Freemont scooted his chair back and started to rise. "That won't be necessary, I can—"

The look he received from Dixie shut down any protest and he returned to his seat.

"Thank you." I grabbed my purse and turned and walked out with Dixie, leaving Freemont with his swordfish.

Chapter 11

Dixie drove me back to the museum while I filled her in on lunch with Freemont Hopewell, or the little bit of it that I'd experienced. I had never been so thankful for drivers who actually stopped at stop signs and red traffic lights in my life. Freemont viewed them as challenges to be overcome, rather than rules to be observed. Back at the museum, I got out of the car.

"Are you sure you're okay to go back to work?"

I nodded. "I'm fine. I think I'll get a cup of tea from the café and a bowl of soup. I'll be fine." I stood outside the car. "Do you want to come in and see where I work?"

Dixie shook her head. "Sorry. I need to get back to my meeting, but I'll call later before I head home."

"I'm so sorry. I totally forgot you said you had a committee meeting today. I didn't mean to take you away. I could have taken a taxi back."

She shook her head. "It's okay. I was glad for the break. I mean, I wasn't glad you nearly choked or that your date with Freemont went downhill. I just meant it was good to get away from the bickering."

"I knew what you meant." I smiled. "Thank you again." I closed the door and walked to the front of the museum. I turned and waved at Dixie, who I knew wouldn't drive away until she saw me safely inside the building.

I stopped by the café. Thankfully, they hadn't delivered the lunch I'd ordered yet, and I picked it up and went upstairs. I had hoped Jacob would still be at lunch, but unfortunately, he was sitting at his desk. As I passed holding my tea and soup, he merely lifted an eyebrow.

"Don't ask."

He nodded and returned to his work.

I sat down and looked at the three vases of flowers on my desk. I hadn't actually gotten a good look at the latest bunch in their blue vase. It was a deep rich cobalt with speckles of red, yellow, and black. The flowers around the rim were delicate and translucent. I was so engrossed in admiring the vase, I didn't hear Linda Kay until she was almost at my desk.

"I'm sorry. I knocked, but you—"

"I was admiring this beautiful vase. I didn't hear you. Please come in."

She motored closer to the desk. "It is beautiful, isn't it? That's one of my favorite Chihulys."

I had just taken a sip of tea and nearly spit it out. "Chihuly? As in Dale Chihuly? The world-famous glass artist?"

Linda Kay smiled and nodded.

Jacob entered and stood behind her. "Cobalt blue venetian with flowers, circa nineteen ninety."

"I don't think I've ever been this close to something that beautiful and expensive."

"Well, you better start getting used to it. You work in a museum," Linda Kay said. "Now, are you okay? When Jacob told me you went to lunch with Freemont, I expected you'd be gone for at least three hours. He likes to show off by taking people to his fancy French restaurant. You weren't gone an hour." She leaned across the handlebars of her motor scooter and waited.

Jacob stood behind her with his arms folded.

I told them about my experience, and Linda Kay's facial expression was everything I could have hoped for in sympathy. After a few moments, I wondered if I had been too hasty in walking out. I shared my doubts with Jacob and Linda Kay.

"Absolutely not." Linda Kay shook her head frantically. "I'm appalled that he merely sat there while you were choking."

"Well, everyone isn't good in emergency situations," I said.

"Maybe not, but he definitely has a cell phone and could have called nine-one-one." Jacob held up his phone with one hand while he stood with his other hand on his hip.

"When I talk about it now, it seems like maybe I overreacted. I mean, it's not like he did anything deliberately wrong."

Jacob and Linda Kay exchanged glances.

"What?" I looked from one to the other.

Finally, Linda Kay sighed. "We didn't want to influence you against Freemont. I mean, he is a horrible accountant, but he hasn't done anything wrong, as far as we know."

"Or that we've been able to find out, anyway," Jacob muttered.

"It's just that there is something that rubs me the wrong way," Linda Kay said. "He's wealthy, and he likes to flaunt his wealth. He's always talking about his custom-made suits from England or his Italian leather shoes."

"Or his cologne that costs three hundred dollars per bottle?" I said softly.

Jacob rolled his eyes. "He drives that Beamer like he's the only one on the planet who's entitled to use the road and all other traffic must yield to him."

I'd seen that behavior firsthand.

"However, he would be a good catch." Linda Kay looked at me as though she were trying to see into my soul.

"I'm not fishing for anything. I was married to my husband for over twenty-five years when he dumped me for a stripper."

"Oh my." Linda Kay gasped. "I thought you said you were a widow?"

"I am a widow, now." I quickly filled them in on Albert's murder, and since I felt Linda Kay deserved to know, I also filled her in on my arrest for his murder and how we discovered the real killer.

Linda Kay and Jacob listened in rapt silence until I finished.

"Wow. You poor thing. You've really been through the wringer." Linda Kay patted my hand.

"I guess that's why I was so flattered that someone was interested enough in me to send me flowers. Albert certainly never sent me flowers."

"Every woman should have beautiful things. You deserve flowers and to have someone treat you like a queen," she said with passion.

I laughed. "At the moment, I'd accept someone who treated me with respect."

We chatted for a few additional minutes, and then Jacob reminded Linda Kay that she had to prepare for a board meeting and they left. My soup was cold, so I tossed it into the trash. I took one last look at the flowers and then got up and gently and carefully moved them to the conference table so they wouldn't be in danger of falling off my desk as I worked. Then I sat down and got busy straightening out the accounting mess Freemont had created.

By the end of the day, my throat was feeling much better, although my neck was stiff from leaning over accounting ledgers all day. I stretched and hurried out. I wanted to get home in time to see Joe before he left.

Traffic was heavy, but thankfully, there were no accidents to delay me. I pulled into the garage and noticed a black SUV parked in front of the house. By the time I got inside the garage door that led past the laundry area, Stephanie was putting Aggie and Turbo out the back door.

Joe was sitting at the breakfast bar with another man, who turned and stood when I entered.

"Hello, you must be Joe's friend." I extended my hand.

"Yes, ma'am."

"Lilly Echosby, this is my friend Dennis Olson." Joe turned to Dennis. "Dennis Olson, Lilly Echosby."

We shook hands.

"Pleased to meet you," I said.

Dennis Olson wasn't what I expected. He was older, probably mid to late fifties. I was expecting someone closer to Joe's age, late twenties. Olson wasn't as tall as Joe. He was probably five feet ten, with a stocky build. His hair was clipped very close in a buzz cut popular with men in the military, and he had light gray eyes. A raised scar went from the top right side of his face down to his mouth.

Stephanie returned. "How was your day?"

"Don't ask." I kicked off my heels. "Mr. Olson, can you excuse me for a minute? I need to change. I'll be right back."

"Mr. Olson is my dad. Everyone calls me Red."

I smiled. "Okay, and please call me Lilly."

I hurried into the bedroom and quickly changed into jeans and a sweat shirt.

Joe and Red were drinking beer, which Stephanie must have picked up at the grocery store for the men since neither of us cared for it and didn't drink it. She had a glass of wine.

"You look like you could use a drink." She moved to the side counter, where I had a small bar setup. "Sex on the Beach?"

I nodded. "Thanks."

Red raised an eyebrow but didn't say anything.

I accepted the glass Stephanie handed me and drank half its contents before I came up for air. "Mr. Ols...ah, I mean Red, thank you for coming by. Did Joe fill you in?"

He nodded. "Your landlord was murdered and your house was ransacked. What do you think they were looking for?"

I shook my head. "I have no idea. Why would anyone go through the flour and sugar canisters unless they were angry and wanted to cause a mess?" I could tell from something in Red's eyes that he had an idea. "What?"

He rubbed the back of his neck. "Well, the one thing that comes to mind is drugs or money."

"Red works with the Drug Enforcement Division of the TBI," Joe said.

"Drugs?" I nearly choked. "You think my landlord was selling drugs?"

Red raised a hand. "Hold up. I'm not saying that. I did, however, run a background check on him. There were never any arrests or convictions for drug dealing."

I stared at Red. "You're holding something back. What is it?"

"My facial mask must have slipped." His eyes were wide in surprise. "Obviously, I need to work on hiding my thoughts better." He hesitated. "Robert Hansen wasn't involved in drugs as far as we can tell; however, he was a person of interest in an investigation."

"What type of investigation?" Stephanie asked.

"I'm not at liberty to say."

"Not at liberty to say?" I stared from him to Joe. "That must mean you're still investigating him."

Red was silent.

"But he's dead. Surely your investigation is over now." I turned to get a full view of Red's face.

However, if he felt his facial mask had slipped earlier, by now he had the mask firmly in place, and neither his face nor his body language gave up any clues.

Joe turned to his friend. "Look, if you know something, I need you to tell us. These are people I care about. If they're in danger, you owe it to us."

Joe and Red stared at each other for several tense seconds. During that time, something passed between the two.

Eventually, Red sighed. "I could lose my job for this. Robert Hansen was being investigated for smuggling and espionage."

"Espionage?" I stared openmouthed.

"Smuggling what?" Stephanie asked.

"We weren't sure."

"Well, considering you work in the Drug Enforcement Division, if he came up on your radar, then it seems like drugs are the most likely possibility." Joe pounded the counter.

A red flush went up Red's neck. "Hold up. Smuggling is more than drugs." Joe started to protest, but Red held up a hand. "Robert Hansen was suspected of smuggling. He hung around with some pretty dicey people, and we weren't sure what legitimate businesses he had and which businesses were just a cover for other things." He held up a hand and ticked off items as he spoke. "He was partners in some land business where he bought a lot of real estate, including a number of lots here." He waved his hand around to indicate the current house. "He was in the business of importing art into the States. He was also a government contractor and might have sold insider information."

"So he's guilty of espionage and smuggling?" Joe looked about ready to explode. "Is that all?"

"Proof. We have no proof."

"Why was he allowed to enter the country without surveillance?" Joe asked.

Red hesitated. "We didn't know he was back."

I had been content to listen to the back and forth between Joe and Red, but when they stopped arguing, I raised a hand. "What was the real estate being used for?"

Red shrugged. "We're not sure. It might have just been his way to launder money. Even the worst criminals have some legitimate businesses."

"Great." I took a sip of my drink.

"But what were they looking for?" Stephanie asked.

Red shook his head.

"I think you ladies need to find someplace else to stay. This house isn't safe," Joe said.

I stared at Red. "Do you think we're in danger?"

He looked back at me with an intensity that made me blush. However, I chalked it up to the Sex on the Beach. "I can order extra protection, but..."

"What?" Stephanie and I asked together.

"I don't know if the bureau will agree. I mean, Hansen was the one under surveillance, and he's dead. I don't know if they'll want to invest in more surveillance. But—"

Joe started to object, but Red held up a hand. "However, I could stay here a few nights and keep an eye on things, on my own time. If you have a spare blanket, I can make sure you ladies are safe until Joe returns, at least." A red flush went up the back of his neck. "You could say I was an old family friend."

Stephanie and I exchanged a glance. For some reason, I found it hard to keep from giggling. Perhaps my Sex on the Beach was stronger than normal.

"Would your wife be okay with you staying here?" I asked as casually as possible.

"I'm not married, so that won't be a problem."

"Good." I took another sip of my drink. After a few seconds, I nodded. "I think that can be arranged. I can put you upstairs in the spare room."

We worked out a few last-minute details, and then Red left to go home and pack a bag. I gave Joe a hug and made a discreet exit to the bedroom with Aggie, who'd had enough of hanging out outside and made her displeasure known.

Stephanie and the golden retriever took Joe and Turbo to the airport. I ordered pizza and made another drink. I took advantage of the time to change the linens in the room Joe and Turbo had used. I put fresh towels in the bathroom and made sure everything was ready for the next guest. By the time Stephanie returned, I was at ease.

Stephanie's eyes were red, and her raccoon eyes indicated she'd shed a few tears on the drive home. When she got home, she declined food and went to her room with a pint of Ben & Jerry's Cherry Garcia Ice Cream and a spoon.

Red arrived a few hours later. I showed him around. He'd brought a duffel bag and said he didn't need anything. He'd eaten before he came back.

With nothing left to do, I went to my room and spent time sending text messages to Dixie, updating her on the latest developments. I didn't want her to be shocked if she saw a strange man at the house. Her response was something along the lines of I seemed to have picked up quite a few men in my short time in Chattanooga. Despite the smile her teasing caused, I denied all allegations.

The next morning was Saturday. I rose early and threw on sweats. I needed to cut my grass. However, Red was already awake and in the kitchen, preparing breakfast.

"What is that glorious smell?" I asked.

"Bacon, eggs, hash browns, and French toast." He smiled. "I took the liberty of checking with Joe last night, and he assured me you both would enjoy a hearty breakfast and that no one had any food allergies or dietary restrictions."

"Nope. We're all carnivores in this house, although I'm not fond of oysters."

"Neither am I."

Red immediately rose two points in my estimation.

"Is that coffee?"

His brow furled. "I should have asked what you'd like to eat, but I didn't want to wake you. I hope this is okay."

"Yes, it's fine."

He smiled and handed me a cup of steaming-hot coffee. "I hope you don't mind that I made myself at home. I ran to the market first thing this morning. I figured cooking was the least I could do to repay your hospitality."

"What are you talking about? I should be cooking for you. You're the one who's being inconvenienced. We really do appreciate your staying, although I hate to inconvenience you simply to babysit." I sipped my coffee.

He smiled. "I don't mind."

I tried to stop salivating over the wonderful smells. "You must like cooking."

"I do. Most people think bachelors can't cook, but I enjoy it."

Stephanie came out of her bedroom in sweatpants. Her hair looked as though she had just awoken and had a hornet's nest on her head. "Oh my God, that smells amazing." She took a big whiff. "Please tell me there's enough for three?"

Red smiled and nodded. "Coffee?"

"Yes, please." She perched on the bar stool next to me.

Red took plates out of the cabinet and divided the food between us.

The golden retriever sat beside Stephanie patiently, but Aggie stood on her hind legs and whimpered.

I was about to get down to let her out when Red held up a hand.

"I can let them outside." He picked Aggie up and gave her a scratch behind her ears, which made her leg jiggle, and she looked at him with adoring eyes. He looked at the golden. "Come on, boy."

The golden took one look at Stephanie and then got up and followed Red outside. The room was open, with a large bank of windows at the back, which allowed us a clear view to the back deck. We watched as Red stood on the deck and waited as the dogs went down the stairs.

"This is delicious." Stephanie shoveled food in her mouth.

"Hmmm. I know."

"A man who can cook is a wonderful thing," she said in between bites. "He may not be rich like your fancy Hopewell suitor."

I snorted. "If I never see Freemont Hopewell again, it will be alright with me."

Stephanie paused, fork midway to her mouth, and stared. "I can't wait to hear what happened."

An explanation would have to wait. Red came back inside with the two dogs.

"You're an excellent cook. Where'd you learn to cook like this?" I asked.

"Thank you. I would tell you, but then I might have to kill you." He laughed.

"Don't tell me the TBI trained you to cook?" I stared.

He took a sip of coffee. "Actually, my mom taught me. I have five older sisters, so I learned a lot of things other boys my age never learned."

"Five sisters? Are you the only boy?" I asked.

He nodded. "Guilty."

We ate in companionable silence for a few minutes. Eventually, I rose and picked up my plate.

"You looked like you were going out earlier." Red took the plate from me. "Why don't you let me take that?"

"Oh no. You cooked. The least I can do is clean up. Besides, I'm just going to load the dishwasher. Although"—I looked around—"the kitchen looks pretty clean."

He took the plate and, with a flourish, loaded it into the dishwasher. "I clean as I go. That way, you're not left with a mess at the end."

"Wow. Tell me why you're single?" Stephanie teased.

He turned his head away to hide a smile, and I noticed a red mark on the back of his neck. When he turned around again, he shrugged. "It's hard to find time to date in my line of work."

Stephanie looked into her coffee cup. "I can understand that."

After an awkward silence, I headed to the garage door. "I was going to mow the grass."

"Would you like some help?" Red eagerly asked.

"I can't have you doing all of my chores," I joked.

"I don't mind. In fact, I like to stay busy."

"Why don't you let him help, Mom?" Stephanie turned so her back was to Red and mouthed, *He's so cute* to me. "You know what they say."

"What?" I asked.

"Many hands make light work." She raised an eyebrow and grinned.

"Well, if you're sure. You can mow, and I can edge—or vice versa."

Red grabbed his jacket, hurried around the counter, and followed me into the garage.

I pointed out the lawn mower and grabbed the edger, a broom, and a package of large lawn and garden bags, while Red checked the oil and filled the mower with gasoline from a container. When we were done, we got to work. Red mowed while I edged. Even though the weather in Tennessee was a lot nicer than in Indiana, the lawn was yellow. I asked if he thought we needed to fertilize.

"No, the grass is just dormant for the winter. It'll be green in the spring and summer months. Actually, this lawn looks pretty healthy. It's just a bit neglected."

We finished quickly.

"Most Southerners aren't that concerned about mowing in the winter. The grass is dormant and doesn't grow very much, but you seemed adamant about mowing. What's up?"

The grass may not grow in the winter, but I wasn't taking any chances it had grown above the required length since I'd moved in. No point in aggravating my grumpy neighbor more than I already had. I went through the long story of how Theodore Livingston measures grass to make sure it fits the restrictive covenant as we returned the equipment to the garage. I glanced at Red as I finished. I might not be very good at reading the face of a professional law enforcer, but I was pretty sure I saw a look of admiration in his eyes, which made me feel warm and fuzzy.

He asked a few questions about my crackpot neighbor, which I answered to the best of my ability.

"This is a nice subdivision. How about we clean up a bit, and then you can give me a tour? It'll help me get the lay of the land."

"I must look horrible." I wiped my forehead and saw the trail of grass clippings I was leaving in my wake.

"Not at all. However, I know I could use a shower and thought you might want one too."

In the house, I peeled off my sticky clothes, tossed them in the laundry basket, and then hopped into the shower. The water was hot and felt wonderful. I washed my hair and allowed the warm water to remove the kinks of the past week. I must have been in the shower too long because after a while, I saw a little black nose move my shower curtain and peek inside.

I smiled at Aggie and used my hand to flick water on her, which caused her to quickly step back.

I dried my hair and dressed in jeans and a bright red shirt, which looked good with my skin tone. Normally, I didn't wear makeup on Saturdays, but today I put on the basics. When I was done, I went into the living room, where Red was sitting on the sofa reading a Rex Stout novel he must have brought with him.

"You like Rex Stout?"

He nodded and closed his book. "I like his Nero Wolfe novels. I rarely get time to read for pleasure, but one of my sisters sent it for my birthday."

I got Aggie's leash and a few plastic bags, and we headed outside. "I love mysteries. I like Rex Stout, but I'm pretty partial to British historic cozy mysteries. I love Agatha Christie."

"That explains it." He pointed at Aggie.

"Guilty." I smiled.

We walked in a companionable silence for a bit. I showed him the gazebo, and then we walked to the area where Aggie had found my landlord.

Whether from curiosity or force of habit, Red stopped and went into the wooded area and looked around. Aggie wanted to go with him, but I refused to let her, and we waited on the nearby park bench until he came out.

"Find anything?"

He shook his head. "I didn't expect to, but I was curious how far the woods went back and if there was any chance the murderer could have gotten in from any other way or if he had to come through the subdivision."

"Well?"

He shook his head. "No other way inside."

"Great."

We walked around the back of the neighborhood and talked about mysteries and our favorite authors. He was intelligent and well read. He knew his mysteries. However, Rex Stout was the only author we both liked. I preferred traditional whodunits, while he, not surprisingly, preferred thrillers with more gore and forensic data. We still managed to have a good debate. The time went quickly as we talked, with few stops for Aggie to take care of business or for cleanup, which Red felt was his duty, despite the fact that she was my dog. We were so engrossed in our conversation, I didn't even notice when Carol Lynn Hargrove approached until she was standing right in front of me.

"Oh hi, Carol Lynn. I didn't see—"

"I don't know how you managed it, but I'm going to fight it."

"Fight what? What are you talking about?"

Carol Lynn's face was red. "Don't pretend you don't know what I'm talking about, you...you...murderer." She ran down the street.

I stared after her for several seconds and then turned to Red. "I wonder what that was about? She can't possibly believe I had anything to do with my landlord's murder."

He shrugged. "Who was she?"

I explained what I knew about Carol Lynn Hargrove, and even though I hadn't intended to, I found myself telling him what I suspected about Carol Lynn and the neighborhood association president, Jackson Phillips.

He listened quietly, asking a few clarifying questions, but I didn't have many answers. Eventually, I shook off the encounter, and we continued our walk. We rounded the corner by the association clubhouse building, the site of my humiliation.

"What happened here?"

"What makes you think something happened?"

"Body language. You looked at the building and blushed. Then you avoided looking at it. You turned your body away from it. Most of the walk,

I've been on the outside." He leaned close and whispered, "Which is how Southern gentlemen were trained to always walk—on the outside—but you just moved to the outside. And, even though you're obviously right-handed, you transferred Aggie's leash into your left hand."

I stopped and stared. "Wow. You're good."

He made a quick bow. "I am a highly trained professional. I get paid to notice things."

I stopped and stared. I moved back to the inside, closer to the building, and made a production of transferring Aggie's leash to my right hand. "Okay, I'll tell you about my day of shame." I shared the events from the association meeting and my run-in with Theodore Livingston. When I was finished, I glanced at Red.

He looked straight ahead; however, after a few seconds, the corners of his lips twitched. Eventually, he burst out laughing.

"That's not funny."

He nodded his head. "Yes, it is. You actually hit him?"

"I'm ashamed to say I did."

He glanced at me closely, and heat rose up my neck. "You are a woman with many talents."

I walked faster. "Come on. You might as well get the full tour." I walked into the community building. It was dark, but the sun shone through the large windows and made the area light and bright.

Behind the building was the neighborhood pool. There was a gate that all the residents had a key card to unlock. This was the first time I'd been to the pool area, so I walked around to get a closer look. The pool was closed, but someone had unstacked one of the lounge chairs and was lying out in the sun. Initially, I thought it was an overzealous sunbather. Despite the fact that it was winter, the temperature was in the sixties, and it was a nice day. However, closer inspection showed me the person lying out was fully clothed and completely uninterested in getting sun.

Aggie grew tense, and her bark deepened. She growled, and the hair on my arms stood up.

Red hesitated a moment, reached into the back of his pants, and pulled out his gun. He motioned for me to stay and then walked over to the lounger. He reached down and felt for a pulse. After a few seconds he stood up. "You better call nine-one-one. He's dead."

Chapter 12

If I thought Officer Lewis had looked suspicious the first time I found a dead body, I was mistaken. That look was nothing compared to the side glances he shot my way today. He looked as though he thought I was a serial killer and responsible for every recent murder in the state of Tennessee. Thankfully, I had been in the presence of Red most of the day. I hated to admit it, but having a TBI agent as an alibi was a big help.

Similar to the previous exercise, the police, several crime-scene investigators, and a myriad of other folks showed up. Instead of waiting on a bench outside this time, I sat on the comfortable sofa in the community building, sipping hot tea. After about an hour, Stephanie and the golden retriever showed up, and not long afterward, Dixie arrived. Officer Lewis reluctantly authorized them to wait with me. Red shot me a questioning look, and I held up my cell phone. "Nine-one-one wasn't the only call I made."

"Who is it this time?" Stephanie flopped down on the sofa next to me.

"Theodore Livingston."

Dixie shuddered. "Good Lord." She dropped into a chair next to the sofa. "How did it happen?"

I shrugged. "Fortunately, Red was there, and he went over and checked his pulse."

"Red?" She craned her neck to look at the group of law-enforcement officials swarming the pool area. "Which one is he?"

I glanced around. "The one in the jeans with the black turtleneck," I whispered. "And the scar."

She took a good, long look and then turned and gave me a thumbs-up. "He's cute."

Heat rushed up my neck, and I took a sip of tea. "I barely know the man. He's only here because he's a friend of Joe's, and Joe was concerned about Stephanie."

Stephanie patted my hand. "Mom, you really are naïve."

I turned to face her. "What are you talking about?"

"He is a friend of Joe's, but he's not exactly concerned about me. He's spent the entire day with you."

I thought about that and forced myself not to smile. "You can't think he's interested in me?"

Stephanie patted my hand again. "He fixed breakfast, cut the grass, and then spent over an hour walking around the subdivision with you. I haven't seen him for more than thirty minutes while I ate breakfast." She laughed. "I think it's safe to say his interest lies elsewhere."

I paused and thought about what she'd said.

"Chattanooga certainly looks like it's going to be good for your love life," Dixie joked.

"Well, things didn't work out so well with Freemont Hopewell."

"I didn't know you knew Freemont Hopewell." Red was behind the sofa, and I jumped.

"Oh my God, you scared me." I turned around. "How long have you been standing there?"

He grinned. "Long enough."

Dixie stood up and extended her hand. "Hi. I'm Dixie Jefferson, Lilly's friend."

"Red Olson." He shook her hand.

Dixie sat back down, and Red leaned on the arm of the sofa nearest where I was sitting. I tried not to notice, but if the glance that passed between Stephanie and Dixie was any indication, they definitely noticed.

"Now, you never mentioned you knew Freemont Hopewell." He looked at me.

"You never asked. I only met him this week and didn't realize it was important."

"How well do you know him?" His tone implied he wasn't just being nosy.

"Not well." I told him about my job at the museum and Freemont sending me flowers. I told him about lunch yesterday.

He listened with a scowl.

"Why? What's Freemont have to do with Theodore Livingston?"

He rubbed the back of his neck. "Maybe nothing, but it seems a bit of a coincidence."

I held up Aggie, who had been sleeping on my lap. "If you don't tell me what's going on, I'm going to sic my attack poodle on you."

Aggie yawned as though she'd had a tough day, which made everyone laugh.

Red reached out and scratched her behind her ear. "Freemont was one of Robert Hansen's business partners."

I looked at Dixie, and she shrugged. "Did you know?"

She shook her head.

"I don't suppose there's a chance Livingston died of natural causes?" I asked.

"Not likely."

We waited for more. Eventually, he sighed. "He was strangled."

I shuddered. I hadn't liked Theodore Livingston, but I wouldn't wish that on anyone.

Officer Lewis joined our group. "Well, another body. You've certainly been busy." His eyes had an intensity that implied he held me responsible. "You've been in Chattanooga less than a month, and already you've found two dead bodies. It's a wonder we found anyone before you arrived."

Dixie and Stephanie objected.

"You can't honestly believe I had anything to do with these two murders." I stared at him.

Red sat quietly for a bit. "I can vouch for Mrs. Echosby from roughly nine this morning until we found the body."

"She never left your sight during that period?"

He shook his head. "For approximately forty minutes while she showered and dressed, but there is no way she would have had time to come over to the pool house, murder Mr. Livingston, and get back without me noticing."

"Thanks, I think."

"Besides, we both know you don't believe she strangled that man, so let's stop wasting time."

Officer Lewis's eyes flashed for a second, and he clenched his jaw in a way that told me he was fighting for control. After a few seconds, he flashed a phony smile. "Well, I may be just a normal cop and not as smart as the Tennessee Bureau of Investigation, but where I come from, you need evidence before you discount potential murder suspects." He grimaced.

Red was about to rise, but I clutched his hand, and he stopped.

"Now, the way I see it, we've got one common denominator in all these murders, and it's you." He pointed at me. "You had a fight with Mr. Livingston in front of an entire room full of people where you were heard threatening him. You also assaulted him."

His initial accusations seemed comical, but I felt shame when he mentioned the fight. However, Officer Lewis showed no mercy. "Until we get the coroner's report back on the time of death, you are a person of interest in this investigation." He pointed his finger in my face. "So don't think about leaving town." He turned and marched away.

"Round one to Officer Lewis," Dixie muttered. "The shrew-faced little troll."

"I'm sorry." Red paced. "If I hadn't made him angry, he might have used his head and thought things through and wouldn't have come down so hard on you."

Stephanie patted my hand. "Well, you better believe I'll be sticking around now. There's no way I'm going to let him railroad you, although I'm not licensed in Tennessee."

"I'm going to call my husband's attorney." Dixie whipped out her cell phone. "He's as slick as a greased pig, but he's a darned good lawyer." She walked over to a corner to make her call.

I leaned forward and rested my head in my hands. "I can't believe I'm being accused of murder, again."

Stephanie rubbed my back and comforted me.

"Not again. I can't believe this is happening to me *again*. I don't want to go through this again. I can't go back to jail."

Chapter 13

"What do you mean 'back to jail'?" Red stared at me.

I was too upset to even talk about it. I gave him a look that said, *Don't even go there.*

He read the look properly and held up his hands in surrender.

Dixie finished her call and hurried over. "That slick shyster is out of town at some convention. He won't be back until Tuesday, but I left a message for him to call as soon as he gets back."

"I could be arrested by then, the way Officer Lewis was behaving, but I appreciate you for trying." I tried to smile, but I didn't think it came across very well.

Dixie plopped down in her chair. "Something is rotten in the state of Denmark and in the state of Tennessee too, if that's how policemen treat new residents."

I loved how Dixie quoted or misquoted famous sayings when she was nervous. For some reason, it made me smile.

Aggie must have sensed my mood. She moved from her position on the sofa next to me and crawled under my arms and into my lap. She then stood on her hind legs with her paws on my shoulders. Unsure of what was going on, or perhaps motivated by a desire to comfort, she reached up and placed her paw on the left side of my neck. It was a touchingly sweet gesture, but then she dug her nails into my shirt and hoisted herself and climbed onto my neck.

"Ouch." I tried to pull her off, but she gripped my hair and shirt with vigor.

Eventually, it took both Stephanie and Red to get me untangled. Stephanie handed Aggie back to me, and I put her on the floor, careful to keep her claws away from my clothes and hair.

Stephanie pulled her cell phone out of her pocket. "I'm calling Christopher. I doubt if he's licensed in Tennessee either, but he may be able to recommend someone." She took a couple of steps, punching numbers as she walked. "Then I'm going to call Joe. Job or no job, he needs to get back here and help."

Christopher Benjamin Williams was a friend of Stephanie's from Lighthouse Dunes who was also an attorney. He represented me when the police thought I'd killed my husband.

Dixie reached over and took over Stephanie's patting and soothing responsibilities.

Red paced. After a few turns around the room, he turned awkwardly. "This is crazy. I can't believe he actually believes you killed him." He mumbled something that sounded like *What a bass,* but then he resumed pacing, and it wasn't really clear. He whipped his phone out of his pocket and walked, dialing.

"He seems nice."

I turned my head to the side and gave Dixie my *You have got to be kidding me* look. Now was definitely not the time.

"Sorry. I know it's not the right time, but it's either that or I'll start spouting off crazy quotes because that's all that's going through my head right now."

"Like what?"

"Lord, what fools these mortals be." She looked sheepish.

"*A Midsummer Night's Dream*," we said together.

We looked at each other for a few moments and then burst out laughing.

Stephanie returned and stared at us. "Are you two hysterical? Let me know if I need to slap you."

For some reason, that made us laugh more.

"Okay, let me in on the joke because I could sure use a good laugh."

I pulled myself together and wiped away the tears. "It's nothing, dear, just the stress."

"Christopher is going to ask around for recommendations, and I couldn't reach Joe." She flopped down on the sofa. "Probably a good thing, since I think I was slightly hysterical and would have burst into tears."

I looked at my daughter and my best friend and realized I was dragging everyone down. Now wasn't the time to have a collapse and fall apart. The last thing I wanted was to bring others down because I was indulging in a pity party, no matter how well deserved it might be. I took a few deep breaths and tried to focus my mind. I sat up straight. "Okay, I'm done feeling sorry for myself." I looked at Dixie and Stephanie. "This sucks. Life isn't fair. Yadda yadda. The bottom line is God helps those who help themselves."

Dixie and Stephanie both sat up straighter.

"Okay, Sherlock, what's your plan?" Stephanie asked.

I looked from Dixie to Stephanie. "We're going to find the real killer."

Dixie slapped her thigh. "Hot damn!" She held out her hand.

Stephanie grinned. "Count me in." She put her hand atop Dixie's.

"Let's do it." I put my hand on top of theirs, and we pumped them twice and then raised them in the air.

Chapter 14

"What's going on here?" Red walked over and stared at our display of solidarity.

"Nothing." I lowered my hand and stood up. "Are they done?"

Officer Lewis stood in a corner near the door talking to a uniformed policeman.

I headed for the door.

"Where do you think you're going?" he asked.

"It's late, and I'm hungry. So, unless I'm under arrest, I'm leaving." I picked up Aggie. I opened the door and looked back. "You know where I live if you have more questions." I looked at Dixie, Stephanie, and Red, who seemed to be frozen in place. "You coming?"

Dixie grabbed her purse and hurried out the door. Stephanie and the golden retriever followed closely behind. I looked at Red, who seemed conflicted.

He stared from me to Officer Lewis. Only the flash of mirth in his eyes indicated he found the situation amusing. "No. You go ahead. I'll be along shortly."

I nodded and walked out.

Outside, Dixie and Stephanie waited.

"That was brilliant." Dixie held up a hand, and we high-fived. "Looks like the game's afoot."

"Where to now?" Stephanie took a bag and cleaned up after the golden relieved himself.

"I was serious when I said I'm hungry. Let's grab some lunch and come up with a plan of action."

We walked the short distance back to the house and gave the dogs another opportunity to take care of business. None seemed inclined; they seemed to prefer to sit on the back deck and look at us through the door. So we let them back in. I headed to the bedroom, expecting Aggie to follow; I was surprised to find she wasn't behind me. Instead, she and the golden sat by Dixie's feet and stared as if in a trance.

"What have you done to my dog?" I asked.

Dixie looked down as if noticing them for the first time. She smiled. "I was training my dogs earlier." She stood up and reached in her pocket. She pulled out a plastic bag. She held up the bag, and Aggie got on her hind legs and danced around like a ballerina on a music box.

"What's that, doggie crack?" Stephanie asked.

Dixie praised Aggie and the golden, who was seated and attentive. "Pretty much. It's hot dogs." She reached inside the bag and held up a small piece.

Aggie sat, then stood, then turned around three times and sat.

"Sit." She held the hot dog in her hand. The golden lifted his butt and then repositioned it.

Dixie immediately gave him a treat. "Good boy." She then turned to Aggie. "Sit."

Aggie bounced around but eventually sat.

Dixie quickly praised her and gave her the treat.

Aggie gobbled the hot dog as if she had been starved. When she was done, she immediately returned to sitting.

Dixie reached in the bag and pulled out more treats. She turned to the golden. "Down."

Instantly, the dog slid back and lay down in sphinxlike fashion, never taking his eyes off Dixie.

"Good boy." She gave him the treat. She then turned to Aggie. "Down," she said firmly.

This time, Aggie seemed confused. She sat. She stood. She turned. Nothing was getting her the treat. She barked.

Dixie gave the command again. "Aggie, down." This time she put the treat in front of her nose and slowly brought it down to the ground.

Aggie followed the treat with her body. The instant her belly hit the ground, Dixie lavished her with praise and gave her the treat.

"Wow." I stared openmouthed. "You're good."

"The power of soul-selling treats." Dixie stood up.

I looked at the dry dog biscuit I held in my hand and realized I'd have to up my game if I expected results. "Point taken." I walked to the refrigerator and got a slice of string cheese.

"Aren't you worried about her getting overweight?" Stephanie asked. "Or, getting...bound up."

I paused.

Dixie shook her head. "The special treats are only used for training purposes. The dog biscuits are fine for everyday. Eventually, she'll figure out what you want her to do, and you won't need to bribe her. However"— she took the cheese from my hand—"she's a small dog, so I'd break off a small amount of cheese. A small piece can go a long way." She pulled off a couple of tiny pieces. "Where's her kong?"

I went to the dog bed and pulled out the red-rubber toy Dixie had encouraged me to buy and handed it to her.

She stuffed the cheese inside the toy and used the dog biscuit to plug the hole and keep it inside. She turned to Stephanie. "Do you have one?"

Stephanie shook her head. "Joe thought I was getting too attached and discouraged me from buying too many toys."

"No problem." Dixie ran out to her car and came back with a large black kong. "I always keep extras in the glove box in case of emergency." She put more of the string cheese inside and took a standard poodle–sized dog biscuit that must have also been a part of her emergency supplies and used it to plug the hole. "There." She handed one to each of us. "They will be able to smell the cheese and will be occupied trying to get it out of the kong."

This time when I called Aggie and walked to the bedroom, she followed. Stephanie patted her leg, and the golden followed her into the bedroom.

Television on and dogs engrossed in trying to get to the cheese inside the rubber toys, we slipped out of the bedroom and closed the door.

We climbed into Dixie's Lexus and headed out. She drove to a chain restaurant near the mall that was known for Asian cuisine and parked.

We were seated at a booth near the back of the restaurant. We ordered cocktails, spare ribs, and lettuce wraps to share for an appetizer and prepared to get to work. I pulled out a notepad and pen. "Now, does anyone believe these two murders are *not* related?" I looked from Dixie to Stephanie.

Both women shook their heads.

"Good. Neither do I." I drew a line down the center of the page and wrote "Robert Hansen" on one side and "Theodore Livingston" on the other. "I think we need to start by listing what we know about each of them."

We rattled off what few details we knew. Unfortunately, the list seemed pretty sparse and contained a lot of words like "mean," "busybody," and "nosy," when it came to Theodore Livingston's side. Robert Hansen's side was even more bare, with words like "under surveillance by the TBI," "Cayman Islands," and "angry I rented the house."

The waiter brought our appetizers and drinks and took our entrée orders. When he left, I set my notebook aside while we ate.

"We don't know much about either of them, do we?" Dixie looked discouraged.

Stephanie sighed. "I don't know if this will be as easy as it was last time."

I thought about that for a minute. "I don't know that figuring out who murdered your father was easy. However, we can't get discouraged. We just need more information, and there's only one way to get it."

They both looked at me with raised eyebrows.

"We have to search for it. Look, Theodore Livingston was mean and hard to get along with. However, that's nothing new. He's probably been that way for a long time and no one killed him." I looked around, and they nodded. "Something must have happened recently to make him dangerous to someone."

"What?" Dixie asked.

"That's what we need to find out." I tapped my fork against the table absentmindedly. "Something changed." Suddenly it hit me. I sat up at attention, and my heart raced. "Dear God. I know what changed."

Dixie and Stephanie waited.

"Robert Hansen was murdered."

"Yeah, we know that," Stephanie said slowly.

I held up my notepad. "My nosy, busybody neighbor, Theodore Livingston, must have seen the murderer."

The reality of what I said must have dawned on both of them at the same time as their eyes grew wide.

Dixie smacked the table. "You're right! That has to be it."

I sighed. "Well, it's logical, and it makes sense. We won't know for sure until we catch the murderer, but at least it'll be a good place to start."

They both nodded.

"Well done, Mom."

I beamed. "Thank you."

"Okay, so we think Theodore Livingston saw the murderer kill Robert Hansen. Either the murderer saw him, or Livingston told him he knew." I paused. "Based on my limited experience with him, my money is on the latter."

Dixie nodded. "Agreed. That crotchety old fool would have enjoyed boasting about how he knew what he did—"

"Or she," Stephanie added. "It could have been a woman."

I nodded. "Good point. We need to find out how he was murdered and whether or not a woman could have done it."

Dixie pointed her fork at me. "You ask your TBI friend how he was strangled." I started to protest, but she held up her fork. "Hold on. I'm not saying you have to date him, just ask him." She shook her head. "Although I don't think he'd mind if you used your womanly ways to get information out of him."

"My womanly ways? I don't think I have those anymore."

"You've got them alright; they're just a little rusty, but we can fix that." She winked. "But back to business. He's staying at your house. It'll be easy for you to talk to him. We need to know if the murderer used their bare hands or if they used something...you know, a..."

"Ligature," Stephanie added.

Dixie nodded. "A ligature. Then I'll check with Dr. Morgan at dog-training class on Tuesday to see how much strength it would take and any other medical-type questions we have."

I nodded. "Okay." I wrote down our tasks in my notepad. "Now, what about Robert Hansen?"

"I think we need to talk to his mother. I've been meaning to call her to talk about the lease and find out how she wants to proceed," Stephanie said. "I just wanted to give her some time. I mean, she just lost her son, and I'm sure she's upset right now. This has to be devastating."

Dixie chewed vigorously and then took a long sip of her martini to wash down the food. "I meant to tell you, but I got distracted by the murder: I saw the obituary in the newspaper. The funeral is Monday. I think we should go. Maybe we can talk to her afterward. At the very least, we can go and pay our respects."

"And maybe we can see if we recognize anyone at the funeral," Stephanie said.

"Great, although..." I sighed. "I have to work. I just started this new job. I can't keep taking off or I'll be unemployed."

"Well, let's see. You can miss work to go to the funeral and track down the real killer and potentially lose your job. Or you can go to work and leave finding the killer up to Detective Lock-Her-Up Lewis and spend the rest of your life in prison for a murder you didn't commit." Dixie stared.

"Good point. I'll call Linda Kay first thing tomorrow." I chewed on my lip.

"What's wrong?" Stephanie asked. "I know that look."

"I just wish we knew more about Robert Hansen and Theodore Livingston."

Dixie nodded. "For that matter, I wish we knew more about the other people in the subdivision."

"Write down the names of some of the people. I'll ask Joe to look them up." Stephanie took a sip of wine. "Just because he's not here doesn't mean he can't still help." She gave me a look as though she were studying me.

"What?" I asked.

"Have you ever considered highlights?" She hurried on. "Aunt Dixie's right, you might need to work on your womanly ways."

"What do highlights have to do with it? I know I've been out of the game a long time, but I don't remember highlights being a factor."

"It's an entirely new game now." She exchanged a look with Dixie that made me nervous.

Dixie picked up her phone. She swiped a few screens and then pushed an app and put the phone to her ear. "I'm on it."

I was more puzzled than ever. I sat and listened to one side of Dixie's conversation, which sounded like she had just made an appointment for something.

She disconnected and smiled. "I pulled a few strings, but she can get us in at four." She looked at her watch. "So, we've got an hour."

"An hour for what?" I asked.

"I made an appointment for you with my hairstylist." I started to object, but she held up a hand. "Don't worry. Just because I like big hair doesn't mean you have to. Kit is a wizard with dye and highlights."

Stephanie's eyes gleamed with excitement. "Can she do something about her eyebrows?"

"What's wrong with my eyebrows?"

"Nothing. They just need a bit of shape and definition."

Dixie nodded. "I told her we wanted the works, so she'll take care of her brows, plus we'll get manicures. She wasn't sure if we could all get pedicures too, but she's going to see if they can fit us in."

"Wait. Hold on. We're trying to solve a murder...two murders. We don't have time for manicures and pedicures." I looked from Stephanie to Dixie. "Besides, what's wrong with my hair and my eyebrows?"

Stephanie patted my hand. "Mom, there's nothing wrong...exactly, it's just that your hair is a bit...dated."

Dixie leaned forward. "A new hairstyle and highlights will help in the investigation."

I tilted my head and waited for her to elaborate.

"You catch more bees with honey than you do with vinegar," she said as though that explained everything.

"What the heck are you talking about?" I slid her martini glass farther away from her.

"What I think Aunt Dixie is trying to say"—Stephanie shot Dixie a glance before continuing—"is we need you to use every weapon at your disposal to get people to talk and share information. Several of those people are men. Men tend to talk to women who look nice."

"That's pretty sexist, don't you think?" Something about the look on her face compelled me to ask. "You don't mean to tell me you use your looks to get what you want?"

Stephanie shrugged. "Unfortunately, it's the world we live in." She took a sip of wine. "I know men think I'm attractive, but I'm also smart. There's still a perception that pretty women aren't intelligent. So if they get distracted by my looks, maybe they'll make a mistake or underestimate me." She sipped again.

"I feel like you two have set feminism back forty years." I stared from my daughter to my friend.

"Honey, you've just got to get over it. It's not like we're telling you to seduce anyone. All we're saying is that when you look nice, people treat you differently. You can use that to your favor."

"Do it for yourself. You've been through a lot over the past year." Stephanie looked sincere. "Dad leaving you for that bimbo and then being accused of murder are a lot. You should spend some time and energy on yourself." She smiled.

Stephanie was right. It had been a difficult year. I knew she and Dixie were only concerned about me, and a new hairstyle might make me feel better about myself. I looked at my nails and couldn't remember the last time I'd gotten a manicure. "Okay."

Dixie's salon was near the mall, close to the restaurant. After we ate, we headed over.

The salon had a Zen-like décor. There was a fountain in the lobby and soft lighting. Dixie was obviously well-known there.

"Hello, Mrs. Jefferson. Perfect timing." The receptionist, a thin woman with short pink hair, greeted us.

"Hi, Angel. This is my friend Lilly and her daughter, Stephanie."

"Nice to meet you." She smiled. "Kit will be right up. Can I get you a glass of wine?"

"Thank you." Dixie took a seat, and I followed.

"Things really have changed a lot. I don't remember being offered wine at the beauty salon." I sat next to Dixie.

"Gotta love the South, honey. This is how we roll." She laughed.

Angel returned with a tray and three glasses, which she placed on a small table in front of us. Then she left. When she came back, she had two bottles of wine. She held them up. "White or red?"

"Yes," Dixie said.

Angel smiled, put both bottles on the tray, then turned and left.

Dixie poured a generous amount of wine into her glass. Stephanie and I followed her lead. Once the wine was poured, we clinked our glasses in a toast.

"To the South." Stephanie took a sip of wine.

I took a sip of wine. "Amen."

Chapter 15

My time at the salon was relaxing, and in spite of my misgivings, I enjoyed myself. It had been a while since I'd pampered myself, and it felt good to sit back and allow someone to cater to me. Kit turned out to be in her late forties. She had white hair, which she wore cut short. Dixie told her to make me look amazing, and she went to work.

They'd had a cancellation, which allowed all three of us to get manicures and pedicures. Between the brow wax, manicures, pedicures, haircut, color, and style, we were at the salon for three hours. However, when I looked in the mirror at the finished results, I barely recognized myself.

"Wow. I can't believe that's me."

"Mom, you look amazing."

"I feel amazing." I stared from various angles. "I can't believe what a difference getting my eyebrows arched has made."

"It really opens up your eyes and helps define your face," Kit added.

"You look beautiful." Dixie smiled.

I hugged her and Stephanie. "Thank you for prodding me into doing this. I feel like I'm making a completely new start in life. I've moved to a new city. I feel like I'm not starting over. I'm starting new. Everything is fresh and different."

Dixie wiped her eyes. "Don't you dare make me cry."

I looked down. "Now I feel like I need a whole new wardrobe."

"Well, we can do that later," Stephanie said. "I think we need to get back and check on the dogs."

When we walked in the door, the first thing that met us was the smell. I sniffed and followed my nose inside. "What is that glorious aroma?"

Red was in the kitchen stirring a pot. "I hope you don't mind. I'm making spaghetti. Cooking helps me think." He dipped a spoon into the rich tomato sauce and held it up. "Want to taste?"

I leaned in and blew on the bubbling liquid and then tasted it. "Hmmm... that's delicious."

He smiled and reached behind and opened the dishwasher door and put the spoon in the tray.

"I'm going to need to work out or I won't be able to fit into any of my clothes when I get back to Chicago," Stephanie said.

"Is that a cake?" I looked on the counter.

He shrugged. "I made a carrot cake too."

"Wow. A man who cooks, bakes, and carries a Glock. If I wasn't already married, I'd probably throw myself at your feet." Dixie pulled a piece of bread from a loaf on the counter, stuck it into the sauce, and then popped it in her mouth. She closed her eyes and moaned.

Red stared at Dixie with admiration. "A woman who knows her weapons...impressive." He reached to the small of his back and retrieved his gun. "Sorry, I forgot to put this away. Joe mentioned you were a bit jumpy about guns."

I shook my head. "It's true. I don't like guns, but I know you're in law enforcement, just like Joe. So it's okay. Don't worry about it."

"Are you sure?"

I nodded, and he put the gun back and pulled his turtleneck sweater out of his pants and used it to cover the gun. "Better?"

I nodded, although whenever he turned back to the stove, my gaze kept darting to the small of his back.

"You look nice."

Heat rose up my neck. "Thanks. My daughter and my friend thought I could use a makeover."

"Well, you look very nice...if you don't mind me saying."

I pretended not to notice the looks that were passing between Dixie and Stephanie. "Thank you...um...I better go and let the dogs out."

I hurried to the bedroom. Both dogs were asleep when I retrieved them from the bedroom. In fact, I had to shake Aggie to wake her up. "Some watch poodle you are." I scratched Aggie's ear as I lifted her off the bed, opened the door, and let both her and the golden retriever out onto the deck to take care of business.

I took a look at myself in the bathroom mirror and couldn't help smiling. I had been joking at the salon when I mentioned new clothes. However, in the same way old furniture could look dated in a new house, my clothes looked outdated and tired with my new look. I took a quick glance in the walk-in closet under the auspices of finding my black dress for the funeral. Apart from the jeans and a few sweaters, practically everything I owned looked as though it belonged in a different decade.

I was just about to give up when I heard a ruckus. There was barking that was too deep to belong to Aggie and a clatter that indicated the golden had crashed through the dog pen. Next, I heard a door and running on the deck.

I hurried to the living room. Dixie and Stephanie were standing in frozen silence staring at the open door.

"What happened?"

Stephanie dialed her phone.

"We heard a noise, and the dogs went crazy." Dixie pointed. "Red took off like lightning out the door."

I walked toward the door.

"He said to call nine-one-one and wait here."

I looked from Dixie to the back door. "But what about Aggie?"

She looked at me as though I'd lost my mind. "Are you kidding? Aggie will be fine. She's the one with the TBI agent with a Glock." She looked around wildly. "I left my gun in the glove box." She looked as though she was going to go for it, but then thought better of it and sat down.

We waited for what felt like hours but was only a matter of minutes. Eventually, we heard sirens.

There was a pounding on the front door. I peeked through the peephole and opened it.

A uniformed policeman rushed inside, weapon drawn. Dixie and I pointed out back, and he headed for the door.

Stephanie yelled, "There's a TBI officer out there in plain clothes with a weapon."

He nodded and hurried through the door.

Eventually, three other uniformed officers arrived. Finally, Officer Lewis waltzed in. Annoyed didn't begin to describe the look on his face. "You again?"

Fear for Aggie, who was outside with a potential murderer, regardless of how many armed policemen were there, ignited a fuse.

Anger bubbled up, and I walked up to him. "Look, I've had about as much of you as I can take. My six-pound poodle is outside with someone who has probably murdered two people. Not to mention my daughter's dog and a friend, the TBI agent. I am a woman on the edge, and I've had about as much cynicism as I can take." I could feel the blood rush in my ears, and my heart pounded. "Now, last I knew, my tax dollars were still paying your salary, so unless you're planning to arrest me, you might want to back off."

Officer Lewis looked shocked more than angry, but I honestly could have cared less.

Stephanie walked over and put her arms around me. "It's okay, Mom." The anger subsided as quickly as it rose, and I burst into tears.

Officer Lewis might have been a hard-nosed, cynical detective, but he must have realized he'd pushed me a bit too far and hightailed it outside.

After a few moments, Red and two of the uniformed officers came up the stairs and stood on the deck talking. The golden trotted along beside him and sat by his side. I craned my neck, looking for Aggie. After a few seconds, he turned, and our gazes met. That was when he turned his body slightly to the left so I could see Aggie perched on his shoulder like a parrot. She dug her claws into his shirt, and he held her with his right hand while his left still held his gun.

I breathed a sigh of relief and cried again.

Dixie stood close by and patted me on the back. "You should marry that man."

I pulled myself together and splashed water from the kitchen sink on my face. "I need a drink."

"I thought you'd never ask," Dixie said. "Make mine a double."

Stephanie took glasses from the cabinet and placed them on the counter next to my makeshift bar area.

"A double what?" I asked.

"Anything."

I smiled. At this rate, we were going to be stone-cold drunk by the end of the evening. We'd each had a cocktail at the restaurant and shared two bottles of wine at the salon. However, the shock of recent events had certainly removed any buzz that lingered. I checked my watch. It had been several hours since we'd left the salon; nevertheless, we needed to come up with another way to steady our nerves or we'd all be in Alcoholics Anonymous before the weekend was over.

The house didn't have a formal dining room, but there was an eat-in area in the kitchen near the back window, where I had a glass-top table and four chairs. I placed a bottle of wine on the table. Dixie and Stephanie sat down, and I grabbed the bread and set the table with four plates.

We sipped wine and waited. The two uniformed officers walked around the house and left. From our positions at the table, we could watch the exchange going on between Red and Officer Lewis, although we couldn't hear what was said. Even though it was dark, the motion lights on the back deck illuminated the area, so we were able to see clearly.

"Looks like a pretty heated exchange." Dixie sipped her wine.

Stephanie sipped hers. "Based on the color in Officer Lewis's cheeks, I'd say he isn't happy."

I merely watched in silence. Eventually, they came inside.

"You look comfortable." Red pulled Aggie off his shoulder and handed her to me.

The golden walked to Stephanie and sat, wagging his tail.

She bent down and hugged him.

I hugged Aggie to my chest and gave her a little squeeze. When I looked down, she had her head resting on my chest, and she looked at me with adoring brown eyes.

"Do you two need a moment?" Red smiled.

Before I could answer, Officer Lewis came in. He nodded to me, glared at Red, and then marched out the front door.

"What's gotten into him?" Dixie asked.

Red shrugged and struggled to hide a smile. "He just got outplayed, and he's still smarting a bit."

Before I could ask for more details, my stomach let out a loud growl. Everyone laughed.

"I'll tell you about it over dinner." He moved to the stove. I directed him to the cabinets with the serving dishes for the spaghetti and sauce. He brought the food to the table and served each of us before sitting and preparing his own plate. I put Aggie down and pointed her toward her bowl of dog food, which someone had generously filled earlier, and then turned to my plate.

"I could get used to this kind of service," Dixie said when Red prepared her plate.

Red sat anxiously and watched our faces as we took our first bites.

The spaghetti was delicious. There were several moans, which brought a smile to his face. Only when we were slurping up spaghetti as though we were starving and hadn't eaten in days did he pick up his fork and eat.

"So, what happened?" I mumbled around a large wedge of bread I'd stuffed in my mouth.

"Officer Lewis—"

"No, start from the beginning. Remember, I was in the bathroom when the chaos started."

He nodded. "I was cooking when someone must have walked into the backyard. The motion detector lights came on."

He looked at the golden, who was eating. Stephanie had bought a large dog bowl, which she'd filled with dog food and set next to Aggie's small purple bowl. However, the two dogs preferred sharing a bowl and took turns eating out of the larger bowl.

He nodded to the golden. "He growled and his hackles rose. He gave one bark and headed for the door." He took a bite, then pointed toward Aggie. "That poodle may be small, but she's got a heart the size of a rottweiler." He laughed. "When I opened the door, she darted out before I could stop her and was down the stairs so fast, I had to run to try and stop her."

Stephanie smiled. "You would have been very proud of her, Mom."

Dixie smiled. "People always underestimate poodles. They think just because they have a foo-foo hair cut that they can't be good protection."

I smiled. "You don't have to tell me. I've seen Aggie in action."

"I can't wait to hear that story," Red said.

"I'll fill you in later. Now, back to this story."

He nodded. "So I asked Stephanie to call the police."

Dixie halted with her fork midway to her mouth, and Stephanie burst out laughing.

Red looked puzzled. "What?"

"Asked?" Dixie said.

"You ordered me to call nine-one-one and then told us to get down and stay down," Stephanie said.

He grinned. "Sorry." He looked sheepish. "By the time I got down the stairs, whoever was there had gone. I saw a shadow and went in pursuit, but he was too far ahead." He looked at the dogs. "Plus, I didn't know how many there were. The last thing I wanted to do was take off chasing one person, only to have someone else circle back and...well, I decided it would be best if I stayed and waited for backup."

I shivered. "This is insane. I can't understand what's going on."

Red shook his head.

Dixie used her bread to wipe up the last bit of sauce from her plate and then leaned back. "That was delicious, but you haven't explained why Officer Lewis was so upset."

Red grinned. "Under normal circumstances, the police have jurisdiction in the state of Tennessee when investigating crime. However, under Tennessee law, the TBI has the authority to investigate any criminal violation if the district attorney general requests it."

Stephanie smiled. "Let me guess. You just happen to know the district attorney general."

He nodded.

"So you've just taken over Officer Lewis's case?" I asked.

He nodded.

"That explains why he looked like he could spit nails." Dixie raised her glass. "Well done."

Stephanie smiled. "I can't wait to tell Joe. I think he'll rest easier knowing you're running things."

"What does that mean?" I looked at him. "Is Officer Lewis off the case?"

"He doesn't have to be. It means the TBI will be leading the investigation." He took a sip of wine. "To be clear, I will be leading the investigation. Officer Lewis and the local police will move to a secondary role rather than the lead."

I mulled that around in my mind. When I looked up, he was staring at me. I took a napkin and wiped my mouth, thinking I must have something on my face. "What?"

"Nothing. I just really like your hair."

My heart rate increased, and my voice sounded breathy, even to my ears. "Thank you." I shook my head to get thoughts out of my mind that had nothing to do with solving this murder. "So what do we do now?"

He raised an eyebrow. "We?"

Okay, he was going to be difficult. "Yes. We." I made a circular motion that included not only him but Dixie, Stephanie, and myself. "It's my future on the line here, and if you think I'm just going to sit back and let Officer Let Me Make My Life Easy by Locking Up the First Person I See and a TBI officer who is nice and a great cook but doesn't know me and may be more interested in his own espionage/smuggling agenda determine my future while I sit back and file my nails, you're sadly mistaken." My speech had me breathing hard, and it had nothing to do with impure thoughts of a carnal nature.

Stephanie sat up straight. "Mom's exactly right. Don't tell me you're one of those Neanderthals who think women are damsels in need of some alpha male to rescue them? Because if that's what you think, you're sadly mistaken."

Dixie smacked her hand on the table. "That's right. Lilly figured out who murdered her two-timing, low-life, snake-in-the-grass husband, Albert, and by golly, I know she can figure out who committed these murders too." She fumed. "And I guarantee you I can outshoot any police or TBI officer if it comes down to it." She was standing with both hands on the table, glaring across at Red. "I'll have you know I was the five-time shooting champion for Bledsoe County."

Red held up both hands in surrender. "Alright. Calm down. I didn't mean to insult anyone."

Dixie sat but turned away so she wasn't looking at him. Stephanie still glared, but she leaned back in her seat. I folded my arms across my chest and waited.

Red released a deep breath and used his napkin to wipe his neck. "Look, I know you want to help, but this could be dangerous."

I started to speak, but he held up a hand. "Please, let me finish."

I sat back and waited.

"This person has already killed twice. As a trained investigator, I've seen a lot of horrible things."

Something in his voice made me look at him closer. I'd always heard the eyes were the windows to the soul. If that was true, then Red's eyes showed his soul was tortured. The pain I saw nearly made me gasp. However, the instant passed quickly, and the window closed. Something in his brief glance pulled my gaze to the scar that traversed one entire side of his face.

"Even professionals can be hurt, and I don't want anything to happen to any of you." He looked at each of us.

I might have imagined that his gaze lingered longer on me than the others, but I didn't think it was my imagination.

He looked down. "Not because you are women and I'm a male chauvinist." He grinned. "Years of dealing with the worst scum of the earth, who would cut their grandmother's throats for five dollars, has me concerned."

"I appreciate your concern, but as long as there is a possibility, no matter how slim, that I could be under suspicion for these murders, then I have to do what I can to figure this out." I looked at him with what I hoped was compassion rather than disdain. "I spent a long time listening to my husband and doing what he wanted. I believed he'd always be there for me, but I learned that I had to look out for myself." I sighed. "Short of arresting me and locking me up, you're not going to be able to stop me from trying to figure out who killed those men."

Red held my gaze for several seconds. Eventually, he sighed. "Okay, if you can't beat 'em, join 'em."

I started to talk, but he wasn't finished. "I've got one stipulation. You keep me informed on everything you're doing." He looked around the table.

Stephanie, Dixie, and I looked at each other. Stephanie nodded. Dixie shrugged.

"Deal, but we've got a condition of our own," I said.

He shook his head slightly but waited to hear our demand.

"The information freeway works in both directions. We'll share with you, but you've also got to share with us."

He took a moment but nodded.

I reached across and held out my hand.

We shook. "Now that's settled. What's your plan?"

Chapter 16

It didn't take long to share our plan. In fact, spoken out loud, away from Chinese food, our plan seemed very tame. Attending a funeral and asking Joe to look into the backgrounds of some of my neighbors was beyond tame. I skipped the note to use "womanly ways" to get Red to tell us how Robert Hansen was murdered.

Red must have agreed that our plan was weak because after he heard it, he visibly relaxed. "I have access to a few more resources than Joe. Why don't I take that one?"

I hesitated, and he added, "Especially since I need to do this anyway."

Glances at Stephanie and Dixie led me to agree. "Okay, but we want to know how Theodore Livingston was killed."

"He was strangled."

"I know that. I saw him." I shivered.

"How was he strangled?" Dixie asked.

"The murderer used a cord, but we won't know more until the coroner files a report. It was pretty well embedded into his flesh, so..."

"Ewww." Stephanie shivered.

"Sorry."

Stephanie took a sip of her wine. "No. I want to know." She gulped. "Could a woman have done it?"

He was silent for a few seconds. "Probably. Livingston was older, and from the look of his hands, I'd say he probably suffered from arthritis. So he probably wouldn't have been able to defend himself."

"Oh God." I put my head in my hands. "I beat up an old man with arthritis."

Red shook his head. "I'm not saying he was weak." He looked at me. "Stand up."

I lifted my head from my hands and looked at him.

He stood and walked around the table and stood behind my chair.

I rose and turned to face him.

He removed his belt and handed it to me. Then he turned so his back was to me. "Put that around my neck."

I reached around him as instructed and placed the belt around his neck.

"When I give you the word, tighten the belt and try to strangle me." He paused until the belt was tighter, but not restrictive. "Now, a man of average strength would probably be able to get away. Go for it."

I tightened the belt, and within a second, he had his fingers between the belt and his throat. He lowered his shoulders and easily flipped me around so I was standing in front of him. He had his arms tight around both of mine, and I was pressed against his rock-solid chest. We stared at each other for a few tense moments. Then he dropped his arms and backed up.

"You made that look easy, but Theodore Livingston wasn't a trained TBI agent," Stephanie said.

"True, but when the ligature tightens and the adrenaline hits, most people fight back. In my opinion, a woman could have killed him."

We stayed up late into the night and talked until Dixie said she needed to go home. I tried to talk her into staying. The thought of her driving up that mountain in broad daylight made me break out into a sweat. I couldn't imagine her doing it at night. However, she merely laughed and said she was used to it.

Stephanie got a call from Joe, and she and the golden went into her bedroom to take the call in private.

That left Red and me alone. I stood and stacked dishes. He tried to help, but I put a stop to it. "You cooked. The least I can do is clean up."

He stepped back and leaned against the counter, watching me.

Knowing someone was watching made me extra fidgety, and I dropped forks and pans multiple times before finally getting the dishwasher loaded and turned on. I wiped my brow, exhausted by the effort to maintain my balance and equilibrium while under scrutiny.

We stood awkwardly for several seconds, but then Aggie came to my rescue by yawning loudly and breaking the silence. We both laughed.

"I better get my little protector into bed." I picked her up and headed for the back door to let her out to potty before bed.

"Maybe I should do that." Red held out his arms. "Though I'm sure whoever was there is gone now, and the local police will patrol this subdivision hourly until we catch the killer."

I nodded, gave Aggie a squeeze, and passed her over. He took her outside, and I noticed he held Aggie's leash with one hand while the other was firmly on his service weapon. The motion lights came on as soon as they approached the stairs. They both went downstairs. I didn't realize I'd been holding my breath until they both came up and I released it.

Inside, he adjusted all of the blinds.

"Thank you." I picked up Aggie and hugged her.

"You're welcome."

I took Aggie into my bedroom and closed the door. After a few moments, I heard Red climbing the hardwood stairs. Aggie was asleep and snoring before I finished my nightly routine. I lay in bed until I got a text message from Dixie letting me know she'd made it home without incident and then rolled over and went to sleep with a smile on my face.

The next day was Sunday. I had yet to find a good parish. Chattanooga was the heart of the Bible belt, but it wasn't a Catholic hub. When it came to Catholic parishes, my options were somewhat limited. However, I'd passed a small Catholic church every day on my way downtown to work. Stephanie and I were going to check it out. I wasn't surprised when I opened my bedroom door to find her up, dressed, and sipping coffee on the sofa with the golden retriever asleep on the rug.

"Good morning."

She looked up. "Good morning."

I walked to the coffee maker and looked around. I couldn't help but notice there were no delicious smells or activity coming from the kitchen. When I turned around, I noticed Stephanie looking at me with a grin.

"Disappointing when there's no yummy breakfast, isn't it?" She grinned.

"Maybe he slept in."

She shook her head. "I don't think so. I heard the shower upstairs earlier, and I think he's gone."

I shrugged. "I suppose he didn't promise to make breakfast every day, and he does have a life of his own and a murder investigation to resolve." I went to the back door and let Aggie in.

We drank our coffee and then put treats out for the dogs. Just as we were leaving, Stephanie got a text message. From the look on her face, I could tell it wasn't good news.

"What's wrong?"

"Someone's claiming the golden is their lost dog." The chill in her voice didn't match the spark that I saw cross her eyes.

"Are you going to answer them?"

She grabbed her purse. "I'll do it after church."

I made sure Aggie and the golden were comfortably set in my bedroom with dog biscuits and television, and then headed out to the car.

The small parish was just what I needed. The people were friendly. The priest, Father Singleton, was a portly older man with a kind face. He reminded me of the priest from the Father Brown mysteries, and I liked him at once. After the service, we decided to go to a nearby chain restaurant for breakfast and then headed back.

Stephanie was uncharacteristically quiet during breakfast and the drive home. However, I knew she had gotten very attached to the golden. I had only had Aggie for a few months, but I certainly wouldn't want anyone to try to take her from me.

Red's SUV was parked out front as we pulled into the garage, and she turned to me. "Look, I know you want to ask, but I appreciate the fact that you haven't pushed." She took a deep breath. "I sent the guy a response to come by at three." She turned to me. "Please don't be sympathetic or try to comfort me because if you do, I'll burst into tears."

I nodded. "I promise to be as mean as possible."

She chuckled. "I just mean it's taking everything I have to hold it together and not burst into tears."

"I understand."

We went into the house. This time our noses were met with more wonderful smells. We followed our noses to the kitchen.

"I hope you don't mind if I make dinner?" Red had several pots going but seemed in total control.

Stephanie mumbled something, opened my bedroom door, called the golden, and then disappeared into the guest bedroom.

"Certainly not. Knock yourself out. What's on the menu?" I sniffed.

"We're having Southern comfort food. Smothered chicken, mashed potatoes, and collard greens."

"We thought you were taking a day off."

"No rest for the wicked. I've been up since five." He paused. "I had to take care of some personal business."

For some reason, the fact that he didn't share what his personal business was bothered me. "Great. I'm going to change clothes." I turned and walked out.

In my head, I knew Red was entitled to personal time, and he certainly didn't owe me any explanations. As I changed clothes, I caught myself thinking out loud. "Whatever he does in his free time is certainly none of my business." I tossed my pants into the clothes hamper. "I mean, it's not like we're dating or anything." I pulled a sweat shirt over my head and put on blue jeans. "I mean, wanting to keep his personal life personal is his choice, right?" I stared at Aggie, who was lying on the bed staring at me.

"We are perfectly content to spend time alone." I leaned toward Aggie. Her tail got faster as she looked lovingly at me. I glanced at my watch. We had plenty of time before the golden's supposed owner arrived. "How about a walk?"

Aggie put her whole body into the tail wag and turned in circles.

I laughed and scooped her up and headed into the living room. I grabbed some plastic bags from a drawer and Aggie's leash. "We're going for a walk. We'll be back soon."

I didn't wait for a response but headed out.

I was halfway down the street before I realized I was being ridiculous. Red was a paid law-enforcement officer. He was here to do a job. Plus, he was a grown man and didn't owe me an apology or an explanation. I slowed down, which I think Aggie appreciated as she no longer needed to run to keep up with the pace I'd set. When I looked down at her panting by my side, I couldn't help but laugh.

"I'm sorry, girl. Let's take a break."

I headed for the gazebo and sat down. I didn't want to analyze my feelings, but they flooded in on me anyway. I admitted to myself that I was attracted to Red. After being married for over twenty-five years and then having my husband toss me aside like a used tissue for a woman less than half my age, I was feeling insecure. I thought Red liked me and felt the same attraction, but maybe he was only in my life to solve the murders. "The best thing would be to get these murders behind us and then see what happens, right?" I looked at Aggie, who was watching a bird perched on the gazebo railing.

"Did you say something?"

I looked up. The association president, Jackson Phillips, looked at me.

"Sorry, I was talking to myself," I admitted. "I don't worry until I start responding," I joked.

"I was walking by and saw you sitting here and just wondered if you had any questions?"

I tilted my head and looked puzzled. "Questions?"

"About being treasurer for the subdivision." He stared. "I thought Carol Lynn told you, but I can tell by your face she didn't."

I shook my head.

He walked up the three steps onto the gazebo and sat near me. "One of the actions we needed to take care of at the last meeting was voting on the officers for the new year. Normally, it's pretty straightforward. However, after the...excitement at the meeting, we ended up holding a special session to vote on the slate of officers."

I waited.

"Since you're only renting, you weren't included," he hurriedly added.

"Okay."

"Like I said, normally it's pretty straightforward and everyone votes in the slate of officers, no questions." He was sweating and wiped his brow.

"I take it this time was different."

He grinned. "Yep. This time Theodore made a number of allegations about our treasurer, which sent the meeting into a tailspin."

"What kind of allegations?"

"Embezzlement. He accused the treasurer of embezzling association funds. He didn't have any proof, and nothing could be substantiated, but the charges were so severe that we will have to investigate."

"Accusing someone of embezzlement is very serious. He must have mentioned some reason why he suspected the person." I shook my head. "I mean, as abrasive as Theodore Livingston was, would he really risk ruining someone's reputation without just cause?"

"Theodore Livingston was a mean, hateful, vengeful man, and I have no doubt he would." Jackson Phillips stood and paced in the small gazebo. "He's done it before."

"You sound like you're speaking from experience."

Jackson stopped pacing. He turned and faced me. "Theodore Livingston and I used to work together."

I must have let the surprise show on my face because he gave me a snide look and then nodded.

"Surprised?" He hesitated but eventually sighed. "I was the chief scientist for the Environmental Protection Agency, and Theodore was a junior scientist." He sneered and took a deep breath. "He accused me of negligence that led to a death."

"What kind of death?" I hated to stop the flow of information, but I was curious.

He shook his head. "A man died when his house was swallowed by a sinkhole." His voice grew soft. "There was a large amount of limestone under the property." His eyes pleaded. "There's limestone underground throughout this area. It rarely causes a sinkhole of this size and magnitude, and rarely does anyone die from it."

"What happened this time?"

He took a deep breath. "Excessive rain and poor drainage led to excess water, which eroded the limestone."

"That doesn't sound like your fault. That sounds like natural causes."

He shook his head. "It was, but I had been going through a rough time. My wife and I were separated, and I was drinking a lot." He gulped. "He accused me of negligence. I was fired. My wife left me. I lost everything."

"I'm so sorry."

He smiled. "The victim's family sued me. Thankfully, the case was eventually thrown out, but I spent every dime I had on attorneys. After that, I couldn't get a job in my field. I finally found a job as an elementary school science teacher."

"How is it that you and Theodore Livingston live in the same subdivision?"

He chuckled. "That is the worst of Theodore Livingston's cruel streak. Just when I'd started to rebuild my life, here he comes. He moved in so he could gloat and make sure neither I nor anyone else ever forgot my shame."

"You don't mean he told your neighbors about...well, everything?"

"Oh yes. He made a point of it."

"That had to make things awkward for you."

He sighed. "Awkward? He made them impossible." He pounded his fist into his hand. "Theodore Livingston was a horrible human being, and whoever killed him did the world a favor."

Chapter 17

My face again registered shock, and Jackson Phillips shook himself and forced a smile. "I guess that makes me a prime candidate for his murderer." He chuckled. "I wish I'd had the guts to kill him, but...I didn't."

I don't think my face looked convincing, but I forced what I hoped was a sympathetic smile. "Well, I'm glad to hear that." I rose from my seat in the gazebo.

"But that's not what I stopped to talk to you about."

I sat back down, picked up Aggie, and held her on my lap as a barrier between Jackson Phillips and me. "Oh yes, the association officers."

"After Theodore's accusations of embezzlement, there will have to be an audit and an official investigation. So we selected an interim treasurer to serve until the investigation is completed."

I stared at Jackson Phillips. "You can't be serious?"

He nodded. "Mrs. Hansen had mentioned you were a CPA, and so you were nominated."

I didn't know how long I stared at him, waiting for the punch line that never came. After what felt like an hour but was just a few seconds, I found my voice. "You have got to be joking. Me? How is that possible? I'm not even an official homeowner, remember?"

He shrugged. "Well, it is an interim assignment, and I think the homeowners appreciated the spunk you showed at the last meeting."

I stood. "Spunk? You mean they liked the fact I struck that poor man?"

"Theodore Livingston was hardly an innocent, but the vote was unanimous." He paused.

It took a minute for me to process the meaning of his words. "Unanimous? You mean Theodore Livingston voted for me?"

He nodded.

"But I have a job...well, it's temporary, but I like it, and I don't have time...I mean, I don't even know how long I'll be staying here." I started to pace. "My landlord is dead, and the police think I might have had something to do with it. Besides, I don't know what Mrs. Hansen will want to do now that her son, who owned the house, is dead. She could decide to throw me out."

He shrugged. "I don't think she will, but there really isn't a lot of responsibility for the person who serves as treasurer. Collect the association fees and write a few checks for things like grounds maintenance and utilities for the community building."

I didn't say anything.

"Plus, it's a paid position, and it is only temporary. Once we prove Theodore Livingston was just being his normal, vindictive self, then you can resign, and we can go back to normal."

I didn't want to accept, but maybe sitting with the other members of the board might help me find out more information that could help me figure out who killed Theodore Livingston. I sighed. "Okay."

He released a breath and smiled. "Great. We have a board meeting Wednesday night. Will you be able to attend?"

I nodded.

"Great. We'll see you at the community building at five-thirty." He started to walk away.

"Wait, can I ask who the current treasurer was that Theodore Livingston accused of embezzlement?"

He turned. "Carol Lynn Hargrove."

Chapter 18

I pondered everything Jackson Phillips told me during my walk back to the house, along with my behavior to Red. I was cold to a man who didn't deserve it because I was hurt that he hadn't shared information about his coming and going, which he was under no obligation to share. I never considered myself to be a jealous woman. However, after the experiences with my late husband, I was insecure. Nevertheless, none of this was Red's fault. We weren't in a relationship, and he was under no obligation to confide in me. I also acknowledged that thoughts of him were intruding, and I didn't have time to deal with a relationship. I needed to figure out who killed my landlord and my next-door neighbor.

With that resolved, I walked into the house in a much better state. Red and Stephanie were sitting outside on the back deck. Dixie's car was parked out front, so I wasn't surprised to see her standing at the deck rail. When I got closer to the door, I saw they were watching the golden and Dixie's two standard poodles in a game of tag. I took off Aggie's leash and opened the door. She flew down the stairs, ready to join in the fun. At first, I'd been concerned about her getting hurt playing with the bigger, nearly sixty-pound dogs. After watching them play, I realized two things. First, the larger dogs were surprisingly gentle with her, a lot gentler when she was in the fray than when it was only big dogs. The second thing I realized was that Aggie was a lot faster than the bigger dogs and able to turn on a dime. Aggie leapt into the yard, and the chase ensued. She quickly left the three larger dogs eating her dust as she darted and dodged around the yard. Dixie had removed the pen, and the dogs raced around the empty lot behind the house.

"Don't worry, I won't let her escape, and if she does, Leia and Chyna will herd her back." Dixie looked at me. "Although you really should get those zip ties to keep her from sliding the latch on the pen. Poodles are smart dogs, and she'll get out if she wants to."

"Sorry, I keep forgetting." I stole a glance back at Stephanie. "Has the owner shown up?"

Dixie shook her head. "Not yet."

The doorbell rang. "That must be him." I started to get up, but Red beat me to the deck door.

"Perhaps you should let me?"

I nodded and watched as he went inside.

Stephanie wiped a tear. "Let's get this over with."

We rounded up the dogs, which proved a lot easier than I thought when Dixie pulled out a whistle and then held up her treat pouch.

The dogs bounded up the stairs. The poodles skidded to a stop in front of Dixie and plopped their butts onto the floor. The golden stood, tail wagging, and then sat. Aggie stood on her back legs and pawed at Dixie's pants.

Dixie unzipped her treat pouch and pulled out some brown, foul-smelling lumps.

"Oh God, what is that?" I scrunched my nose.

"Dried liver." Dixie tossed pieces to Leia and Chyna, who caught the treats in midair and scarfed them down. The golden also got a treat. "Sit." She held up a piece of liver in front of Aggie's nose and then moved the treat backward and down. When her butt hit the ground, she immediately gave her the treat and praised her profusely.

We glanced inside. Red was talking to a man who looked to be in his middle thirties with long dreadlocks pulled back into a ponytail. The two men headed to the back. Red opened the door.

The golden turned and headed to the stranger, tail wagging. He got on his back legs and placed his front paws on the man's chest.

"Rusty, good boy." The stranger hugged the dog, who clearly recognized him.

Stephanie swallowed hard, stood up, and walked over to the man. "Obviously, he knows you." She looked lovingly at the golden. "But we don't."

The stranger looked up. "Sorry. Call me Barry."

Stephanie looked suspiciously at the stranger. "Just Barry?" The lack of a last name hung in the air.

The man got down on one knee and buried his head in the dog's coat.

I looked at Red, who shrugged and shook his head. "Barry, my name's Lilly."

Stephanie wasn't quite ready to give up graciously. "Perhaps you can tell us how you happened to lose Rusty?"

Barry continued to pet the golden, who was now lying on his back while the man scratched his stomach. He waited so long, I didn't think he'd answer. However, after a long pause, he sighed and rose to his feet. "I didn't know I'd have to submit to an interrogation to get my dog back."

"Well, now you know." Stephanie put a hand on her hip and stared the stranger down. "I want to know how you misplaced your dog and why he was found injured and cowering under our deck?"

Barry's eyes darted from Stephanie to Dixie and me. If he hoped to find help in our expressions, he was sadly mistaken.

"Animal abuse is a crime in Tennessee." Dixie stared, hand on hip.

"Hey, I never abused my dog."

"Really? Prove it. We found him starving with a badly damaged paw hiding under the deck. No microchip. No tattoo." I used my mom voice and was happy to see him squirm.

"We put flyers up all over the neighborhood, veterinarians' offices, shelters, and on Facebook and reported him to every rescue-dog organization within fifty miles. Yet you were nowhere to be found, and then you think you can just waltz in here and take him away like that?" Stephanie snapped her fingers.

"You're crazy." He grabbed the golden's collar and turned to walk away but ran into Red, who stood like a brick wall between him and the door.

Red stood, arms folded, feet planted. His face was solid stone, and his eyes were granite. He slowly pulled out his shield and flashed it to the stranger. "I think you need to answer the ladies' questions."

Fear crossed the man's face but vanished in a flash. He tried a change of tactics. He laughed. "Hey, I don't want any trouble. I just came to get my dog."

"Hey, is everything okay?"

I looked around and saw Michael and Charity Cunningham walking down the street. "Do you know him?" I pointed. "Because he claims Rusty is his dog." I turned back to the wayward dog owner.

Barry's face was as white as a sheet, and I saw panic reflected in his eyes. Before anyone knew what was happening, he pushed Stephanie to one side and raced down the deck stairs.

Red hurried after him but was slowed by the fact that Stephanie, three poodles and the golden, and I were blocking his path.

He looked at me. "You okay?"

I nodded, and he took off in pursuit.

When Michael and Charity Cunningham saw Red on the chase, rather than rubbernecking, hiding, or using their phones to call 9-1-1, they took off in pursuit.

We watched the action from the deck.

"What was that about?" Dixie asked.

"No idea." I turned to Stephanie. "Are you okay?"

She nodded.

In a few minutes, Red came back and ran up the stairs. "Sorry, but he got away."

For a brief moment, I wondered if he meant Barry or Michael Cunningham.

"Did you want us to call the police?" I asked.

He shook his head. "There's no need. I've got to go back to work anyway."

"Back to work?" I asked.

He nodded. "I went in early to take care of paperwork and get caught up on a few things." He rubbed the back of his neck. "I didn't want to leave you ladies alone too long."

I felt ashamed for my earlier behavior and wished I could have a REWIND button.

Stephanie petted the golden we now knew as Rusty. "What's wrong with your owner, boy?"

The golden wagged his tail and placed his head on her lap.

Red looked at his watch several times in less than a minute.

"You should go. We'll be fine. We've got four dogs who, I have no doubt, will deter and defend if necessary." I picked Aggie up and gave her a squeeze.

Red reached over and scratched Aggie behind her ear, causing her back leg to jiggle. "I have no doubt this little one will defend you with her last breath. She's got the heart of a pit bull."

Dixie leaned over. "In addition to the four dogs, I've got two guns in my car. When you leave, I'm bringing them in. If Barry comes back, I'll turn him from a tenor to a soprano with one shot."

Red smiled. "I hope you have a license to carry those weapons."

"Of course I do." Dixie folded her arms across her chest. "I pity the fool who tries to take my guns away."

Red held up his hands in surrender. "No, ma'am, I wouldn't dream of it." He grinned. "I guess I'd better get to work."

"Work. Oh my, that reminds me. I ran into Jackson Phillips when I was out walking Aggie."

Red sat down and listened eagerly.

I told them what I'd learned from the association president and about my new job as subdivision treasurer.

"If Theodore Livingston accused Carol Lynn Hargrove of embezzling funds from the association, I'd say that gives her a pretty strong motive for murder." Stephanie turned to Red. "Wouldn't you agree?"

He nodded. "That explains her strange behavior when we ran into her the other day."

"I'd forgotten about that." I quickly told Stephanie and Dixie about the encounter I had prior to finding Theodore Livingston's body.

"Sounds like Carol Lynn Hargrove is one angry woman," Dixie said.

"Sounds like she's not the only one with a motive." Red pulled out a notepad and scribbled a few notes.

"You mean Jackson Phillips?" I asked.

He nodded. "That story about how Theodore Livingston caused him to lose his job might have made him angry enough to commit murder."

"The question is did they have the opportunity?" I asked.

Red stood up again. "That's what I intend to find out."

Chapter 19

The rest of the day was uneventful. Dixie, Stephanie, and I picked apart our suspects like vultures on a carcass left in the desert until there wasn't anything left to pick. We then went inside and picked apart the delicious chicken Red had prepared for dinner. It was well seasoned with a bit of a kick. The mashed potatoes were creamy, with just the right amount of lumps to indicate they were real potatoes and not instant, and the collard greens were tasty.

"He's a really good cook." Dixie sucked a chicken bone. "I like him."

I let the opportunity to agree with her pass and pretended to be engrossed in the sweet tea I was drinking.

"I asked Joe about him. If you're interested." Stephanie raised a brow and struggled to hide a smile.

I shrugged.

"Well, I want to know." Dixie wiped her hands. "Spill it."

Stephanie hesitated, but then sat up and took a sip of tea. "He and Red met in the military."

"I didn't know Joe had been in the military," I said.

She nodded. "He enlisted after high school because he didn't know what he wanted to do with his life." She took another sip of her tea. "Anyway, Red was his commanding officer. He was engaged, so this was going to be his last tour of duty. They were stationed in the Middle East." She talked slower. "Joe doesn't like talking about it, so I'm hazy on some of the details. But they were supposed to go into a village and rescue civilians, and it was a trap. They came under heavy fire." She grew very quiet. "Joe said the only reason they got out alive was because of Red. He fought like a crazy man for two days. Eventually, a helicopter found their location and rescued them...most of them."

"What do you mean?" I asked.

She swallowed. "Red didn't make it. He stayed behind and fought to give the others a chance to get away."

"Oh my goodness." Dixie stared, mouth open. "How did he get out?"

Stephanie shook her head. "He won't talk about it. Joe said they looked for him for two weeks. Eventually, someone fitting his description was found almost dead in an abandoned cave. He was airlifted to Germany." She paused. "Joe said he'd been tortured."

"Is that how he got the scar?" I asked.

She nodded. "Joe says he's got a lot of them."

"Wow. So Red is a hero." Dixie wiped a tear.

Stephanie sighed. "He has a lot of medals, but he doesn't like to talk about it, and Joe said we aren't to mention it."

We nodded.

Something she'd said was bothering me. "What happened to his fiancée? You said he was engaged."

"That's the sad part. Apparently, when she saw him, she broke off the engagement."

"What a...well, if I wasn't a lady, I'd say exactly what she was," Dixie said.

Stephanie took a deep breath. "Joe said it took a long time for him to recover. When he did, he became a daredevil. He took on more and more dangerous jobs. He went into covert operations. A few years ago, his mom got sick, and he moved back to Tennessee and joined the TBI."

We sat in silence for several moments.

When we heard the front door, we readjusted our faces to hide the guilt and pity that signaled we'd been talking about anything other than happy topics.

I knew our efforts weren't successful when the first words out of his mouth were, "What are you ladies talking about that you don't want me to know?"

"I don't know what you're talking about," we all chimed in.

He stared suspiciously from Stephanie to Dixie to me. "Right? You have guilt written all over your faces. What's up?"

"Nothing. We weren't talking about anything, were we?" Dixie said too eagerly.

"Hmmm...wanna try again?" Red stared.

Stephanie and Dixie turned to me.

I thought quickly. Lying wasn't my strong suit, but the best defense was a good offense. "We were talking about something you aren't going to like." I licked my lips, which were suddenly very dry.

"I figured that much." He folded his arms. "Spill it."

I took a sip of tea. "We were talking about sneaking next door and searching Theodore Livingston's house."

Stephanie and Dixie's faces both registered shock and then relief.

"*What?*" Red exploded.

"It's not like it's a crime scene or anything. Maybe we could find a clue that might help us figure out who else wanted him dead."

"No. No. Absolutely *not*! You can't go breaking into the house of a murder victim and looking around for clues. Are you crazy?"

"Why not?" I decided to string things out longer. Since I had no intention of searching Theodore Livingston's house, I was perfectly okay conceding this argument but didn't want to give things away by giving up too quickly.

"Look, I know you like to read mysteries, but this isn't a book, and you're not Nancy Drew. You need to leave this to the trained professionals. This is real life, and whoever killed Theodore Livingston and Robert Hansen won't hesitate to kill you." He allowed his gaze to linger on each of us. "Besides, breaking into someone's home is still against the law." He looked at Stephanie. "You're a lawyer. I'm surprised at you."

Stephanie blushed and looked down.

"Even if they're dead?" Dixie asked.

"Yes! Even if they're dead." He rubbed the back of his neck. "You need to promise me you won't try to break into Theodore Livingston's house under any circumstances." He looked stern. "I mean it."

I sighed. "Alright. I promise."

"Cross my heart." Stephanie followed up by marking an X across her chest.

Dixie held up three fingers. "Scout's honor."

He looked at each of us again and then shook his head. "I don't know if I should believe you or not."

"We gave our word." I sighed. "I guess, we'll have to come up with another idea."

He looked as though he was ready to blow his lid again, but I halted the explosion by holding up my hands in surrender.

"Just kidding. Now, why don't you sit down and let me fix you a plate and you can tell us what you found out."

He looked at me with skepticism but didn't push his luck. Instead, he sighed and sat down.

I prepared a plate while Stephanie poured him a large glass of sweet tea. He still looked suspicious when I placed the plate in front of him, but he didn't say anything and eventually picked up his fork and started to eat.

I waited until he'd taken several bites before resuming the conversation. "Did you find out anything about Barry?"

He nodded. "Surprisingly, I think I did." He took a sip of tea. "What do you know about your landlord?"

I was slightly taken aback by the question but took a moment and explored the recesses of my brain. Even though I hadn't been in this rental for much more than one week, a lot had happened since I'd first talked to my landlord's mother in that café, and as Dixie liked to say, *I'd slept since then.* "When we met Jo Ellen Hansen, she said her son had left the country unexpectedly." I turned to Dixie for confirmation.

She nodded.

"She said she came to check on things and found the front door open." I thought back. "He left quickly. He didn't move his furniture or turn the utilities off; I just got them transferred into my name."

I repeated what his mother had said to us about her son when we met her at the café, which wasn't much.

Stephanie shared the information from the text messages she'd exchanged with him prior to his death, although Red was already well aware of them.

"What's this about?"

He held up a hand. "One more, what about Theodore Livingston?"

Again, I recounted every encounter I'd had with my neighbor—from our disagreement over dog poo to my humiliation at the association meeting and, lastly, our brief conversation when I took him shortbread cookies and apologized. When I finished, I gave him a cold stare. "Now it's your turn."

He sighed. "I learned Theodore Livingston had a younger brother, named Martin."

We stared at him, waiting for him to connect the dots.

"Apparently, the two didn't get along."

Dixie snorted. "Theodore Livingston didn't get along with anyone."

"This time he may have been justified." He shifted in his seat. "Turns out Martin had been in and out of prison his entire life."

"What did he do?" I asked.

"What didn't he do?" Red pulled out a notepad and flipped through some pages. "Assault, grand theft, extortion."

"Sounds like a real loser," Dixie said.

"Okay, so Theodore Livingston had a brother." I frowned. "What's the big deal?"

Red leaned forward. "The brother got out of prison a few days ago and came knocking on his brother's door. Theodore agrees to let him stay, but then one night he just disappears."

"Maybe he found someone else to mooch from," Dixie said.

"He left his things. After a few days, Theodore filed a missing persons report." He shook his head. "The police didn't pay too much attention. He was a crackpot who had called the police too many times."

I stared at Red. "You think Martin killed Robert Hansen?"

He shook his head. "I don't know what to think, but it's suspicious that Robert Hansen is murdered around the same time that Martin Livingston disappears."

"Is that it?" I asked.

"I also learned that Robert Hansen had a dog." Red put his notebook back in his pocket.

I smiled. "I could have told you that. His mother mentioned it when we moved in."

"You didn't tell me that," he said.

I shrugged. "I didn't think it was important."

He smiled. "Did she tell you what breed of dog?"

I looked at Dixie, but she merely shook her head.

Stephanie had been staring down at Rusty. "But I don't understand? Who is Barry? Why did he leave his dog? Why did he run?"

Red shrugged. "I'll ask him the next time I run into him."

Something from earlier was nagging in the back of my mind. "Didn't you think the Cunninghams were odd? I mean, did you see the way they took off after you?"

Dixie nodded. "I wondered who they were chasing."

"Maybe you should look into them." I turned to Red. "They seem shady to me."

Red ate his food. "What makes you say that?"

"The way they just flew after you. Most people would have stayed as far away from that scene as possible," Stephanie said.

"Plus, they've got those brighter than sunlight veneers. I never did trust them," Dixie said.

Red chuckled. "I can't arrest people for having veneers."

"Maybe not, but you could look into their backgrounds." I felt a bit hurt that he didn't seem to be taking my suggestion seriously. Then it hit me. "Wait, you know them." I stared hard.

Red ate silently.

"They're working for you. They're undercover agents with the TBI."

He didn't say anything, but the vein throbbing at the side of his head told me I was right.

Stephanie looked from me to Red. "She's right, isn't she?"

He sighed. "Okay, yes."

"I knew it."

"Hot damn!" Dixie smacked the table. "How's that for Nancy Drew?"

He grinned and held up his hands. "They are working undercover, and I could lose my job for telling you that."

"You didn't tell us anything. She guessed." Dixie pointed to me.

"How'd you guess?" He looked at me.

I struggled to put my finger on it but couldn't think of one definite moment when I knew. "I don't know. I remembered you said Robert Hansen was under investigation, and then when they took off after you, it wasn't like nosy neighbors." I thought back. "They ran with authority, like you did." I shrugged. "I guess it's all my Nancy Drew books."

He shook his head. "You're never going to let me forget that, are you?"

"Nope!" I grinned. "Just remember, Nancy Drew may not have been a trained professional, but she's got a perfect record, and just like the Canadian Mounties, she always gets her man!"

The rest of the evening was uneventful, but I noticed Red seemed more on edge.

The next morning, I phoned Linda Kay and explained that I wanted to go to my landlord's funeral. She was, of course, very agreeable. Even though I promised to come in for the afternoon, she suggested I take the entire day.

When I was dressed, I let Aggie out and then headed into the living room area. I wasn't surprised to see Red in the kitchen but was surprised to see the blanket on the sofa. Obviously, if he'd slept at all, it had been on the sofa, rather than in the bed upstairs. From the color of his eyes, which looked red and tired, I didn't think he'd slept.

"Good morning." Despite having tossed for quite some time with thoughts that made me blush in the light of day, I was in a good mood.

He handed me a cup of coffee and the bottle of creamer I kept in the fridge, along with two packets of artificial sweetener.

I was momentarily taken aback by his attention to detail. He had obviously watched me prepare my coffee and knew what I liked. "Thank you."

He nodded and then slid an omelet onto a plate. "You look nice."

"Thank you." I perched on a stool at the breakfast bar and shoved a forkful of fluffy golden deliciousness into my mouth.

"Okay?" He stared at my face for the answer.

I closed my eyes and savored the yummy goodness. When I opened my eyes, he smiled and nodded.

"That's the reaction I like."

Stephanie came out wearing a simple black wrap dress, which floated onto her hips and hugged her curves. "That smells delicious. Is there one for me?"

Red nodded. "Coming right up." He handed her a cup of steaming-hot coffee and returned to his skillet. Within seconds, he slid another omelet onto a plate, and we both sat, eating and drinking coffee.

I looked up. "Aren't you going to eat?"

He sipped his coffee. "I've already eaten." He looked at his watch. "I need to go downtown and talk to Officer Lewis." He folded his arms across his chest. "I don't suppose I can talk you out of going to the funeral."

We shook our heads.

"I didn't think so. Then can I remind you to please be careful?" He looked at his watch. "I'm going to ask Officer Lewis to send someone to cover the funeral. I don't anticipate trouble, but I'd feel better if there was someone present. Sometimes a uniformed officer can deter criminals, and deterrence is exactly what I'm hoping for."

He gave a few other cautions and then made sure we had his number programmed into our phones. Eventually, he left.

Stephanie smiled. "He's a nice man." She looked at me out of the corner of her eyes. "And he's a great cook."

"No argument from me."

"So what're you going to do about it?"

"Nothing."

"Mom, come on. I know Dad was—"

"This has nothing to do with your dad."

By the skeptical look in her eyes, I knew she didn't believe me.

"Okay, maybe deep down it does. However, I have several good reasons for not getting involved with anyone right now."

"Name two."

"I don't believe in counting my chickens before they're hatched."

She got down from the bar and collected our empty plates and cups. "What does that mean?"

"It means, I'm not thinking about a relationship with a man who hasn't asked me for a date, let alone anything remotely resembling a relationship. I barely know him."

Stephanie loaded our empty plates into the dishwasher. "Okay, it's a reason. Not a good reason, but it's a reason. What's the other reason?"

"I think we need to focus on solving these murders. If I'm in jail for murder, it won't matter how nice I think he is."

"Good point."

Chapter 20

Dixie picked us up and headed down Interstate 75 south toward Georgia. Robert Hansen's mom lived in Stone Mountain, which was about two hours away by normal driver standards. We made the trip in a little over an hour, with Dixie's lead foot weaving in and out of traffic and whizzing past semis and practically anyone content to drive the speed limit.

To get to the church, which was just north of Atlanta, she pulled off the interstate and headed down back roads until she pulled up in the parking lot of a small, red-brick building with a large steeple and stained-glass windows.

Stephanie and I unfolded ourselves and stretched.

"Aunt Dixie likes speed more than your average NASCAR racer," Stephanie whispered as we followed Dixie into the building.

I leaned close to avoid being overheard. "She considers the seventy miles per hour speed limit more of a suggestion than a requirement."

We went inside the building and signed the guest book. The church had wooden pews with red cushions on either side of a main aisle. At the front, a white casket was draped in floral sprays. I wasn't the only one of our group who released a sigh of relief at seeing that the funeral would be one with a closed casket. I shivered at the memory of looking at the body, and while I'm sure the undertaker would have done his best, I wasn't anxious to see that face again.

There was an enormous display of flowers at the front of the church.

I whispered to Dixie, "We should have sent flowers."

"We did. I ordered them online, and the florist promised they'd be here in time." She craned her neck and then pointed to a nice vase with yellow roses. "There it is."

She was good at the details. I would have to remember to do something to repay her. I knew her well enough to know she wouldn't accept money, but I'd think of something.

There was a small section at the front left of the church reserved for family. We moved to the right, slid down a pew to the end so we had a good view of the family, and waited.

The viewing, or what used to be called "the wake," was first. A few people came in and walked to the front. They spent a moment or two, and then turned and left; some, like us, found a seat to wait for the actual funeral.

The funeral itself was small. Jo Ellen Hansen was distraught and broke down multiple times during the short ceremony. However, there were several people around who comforted her. Personally, I didn't want to imagine the grief she must be feeling. No parent was ever prepared to bury their children. I glanced at Stephanie and got choked up thinking about what I'd do if anything ever happened to her or David.

Thankfully, the service was short, and the church had a cemetery behind the sanctuary, so there was no long automotive procession. We merely walked out back and listened while the minister prayed and recited the traditional "ashes to ashes" quote from Genesis. Afterward, Mrs. Hansen was escorted to the basement. Food was provided, and we stayed to pay our respects.

Dixie was the first person to approach her. I wondered what she would say, but I needn't have worried. She walked up and embraced Mrs. Hansen.

The older woman put her head on Dixie's shoulder and wept. The two stood like that for several minutes. Eventually, Dixie helped her into a seat.

"I'm so sorry. I just can't seem to stop crying."

"Honey, don't you dare apologize. You cry as much as you need to." Dixie patted her back and sat in the chair next to her and kept her arm around the grieving woman while she cried.

When the tide of tears slowed, Stephanie and I gave our condolences and hurried away, leaving Dixie to deal with Mrs. Hansen.

We sat at one of the tables and were quickly handed a plate of food.

"Nothing like fried chicken during a time of grief." Stephanie drank Hawaiian Punch from a Styrofoam cup.

I was just about to take a sip of punch when I looked up and spotted Freemont Hopewell approaching Dixie and Mrs. Hansen. I nudged Stephanie. "Look, that's Freemont." I pointed with my head in their direction.

Stephanie looked over and whistled. "He's handsome...too handsome."

"Agreed." Freemont, with his fancy suit and manicured nails, looked out of place at the plain, red-brick church. The contrast of his immaculate clothes and fastidiously groomed hair looked phony when viewed in the context of the simple elegance and honesty of the small country church.

I couldn't imagine Freemont eating fried chicken, green beans, and mashed potatoes on a paper plate with plastic cutlery and drinking fruit punch from a Styrofoam cup. I was surprised when he spotted me and headed to the table.

He flashed a large smile, which showed nearly all of his teeth. "May I join you?"

I shrugged.

He must have taken that as consent because he pulled out a folding chair and sat down. He turned to Stephanie. "This beautiful lady has to be your daughter. She has your eyes."

Stephanie nodded but didn't extend her hand.

"Yes, this is my daughter, Stephanie." I turned to her. "Stephanie, Freemont Hopewell."

He smiled again as she picked up a chicken leg and bit into it. The look on his face made me want to laugh.

He forced another smile and then turned to me. "I wanted to apologize for my behavior the other day at lunch. I'm sure my manners were appalling, and I want you to know I can only say I'm terribly sorry."

Something in the way he apologized told me he had no clue why he was apologizing but knew it was something that needed to be done.

"Please tell me you'll forgive me?"

I nodded.

He smiled.

Before he could say anything else, I asked, "Did you know Robert Hansen well?"

"Not well. We were business associates, nothing more."

Stephanie wiped the chicken grease from her mouth. "Really? Two hours is a long time to drive for a funeral of a business associate you aren't close to."

A vein on the side of his head throbbed. He examined his perfectly manicured fingernails for several seconds. When neither Stephanie nor I said anything, he looked up. "We were business associates. He was an investor in my art and antiques shop, and I was an investor in his real estate ventures."

I put down my chicken and stared hard so I could watch Freemont's eyes. "What real estate ventures?"

He shrugged. "Robert saw himself as some...I don't know, real estate tycoon or something. He wanted to buy land and develop and sell it for military bases and airports. He had a lot of big dreams." He shook his head. "He bought a lot of land in the subdivision where he lived, and whenever any of his neighbors' houses went on the market, he snatched them up."

"But the subdivision is in an area that's already residential. How was he going to have it developed?" I asked.

Freemont sighed. "He had a contact who gave him inside information about something that was going to happen, so..." He shrugged.

"I heard you own an antiques shop. And aren't you also an artist?"

For some reason, something flashed across his face.

I tried to sort out what it was I'd seen but was distracted when I looked up and saw Red walking toward me. Our gazes met. He made a barely perceptible shake of his head.

He sat at the long table with one manly courtesy seat separating him from Freemont. He nodded and then turned to smile at the older woman who placed a plate of food in front of him before he picked up his plastic tableware and started to eat.

I turned back to Freemont, who was still talking.

"I studied at the Royal College of Art." He picked a nonexistent piece of lint from his sleeve.

Stephanie feigned surprise. "Really? The Royal College of Art is one of the most prestigious art schools in the world. You must be really talented to have gotten a degree there."

Freemont sat up straight and smiled. "Well, I don't like to brag, but I was one of the few Americans admitted, and I finished at the top of my class."

"So, you graduated from the Royal College of Art?" Stephanie asked.

I stole a glance at her from the corner of my eye. Something in her manner and voice alerted me to the fact that she was up to something. So I watched Freemont more cautiously than I might have done otherwise.

He preened a bit. "Yes, I got my undergraduate degree there."

"Very interesting." Stephanie smiled. "Especially since the Royal College of Art doesn't have an undergraduate program. It's strictly for postgraduate study."

Freemont's face grew beet red. He narrowed his eyes and looked as though he would have liked to jump over the table and strangle Stephanie. In fact, he stood up and leaned across the table and glared. Before he could open his mouth to speak, Red was standing next to him.

He smiled and said softly, "Sit down, or I'll be forced to cuff you and drag you out of here like the lying piece of—"

"Red, remember you're still in church," I said.

He sighed. "The lying con man that you are." He looked at me.

I nodded.

As quickly as the color appeared in Freemont's face, it drained, leaving him white as a sheet. His eyes darted around like a trapped rabbit.

In the hand that wasn't clutching Freemont's hand, Red discreetly flashed his shield. "Sit down."

Freemont paused for a second, then dropped back down into his seat.

Red slid over into the chair next to Freemont and sidled up next to him so they were shoulder to shoulder. "Now, let's have a nice quiet conversation."

"What is this? Who are you?" Freemont picked up the Styrofoam cup he'd snubbed earlier and took a drink of punch. His hand shook, and he spilled the punch on the white paper tablecloth.

"This is a conversation. I'm going to ask you a few questions, and you're going to answer them." Red stared.

"I don't have to talk to you without my attorney."

He shook his head and sighed. "I'm sorry to hear you say that. See, I was hoping we could do this the easy way, but"—he shrugged—"it looks like you want to do things the hard way." He opened his jacket and showed a shoulder holster and handcuffs. He slowly reached for the cuffs and slowly stood up.

"No, wait." Freemont looked around. "Sit down."

Red sat down.

He sighed. "What do you want to know?" He picked up his paper napkin and wiped his forehead, which was beaded with sweat.

"That's better." Red placed his elbows on the table and leaned close. "I want to know what you and Robert Hansen were really involved in."

For a split second, Freemont looked as though he would protest; however, something in Red's face made him stop. I'm not sure if it was the set of his jaw, the vein that pulsed at the side of his head, or the stony-hard look in his eyes, but whatever it was, it worked.

Freemont glanced at Red and sighed. "Okay." He looked around to make sure no one was standing nearby. "Robert was involved in a lot of...stuff. He *was* into real estate. He was also involved in importing...antiquities and...other items—"

"What kind of items?" Stephanie asked.

"Everything from Egyptian art and pottery to documents."

I leaned forward. "Documents? What kind of documents?" I tried to imagine what types of documents my former landlord could have been importing, but my imagination failed.

He looked at each of us and sighed. "Information. Robert was a government contractor. He had access to information about upcoming government projects. He knew people and knew information that, in the right hands, could have given one company an advantage."

"You mean he was selling insider information about bids that would allow a company to outbid the opposition and secure lucrative government contracts." I tried not to scowl, but I felt my brow furrowing with distaste.

Freemont nodded. "It sounds so ugly when you put it like that."

I picked up my napkin and wiped my hands. "It *is* ugly." I felt a need to bathe.

Red nudged Freemont. "Okay, so he was cheating the government and the American taxpayers. Where do you fit into this?" He hurriedly continued before Freemont could protest. "Before you deny involvement, let me just say we've had Robert Hansen under surveillance for a long time."

Freemont paused for several seconds and then nodded. "It's hard to sell objects without proof of provenance, and not all of the antiques Robert imported had the proper documentation, if you get my meaning." He glanced at Red.

He nodded. "So Hansen provided the objects, and you forged the provenance?"

"Wait, if you have this lucrative forgery business going, why were you working at the museum?" I asked.

Freemont shifted uncomfortably in his seat.

"Go on; the lady asked you a question." Red nudged him.

He refused to make eye contact with me but looked at his hands. "I needed access to the museum's records so I could make copies of some of the documents."

"Why did you quit?"

He shrugged. "I don't know anything about accounting—"

"That's obvious," I mumbled.

He bristled. "Well, I started getting letters from the IRS, and then I overheard Linda Kay talking about an audit, and I panicked."

"You didn't give any of your shady antiques to the museum, did you?" I stared at him and tried to remember the exact moment when my feelings for Freemont changed from attraction to revulsion.

He shook his head. "Linda Kay looks like a sweet Southern belle, but she's sharp as a razor. Plus, that eagle-eyed assistant of hers barely left me alone for five minutes. You saw how quickly he came into your office that day I came to take you to lunch."

I hid a smile and made a mental note to take Jacob a couple of his favorite pastries from Da Vinci's tomorrow.

THE PUPPY WHO KNEW TOO MUCH

"You were never interested in me, were you?" I stared at him. "You just wanted to use me to gain access to the museum's records."

Freemont shook his head, but his eyes told me everything I needed to know. I felt grateful I hadn't allowed myself to be used by him.

Stephanie reached over and gave my hand a squeeze, but when I evaluated my feelings, I realized I didn't feel anything for Freemont.

Red asked a few additional questions, which Freemont answered, although he made sure to place the greatest amount of blame on Robert Hansen, while making himself seem like a poor, innocent dupe who was just following along. Up to this point, Red had been stern but relatively calm. However, as though an internal switch had flipped, something changed. Something behind his eyes grew cold, and I shivered as though the temperature had dropped. His gaze was glued to his prey like a cat stalking a mouse. He leaned forward. "Did you kill Robert Hansen?"

The blood drained completely from Freemont's face, and his hands shook. "No. No. I swear. I didn't kill him. Why would I?" His voice went up two octaves.

"Shhh." I looked around and noticed that the few people who had stayed for the meal had all left and the ladies who'd served us were anxiously waiting for us to finish. "I think we need to leave."

Stephanie and I gathered our belongings.

Red stood. "Come on, Hopewell. I'm taking you in."

Freemont Hopewell's eyes pleaded. "Come on. I swear I didn't kill him. I cooperated. I told you everything I know." His eyes darted around like a trapped rat. "Besides, I'm not even sure Robert is really dead."

"What do you mean you're not sure if he's dead? You're at his funeral, aren't you?" I asked.

Freemont shrugged. "I never saw the body."

"Now you're just grasping at straws, and I don't have time for this," Red huffed. "You can tell it again downtown. Let's go."

"What about my car?"

"Maybe you can convince one of the ladies to drive it back for you."

Based on the stricken look on his face, it was clear Hopewell would have rather eaten dirt than allow anyone else to drive his car.

"Or I can have it towed back to Chattanooga and you can pick it up from the impound lot."

Freemont rolled his eyes. "Do either of you know how to drive a stick?"

My husband had owned a car dealership, so both Stephanie and I were well aware of how to drive a manual transmission. However, I wasn't interested in folding myself into that tiny toddler Power Wheels toy car again.

After a few seconds, Stephanie sighed. "Alright." She held out her hand.

Freemont handed over the keys. "Now, be careful shifting gears and don't press too hard on the clutch or it'll stick."

Stephanie's eyes narrowed. "Is the clutch the pedal on the left or the right?"

A look of sheer terror crossed Freemont's face. For a split second, I thought he was going to reconsider having his car towed rather than allow a woman who didn't know which pedal was the brake and which the clutch to drive his car. "Maybe I should—" He held out his hand for the keys.

Stephanie smiled. "Just kidding."

Red's eyes flashed, and his lips twitched briefly. He plastered on his serious law-enforcement mask and grabbed Freemont by the arm. "Come on. Let's go."

Chapter 21

Stephanie followed Dixie and me back to Chattanooga. Dixie stayed under the sound barrier on the return trip since she knew Stephanie was following. We drove into downtown Chattanooga and pulled up to the police station, where Red had told us to leave Freemont's car. Stephanie left the keys with the desk sergeant.

"Where to now?" I asked once Stephanie was in the car and we were headed down the interstate.

"I'm hungry," Dixie announced.

I hadn't eaten much of the food provided at the church, especially once Red arrived and things got interesting, but Dixie had spent the entire time with Mrs. Hansen and hadn't eaten at all.

She sped around the city, getting off the interstate at the area known as East Ridge. Dixie was born and raised in this area, and she knew all of the best places to eat. She'd taken us to numerous restaurants, but I was surprised when she pulled her Lexus into the parking lot of what I could only describe as a dive.

She hopped out and stretched.

Stephanie and I were slower to leave the safety of the car. Eventually, when it became clear this wasn't a joke, we reluctantly climbed out.

"Well, come on." Dixie marched toward the door.

Stephanie whispered, "Is Aunt Dixie serious?"

I shrugged. "I guess so, but let's stay close to her. She's the one with the gun."

We hurried to catch up to Dixie, who had made it to the door and was waiting for us.

We entered the restaurant and stood huddled by the door. Dixie marched past us to a wooden seat near the window. She plopped down. We followed her example.

She picked up the laminated menus and handed one to each of us. "Best greasy burgers and shakes you'll ever eat."

An exceptionally thin teen with jet black hair, skintight black jeans, a black T-shirt, black lipstick, and black polish on his nails came over to our table. He placed napkins and a knife down for each of us. He had tattoos on every visible surface of his skin and earlobe expanders in each ear. "What can I get you ladies?"

"They're going to need a moment, but can you bring us three waters and an order of fried cauliflower while they look?"

He nodded and left to place the orders.

"They have burgers with peanut butter?" Stephanie frowned.

I shook my head. "I'm more concerned with the liquid nitrogen they put in the milkshakes."

I accidentally knocked over the salt shaker, scattering salt all over the table.

"Don't knock it until you've tried it." Before the waiter could get back to clean our table, Dixie reached into her purse and pulled out a package of hand wipes and cleaned the surface. When she was done, she looked at our faces and burst out laughing. "You two look as though you think I've lost my mind."

"I had wondered. This place doesn't exactly seem like your style." I stared at my friend.

She laughed. "It's not the fanciest place in the Scenic City, but it really does have the best burgers and shakes. Trust me."

I put the menu down. "Okay, I trust you."

Our Goth waiter returned with the waters and fried cauliflower and stood waiting for us to order.

Dixie took a moment and glanced at us and then ordered burgers and shakes for each of us.

Orders placed, Dixie turned to me. "Okay, fill me in on what happened with Freemont, and I'll fill you in on my conversation with Mrs. Hansen."

We quickly told her what we'd learned. When we finished, the waiter brought our shakes.

Dixie watched our faces as we sipped.

"That's amazing." Stephanie's eyes were huge saucers as she sucked the chocolate goodness of her Shock-o-matic.

I might have moaned as the cashews and Himalayan pink salt of the Cat-man-du froze my insides.

Dixie's face broke into a huge smile. "See, I told you." She sucked on her own shake, which included Chattanooga's specialty, moon pies.

After a few seconds, she popped another piece of cauliflower into her mouth and then wiped her lips. "Okay, so while you guys were trying to wring a confession out of Freemont, I got a chance to talk to Mrs. Hansen." She shook her head. "Poor thing is devastated. Robert was her only son, and she doted on him." She halted while the waiter brought our burgers and onion rings.

She waited while we bit into our burgers. "First, I found out that Mrs. Hansen is perfectly okay with you staying in the house for as long as you want. She's too upset to try and deal with it."

I nodded, grateful Dixie had thought to check with Mrs. Hansen about that, although given the recent death toll in the subdivision, I wasn't sure I wanted to stay, even if the police didn't arrest me for the murders.

"Did she know of anyone who would want to kill him?" Stephanie asked.

She shook her head. "No. She was so gaga over her son, she can't imagine anyone wanting to harm him." Dixie bit into her hamburger.

"Did she know about his...extracurricular activities?" I asked.

Dixie shook her head. "No. She thinks he was a legitimate businessman. However, she did say something curious." Dixie wiped her mouth and started digging in her purse. "She hadn't known her son was back in the country, but she did say a couple of days ago, she got an envelope with a business card with the East Brainerd post office's address on it and a key." She pulled out a small key and handed it to me.

Stephanie leaned close and stared at the key as though she expected it to suddenly take wings and fly. It was a regulation key. Nothing special.

"Why didn't she go to the post office and see what was in the box?" Stephanie asked.

"The poor woman's a basket case. She's just buried her son. She wasn't in any state to drive on the interstate to the East Brainerd post office. I told her we'd be happy to go and get whatever was in there and send it to her."

I stared at my friend. "We? Are you kidding? Red is going to be furious when he finds out you have this and didn't tell him."

Dixie shrugged. "Okay, do you want to tell him?"

I hesitated. "Noooo."

"I didn't think so." Dixie finished her burger. "I figured we'd pick up the package and *then* we'd tell him about it. I mean, it could be nothing."

"Right, it could be a notice saying he won a million dollars from one of those national magazines." Stephanie smiled. "It's hardly likely to be a signed confession from the murderer."

Our waiter returned with our bills.

Dixie snatched them up and hopped up. "I'll go to the counter and take care of this while you two decide what you want to do."

Stephanie and I sat for several seconds, staring at the key.

"You know, Aunt Dixie's right. It could be nothing."

I shook my head. "You're probably right, but I don't want to be the one to tell Red about it."

Chapter 22

Despite the fact that I felt like a criminal, the excursion to the post office was uneventful. We all walked in together, although I was tempted to stay in the car with the motor running in case we needed to make a quick getaway.

Robert Hansen had one of the larger post office boxes, and it was stuffed with everything from promotional circulars to letters declaring he was preapproved for large amounts of credit. Fortunately, I always carried a big purse. We dumped the contents of the post office box into my purse and hurried back to the car.

Dixie drove under the speed limit, which was so disconcerting, I found myself constantly checking the rearview mirror to see if there was a patrol car tailing us.

When we got home, we hurried inside. Stephanie let the dogs out, and I dumped the contents of my purse onto the dining room table. I sorted through the items and set aside the items that belonged to me—wallet, credit cards, cell phone, toiletries, and snacks.

Dixie and Stephanie watched me sort through the items.

"Mom, what's with all of the artificial sweetener?"

"This is my 'in case of emergency' supply." I straightened the packets and returned them to my purse. "Every restaurant doesn't carry the blue packets. I don't like the pink, yellow, or green packets. So I keep some of the blue ones in my purse." I didn't need to look at her to know she was smirking.

Dixie took the newspaper circulars and tossed them in the trash. I gasped. Something about tossing someone else's mail seemed disrespectful, but she merely shrugged. "I'm pretty sure Robert Hansen isn't going to need these offers or preapproved credit cards."

What was left after the purge was mostly bills. There was one envelope, on which the address was handwritten; it stood out from the others because it was addressed to Mrs. Hansen, rather than Robert. I stared at the envelope for a long time. "What do you think we should do?"

Dixie leaned over my shoulder. "I think we should open it."

I turned to Stephanie. She shook her head. "I think we should give it to Mrs. Hansen. It belonged to her son, and by giving you the key, she gave you permission to pick up her mail. She didn't give you explicit permission to open or read her mail."

Dixie stuck out her tongue. "Party pooper."

Stephanie shrugged. "Tampering with mail is a federal offense. Not even the TBI should open this letter without a warrant."

I sighed. "I agree. We need to get these items to Mrs. Hansen." I stacked the envelopes together. When I looked up, I noticed that Stephanie was scowling at a plastic bag.

"What's this?" She held up the bag.

I stared at the plastic bag. "Oh, I know what that is."

"What?" Dixie frowned.

"It's what the golden retriever had swallowed. The vet from the emergency clinic gave it to me after the surgery."

"Eww..." Dixie frowned and shivered.

Stephanie's frown was more of the inquisitive type than the disgusting one on Dixie's face.

She stared so long that I wondered what was so fascinating. "What is it?"

"It looks like a flash drive." She glanced from Dixie to me. "And the bigger question is, what's on it?"

I looked at Dixie. She was staring at a piece of paper that had fallen out of my bag when I dumped the contents on the table. Something about the look on her face made me ask, "What's wrong?"

Dixie held up the paper. It was one of the programs from the funeral. "Did you look at this?"

I shook my head. "Frankly, no. I just shoved it in my purse when we got to the funeral. Why?" I went around the table and stood over her shoulder so I could see what she saw. I stared at the paper. "How? Who?"

She looked at me. "According to the program, that's Robert Hansen."

I stared from Dixie to the program. "That can't be Robert Hansen. That's not the man who was buried in the woods."

"I know."

"That's the man who came by claiming to be the owner of the golden." Dixie nodded. "I know."

Our gazes locked.

I pointed to the program. "If that's Robert Hansen, and he was here yesterday pretending to be someone else, then whose funeral did we just attend?"

Dixie shook her head. "I have no idea."

Chapter 23

"I think we need to open the letter." Dixie reached for the letter, but I moved it out of reach.

Something was stirring in my head. Like tennis shoes in a dryer, ideas were tumbling around whacking against the side of my brain. "It makes sense. It all makes sense."

"I'm glad it makes sense to somebody." Dixie folded her arms and leaned back.

Aggie went to the door that led out to the laundry room and the garage, and barked.

I turned and saw that, while the golden retriever was also at the door, his posture was completely different. Where Aggie barked, lunged, and scratched at the door, the golden stood, tail wagging. "Stephanie, can you let Aggie outside, please. That barking is working my nerves."

Stephanie walked over and picked her up. Uncharacteristically, Aggie didn't settle down but grew more restless. "What's the matter, girl?" Stephanie scratched her ears.

"It's probably just a field mouse in the garage or Rusty would be barking too." Dixie turned her attention back to me. "Now, what is it that makes sense?"

Stephanie opened the door that led onto the back deck and put Aggie outside.

"Remember when Mrs. Hansen said 'My son had a dog.'? Remember the dog's name?" I waited and watched the lightbulb go on in Dixie's head.

She smacked herself in the forehead. "Rusty."

I nodded.

"Okay, that makes sense, but that doesn't explain why there's a dead man in a coffin in Stone Mountain, Georgia, who isn't Robert Hansen."

I paced. "Red said someone at the TBI had been watching Robert Hansen, so what if he found out and got scared."

Dixie nodded. "And he hightailed it out of the country."

"But he wasn't out of the country," Stephanie said.

"Right. He only *told* his mother he had to leave the country, but he didn't leave. Instead, he faked his death to confuse the authorities."

Dixie and Stephanie both looked skeptical.

"What's wrong?"

Stephanie shook her head. "I can accept the fact that he wanted the authorities to believe he was dead, but he didn't just pretend to have drowned in the ocean or something."

"He killed someone and stole his identity." Dixie shivered. "That's a bit extreme."

I paced. "I know, but it all fits. Remember what Red said?" I looked from Stephanie to Dixie. "He said Theodore Livingston had a brother, Martin. Martin came to live with Theodore and then disappeared."

They were silent but I could tell the pieces were falling into place for them just as it had for me.

"Martin didn't disappear, did he?" Stephanie asked.

I shook my head.

"I think Robert Hansen killed him."

"Why?" Dixie asked.

I shrugged. "I don't know. Maybe he was the right size." I paced. For whatever reason, he wanted Martin dead. "He got lucky when we found the body."

"Lucky?" Dixie asked.

"We'd never seen him before, so we wouldn't be able to say it wasn't my landlord." I paused. "He must have had a backup plan. There had to be someone else who was supposed to find the body." I walked faster as I thought. I stopped when I remembered. "His girlfriend, Lynn. Remember his mother saying his girlfriend lived here too."

Stephanie walked over to the golden. "What's wrong, boy?"

Dixie nodded. "That's right, but I don't know anyone named Lynn. Do you?"

I shook my head. "It doesn't matter. I'm sure Red will find her." I picked up my cell phone and dialed his number.

He picked up quickly, but I didn't bother to let him talk. Instead, the words tumbled out of my mouth. "Red, I figured it out. It was Robert Hansen. He's not dead. We need you to—"

"That'll be enough."

I turned.

Robert Hansen was standing in the living room. He had his arm around Stephanie's neck and a gun pointed at her head. "Hang up now or I'll kill her."

I could hear Red talking, but I couldn't focus on anything except the gun pointed at my daughter's head. I ended the call.

"Good. Now, put the phone down on the counter and go stand by your friend."

I followed instructions and stood by Dixie near the window. We clutched each other's hands for support. For a brief moment, Dixie's nearness gave me courage. I looked around for her purse, knowing she most likely had her gun with her. My eyes saw it on the counter at the other end of the kitchen.

"Please, don't hurt my daughter."

Robert Hansen grimaced. "I don't want to hurt anyone. I just want to get what I came for and get out of here."

"What did you come for?" I barely managed to squeak the words out.

He propelled Stephanie forward toward the table. Before he could reach out and take what he wanted, we heard a noise in the garage. Hansen stiffened. He grabbed Stephanie tighter and pulled her closer to his body.

She winced as he pressed the gun into her head.

With his mouth inches from her face, he whispered, "Don't do anything stupid or you're dead."

The door opened, and Carol Lynn Hargrove stood just inside the laundry room. She stopped suddenly at the sight of Robert Hansen and froze for a split second.

I released a sigh. Surely he wouldn't be able to control all of us.

For a split second, there was tension in the air that was only broken by the sound of Aggie's barking from the back deck as she lunged and pawed at the door.

My relief at seeing Carol Lynn vanished when she smiled.

"What took you so long?" Hansen asked.

Too late, I realized the truth. "Carol Lynn...Lynn. You're his girlfriend?"

She proved the point by walking over to Hansen and reached up and kissed him. "My family and close friends always called me Lynn."

"You're involved in this whole thing with him." I didn't even try to hide the disgust in my voice.

She smiled. "It was a beautiful plan. Robert bought up all of the houses and vacant lots." She leaned across the breakfast bar. "I was even able to use the association's money to help pay for it." She frowned. "Until that batty old fool started snooping around."

"I thought she was involved with the association president," Dixie said.

The counter behind us served as a bar. There were glass-fronted cabinets where I stored wineglasses. On the counter, I kept a corkscrew, ice bucket, and various alcoholic beverages. The bottom of the cabinet was fitted with a wine rack.

Carol Lynn laughed. "That fool. I just needed him in case anyone requested soil samples."

"Enough talking. Grab the letter and the file and let's get out of here." Hansen pointed to the table.

"What's so important in that letter that you risked coming back here to get it?" Dixie asked.

He smiled. "Ask your smart friend. She seems to have all the answers."

"If I had to guess, I'd say it's the fake credentials Freemont made for you—passport, airline tickets, and identification to help you get out of the country."

He looked at me with respect in his eyes. "You really are smart."

Dixie and I leaned against the counter. Shoulder to shoulder as we were, I could feel as she slowly reached for the corkscrew. I knew Dixie was tough, and she wouldn't go down without a fight.

"Why send it to your mother?" I needed to keep him talking.

"If you can't trust your mother, who can you trust?" He laughed. "Besides, this way she would know I was okay."

Dixie bristled. "I think you're despicable. Your poor mother has been devastated thinking you're dead. What kind of person would do that to his own mother?"

Anger flashed across his face but quickly dissipated. "She'll get over it. I had planned to tell her earlier, but once you stumbled across the body before Lynn could get there to identify the remains, I couldn't just walk in and say, 'Hey, Mom, I'm home.'"

I nodded. "So, Carol Lynn...Lynn was supposed to find the body."

"Yep, you beat me to it." She grinned. "But it all worked out in the end." She grabbed the envelope and the plastic bag from the table. "It would have worked out perfectly if that nosy old geezer hadn't been snooping and saw us moving Martin's body."

I nodded. "So it's Martin Livingston in the coffin?"

"He claimed he had proof that could cost me my life." He chuckled. "The United States government is all about free enterprise until they're the ones getting duped." He smiled. "I couldn't stand by and let that happen. Not when we were so close."

The room grew silent as Aggie gave up on barking and scratching at the back door. She ran down the deck stairs. After a few moments, I heard her barking as she ran around to the front of the house. I had forgotten to get the zip ties to lock the sliding latch on the dog pen, and she must have used her nose to open the latch.

One arm behind my back, I slowly felt for the bottle of wine I knew was immediately behind me.

Carol Lynn picked up the plastic bag. "We've been looking all over for this." She smiled at me. "Dropped it in all of the confusion when we killed Martin." She looked at me. "I searched this place from floor to ceiling. Where was it?"

I pointed to the golden. "The dog ate it."

She stared at the plastic bag and gave Rusty a frown. "I never liked that dog."

"Just grab the stuff, and let's get out of here."

"What are you going to do with them? You can't leave them. They'll be on the phone with the police before we can get out of the driveway."

He pondered this for a minute. "We'll have to take them with us."

"You can't be serious. We can't get out of the country with three women and a dog in tow. Besides, she's gotten really friendly with that TBI agent." She pointed to me.

We heard a loud noise at the front door.

It was now or never. I grabbed the bottle.

Everyone turned toward the front door.

Aggie rushed through the laundry room door.

Robert Hansen relaxed when he saw her, which was his undoing. Red rushed through the laundry room door with a weapon aimed at Robert Hansen. He yelled, *"Drop it!"*

One of Hansen's arms was still wrapped around Stephanie. With his other arm, he pointed the gun toward Red.

I grabbed the bottle and brought it down hard on top of Robert Hansen's head as Dixie lunged for him and jabbed the corkscrew into his cheek.

Stephanie gave him an elbow to the solar plexus and wound out of his reach.

Aggie leaped into the air. She pounced at just the right place on his knee, which caused his legs to buckle.

Hansen dropped to the floor.

Aggie attacked his leg.

Hansen shook his leg in an attempt to dislodge Aggie. He looked at Rusty and pointed to Stephanie. "Fass!"

Rusty followed the direction of his owner's finger.

The word sounded like "fahs," and I recognized the command to attack from a video Dixie had shown me online when she was explaining Schutzhund dog training.

The color drained from Dixie's face. "Oh my God!"

Rusty looked from Hansen to Stephanie.

Hansen tried again. "Fass!"

Carol Lynn stood dazed for a moment and then reached down to pick up the gun that Hansen had let slip from his hand.

Dixie kicked the gun out of reach.

Michael and Charity Cunningham crashed through the back door. Guns raised. *"TBI! Drop your weapons!"*

Rusty slowly walked to Stephanie and sat by her side.

Charity Cunningham took over for Red. She put her knee in Robert Hansen's back and handcuffed him.

Michael had Carol Lynn bent over the table, hands behind her back.

Officer Lewis and several other policemen, some in plain clothes, some uniformed, poured into the house.

Red stared at me with a wild look in his eyes. "You okay?"

Unable to speak, I nodded.

He looked for a few more seconds, then turned and said, "Secure the premises."

Chapter 24

It took hours for the police, EMTs, the TBI, and a host of other law-enforcement people to finish asking questions, even after Robert Hansen and Carol Lynn Hargrove were taken away.

We'd answered the same questions so many times, my answers became automatic.

After the initial shock of the situation wore off, my teeth chattered, and I noticed my hands shaking.

Red was standing nearby. "That's enough," he said to the officer questioning me. He inclined his head toward the door, and the officer packed up and left.

I stared in awe. "Thank you."

Stephanie headed to her bedroom. "I'm going to lie down and call Joe." She looked at the golden. "Come on, Lucky. Let's go."

"Lucky?" I asked.

She smiled. "I'm so lucky to have him in my life." She looked at Dixie. "You can change a dog's name, right?"

Dixie nodded. "Yep. I think Lucky will be the perfect name for him."

They walked into the bedroom and closed the door.

Dixie stared at the door. "That's one lucky girl too."

"What do you mean?" I asked.

Dixie shook her head. "That dog was trained in Schutzhund. You saw how well trained he was."

I nodded.

"I've never known a well-trained dog to disobey a direct order from his handler, but Lucky did."

I took in a deep breath. "So I wasn't mistaken."

Dixie shook her head slowly.

"I wish someone would fill me in." Red looked from me to Dixie.

Dixie looked at me, but I couldn't have spoken if my life depended on it. She took a deep breath. "Robert Hansen gave Rusty a direct command to attack Stephanie: Fass." She paused for the weight of her words to sink in.

"But he didn't attack?" Red looked from Dixie to me.

She shook her head. "He didn't attack."

I found my voice enough to whisper, "Why?"

She shrugged. "If I had to guess, I'd say something changed. In that moment, he switched from being Robert Hansen's dog to Stephanie's. His allegiance changed, and he went from Rusty to Lucky." She shrugged again. "Dogs are very sensitive. Maybe he smelled that something wasn't right about him. Or he might have sensed Hansen was evil and knew what he was asking him to do was wrong." She paused. "All I can say is that in all of my years of training dogs, I've never known a dog who was trained as well as Rusty to deliberately disobey a direct command from his master."

We sat in silence for several moments and allowed the impact of her words to settle in. After a few moments, she shook herself and stood. "I'd like to stay and hear all of the details, but I'm worn out."

"Maybe you should stay over. I don't know if you should try driving up that mountain after everything you've been through." I looked to my friend.

"Nope. I'm fine. I'm going home and get in the bathtub and soak. I may not leave until tomorrow night when it's time for class." She hugged me. "Good thing you forgot the zip ties." She smiled at Aggie. "But you will need to get her trained. Don't forget, we've got obedience class tomorrow." She grabbed her purse off the counter and left.

I got up and went to the sink and wet a towel. We had removed the glass shards from the bottle I broke over Robert Hansen's head, but the wine had dried and left a sticky film on the floor. Aggie had tried to lick up as much of the liquid as she could before I picked her up and confined her to her crate. According to Dixie, grapes were poisonous to dogs, and I didn't want to take a chance on the effects of the toxins or fermentation on my six-pound poodle.

I scrubbed the floor to the best of my ability. When I rose, Red was staring at me.

"You okay?"

I nodded but realized I wasn't and shook my head. I didn't realize I was crying until the first tear fell. Once the tears started, the flood gates opened, and I stood in the kitchen bawling. I wasn't one of those pageant contestants who was able to cry and still look cute. So I put my head down and turned away.

Red's hands rested on my shoulders as he turned me toward him. His arms locked around me as he held me close.

I rested my head against his chest and cried until I had nothing left inside. I had no idea how long we stood there, me crying and him silently comforting me. When all of my tears were spent, I sighed. "I'm sorry."

He reached down and lifted my chin so I was forced to look up. "Don't apologize. If you hadn't started crying, I might not have had the courage to do this." He bent down and kissed me on the lips. At first his kiss was gentle and questioning.

It had been quite a while since I'd been kissed, especially by someone who wasn't my husband. However, after the initial shock, my response was ardent. I wrapped my arms around his neck and pressed my body closer. What started off as tentative turned into a passionate heat, which left both of us panting.

Red was the first to pull away. He stared into my eyes, and I saw a fire kindling inside. "Wow."

I smiled. "Wow, indeed."

The doorbell rang.

Red swore under his breath, and I giggled.

I started toward the door but stopped when he grabbed my arm and pulled me behind him. Momentarily puzzled, I looked at him.

His face was solemn. He removed his gun from its holster, motioned for me to remain where I was, and headed for the door. He cautiously approached the door and then looked out the peephole. After a beat, he lowered his weapon. His shoulders relaxed, and he unlocked the door.

Officer Lewis entered. The two men exchanged greetings.

I waited while the men joined me in the kitchen.

"I wanted to let you know Robert Hansen made a full confession."

I sighed. "That's good, right, so I won't have to testify in court?" I motioned for Officer Lewis to sit.

"The district attorney and all the military lawyers are working on a plea deal. If Hansen spills his guts, he can spend the rest of his life in a prison cell courtesy of the state of Tennessee, rather than facing a harsher trial and penalty through the military."

"What about Freemont Hopewell and Carol Lynn?" I asked.

"Hopewell had already started to sing. When he found out we had Hansen, he sang even louder." Officer Lewis shook his head. "He claims he didn't know anything about the killings." He shrugged.

"I don't think he did," I said. "I think he told us the truth when he said he forged documents for Hansen. However, Freemont would never want to get his hands too dirty with something like murder."

Red joined us at the dining room table. "And the girlfriend?"

"Claims she didn't actually pull the trigger. She embezzled the money from the association and helped Hansen take the body into the woods, but she claims he's the one that killed Martin."

"She may not have killed Martin, but she did kill Theodore Livingston."

Both men stared at me. Officer Lewis broke the silence. "How can you be sure?"

"She was there. I met her when Red and I were walking. She seemed flustered and angry, but that was mostly a show. The meeting to oust her as treasurer had already happened. I'd never seen Robert Hansen before the day he showed up to claim his dog."

"He could have been in a car," Red suggested.

I shrugged. "Maybe, but I remember at the association meeting when Theodore Livingston made a comment, 'I know all the dirty secrets.' I didn't think much about it at the time. I thought he was just being his normal, hateful self. Now I think he was sending a message to Carol Lynn." I stared from Red to Lewis. "Besides, I don't think Robert Hansen would risk running into someone who recognized him after he was supposed to be dead."

"He took a big chance coming for the dog," Red said.

I nodded. "That's why he was so skittish. When you threatened to take him to the police, he took off. He couldn't risk you running his fingerprints and finding out who he really was."

We sat in silence for a few moments. Officer Lewis's gaze darted around as though he couldn't figure out who to look at. Eventually, he took a deep breath and blurted out, "I'm sorry."

I stared. "For what?"

"I'm sorry I didn't believe you when you said you hadn't killed Robert Hansen or Theodore Livingston." He sat up straight and looked at Red. "And I'm sorry for the things I said to you at the community building. I was out of line."

Red's lips twitched, but he got them under control. "No apology needed."

The two men looked at each other, and some type of exchange took place. Officer Lewis rose. They shook hands, and then Red showed him out.

"What just happened here?" I asked when he returned to the table. "You two just had some kind of silent male bonding moment or something."

He smiled. "Let's just say we came to an agreement. He was wrong. He apologized. I accepted his apology, and now we're fine. No harm done."

"All that passed in that brief look?"

He chuckled. "Men don't need to talk as much as women. I don't need to hear about his feelings. It's all good."

I playfully punched him in the arm. "Fine." I stood up and stretched. "Okay, I'm going to bed. See you tomorrow." I released Aggie from the crate I kept in the kitchen.

She stretched as though she'd had a hard day. I looked at her and smiled. She was a fierce little dog and had fought valiantly. She deserved some extra treats and a lot of extra love tonight. I foresaw a trip to the pet store in her future.

"Wait. You're just going to walk out?" He paused. "Just like that?"

I shrugged. "Why not? I'm tired, and it's late." I picked up Aggie and snuggled her close.

He stood. "Just like that."

"Just like that." I moved closer to the bedroom.

"But you can't. We have to talk."

"What's left to talk about?"

"Oh, I don't know. How about that kiss?" He smiled.

"I thought you didn't want to hear a lot of talk about feelings?" I joked.

He walked over to me. "Okay, very funny." His gaze searched my face. "Are you okay? Are we okay, I mean...I didn't ask for permission, but you responded, and I assumed...I mean, I hoped that maybe you felt..." He sighed.

"Did anyone ever tell you, you talk too much?" I reached up and kissed him.

"So, this means...we're okay?"

I nodded. "We're okay."

He smiled. Aggie was between us, and she reached up and gave his face a lick.

He smiled and scratched her ear. "This is one tough little poodle you have here." He looked at me. "Just like you."

I snuggled her close. "She is tough."

"I think I better go home." He kissed me again. "How about dinner tomorrow?"

I nodded.

He turned to leave but stopped. "Oh, I forgot, you have training class tomorrow." He gave Aggie another ear scratch. "You've done a great job already training her."

"Actually, I think she's the one who's training me."

Mystery bookstore owner Samantha Washington is trying to keep her grandmother from spending her golden years in an orange jumpsuit...

The small town of North Harbor, Michigan, is just not big enough for the two of them: flamboyant phony Maria Romanov and feisty Nana Jo. The insufferable Maria claims she's descended from Russian royalty and even had a fling with King Edward VIII back in the day. She's not just a lousy liar, she's a bad actress, so when she nabs the lead in the Shady Acres Senior Follies—a part Nana Jo plays every year in their retirement village production—Nana Jo blows a gasket and reads her the riot act in front of everyone.

Of course, when Maria is silenced with a bullet to the head, Nana Jo lands the leading role on the suspects list. Sam's been writing her newest mystery, set in England between the wars, with her intrepid heroine Lady Elizabeth drawn into murder and scandal in the household of Winston Churchill. But now she has to prove that Nana Jo's been framed. With help from her grandmother's posse of rambunctious retirees, Sam shines a spotlight on Maria's secrets, hoping to draw the real killer out of the shadows...

Please turn the page for an exciting sneak peek of
V.M. Burns's
THE NOVEL ART OF MURDER
now on sale wherever print and e-books are sold!

Chapter 1

"What the blazes do you mean I didn't get the part?" Nana Jo's face turned beet red, and she leapt up from her chair.

I had never been so happy for a slow morning crowd at the bookstore as I was at that minute. My grandmother was about to blow a gasket, and while it might prove entertaining, I preferred keeping the drama contained to family and friends.

"Josephine, calm down." Dorothy Clark was one of my grandmother's oldest friends, which was probably why she was nominated to break the bad news to her.

"Don't tell me to calm down. I am calm. I'm always calm." Nana Jo pounded the table with her hand. The mugs shook and splashed coffee on the table. "If I want to kick up a ruckus, I'll kick up a ruckus." She pounded the table again and then marched over to the counter and grabbed a dishcloth to wipe up the mess.

Ruby Mae Stevenson, another of Nana Jo's friends, shook her head and moved her knitting out of the way of the spills. "I told you she wouldn't take it well."

"I've had the lead role in the Shady Acres Senior Follies for the past ten years. That role was created specifically for me. I don't just play the part of Eudora Hooper, retired schoolmarm dreaming about becoming a famous showgirl. I *am* Eudora Hooper." Nana Jo wiped up the spilled coffee.

"I know, and you've played the role splendidly." Dorothy's face reflected her sincerity.

Amazingly, Dorothy didn't seem to be humoring my grandmother. Nana Jo's performance was inspired, and each year she got better and better.

Nana Jo looked at her three closest friends. "Who got the part?"

Ruby Mae put her head down and refused to make eye contact.

Irma Starczewski reached for her mug, but it was empty, so she pulled a flask out of her purse and took a swig.

Nana Jo put her hands on her hips, narrowed her eyes, and stared at Dorothy.

For a large woman, almost six feet tall, Dorothy shrank as she stared at Nana Jo. "Maria Romanov."

I thought Nana Jo's face was flushed before, but the beet-red coloring from earlier was nothing compared to the purple red that crept up her neck.

"Maria Romanov? That two-bit hack's only acting talent is in her ability to convince people she's a decent human being." Nana Jo pounded the table again, rattling the mugs.

Just as quickly as the anger flared up, it vanished. Nana Jo flopped down in a chair. Nearly as tall as Dorothy, Nana Jo went through a transformation. Instead of the vibrant, active, five-foot-ten, sharp-shooting, Aikido-tossing woman I knew and loved, there was a seventy-something old woman in her place.

She took a few deep breaths. "If that's what Horace wants, then I guess I wasn't as good as I thought I was."

"Bull—"

"Irma!" we shouted.

Irma coughed and clamped her hand over her mouth. Years of heavy smoking, drinking, and hanging out with truckers, if Nana Jo was to be believed, had left Irma with a deep cough, a salacious sexual appetite, and a colorful vocabulary.

I leaned over and gave Nana Jo a hug. "Your performance was amazing, and I'm not just saying that because you're my grandmother."

She absentmindedly patted my arm. "Thank you, Sam, but Horace Evans is a top-notch director. He once directed Ethel Merman."

"He even won a Tony Award. I've seen it. He keeps it in his bedroom." Irma smiled and then broke out in a fit of coughing.

The fact that Nana Jo didn't acknowledge Irma's quip about the location of the award was an indication of her state of mind. "We've been fortunate to have someone with his experience and credentials at Shady Acres."

"Really? I didn't know he had a Tony Award. They always run something about the Senior Follies in the newspaper, but they've never mentioned it."

"He likes to keep it low key." Dorothy nodded. "He worked on Broadway for more than twenty years."

"How in the world did he end up in Michigan?" I asked.

"He wanted to be close to his family." Ruby Mae looked up from her knitting. "I think his son was an engineer for one of the car companies."

North Harbor used to have a lot of manufacturing plants that supplied parts for the Detroit automobile industry, but when the economy went south in the seventies, so too did most of the manufacturing jobs.

"I appreciate the kind words, but Horace is an expert. If he thinks Maria Romanov will make a better Eudora Hooper than me, I'll just have to accept his decision."

We tried to cheer Nana Jo up, but nothing we said had any effect. She smiled and continued to shrink. Only once did she perk up and demonstrate the flash of fire that normally characterized her personality.

The door chimed, and a customer entered the bookstore.

Nana Jo rose from her seat. "It's time to face the music. On opening night, I hope you all break a leg." She pushed her chair in and headed to the front of the store. "And I hope Maria Romanov breaks her neck."

Chapter 2

Market Street Mysteries was a small bookstore that, as the name implied, specialized in mysteries. It didn't get a ton of business, not like the big-box bookstores. However, neither North Harbor nor its sister city, South Harbor, had a big-box bookstore. Southwestern Michigan book lovers either traveled forty-five minutes to get their book fix or ordered online. In the six months since I'd retired from teaching English at the local high school, I had built up a nice clientele that was enough to keep my dream afloat.

Weekdays weren't especially busy, so Nana Jo was well able to handle things while I took a break. When I left, the girls were still trying to convince her to continue with the Senior Follies, even if she took a lesser role, but I knew my grandmother well enough to know they were fighting a losing battle. Losing the lead role had wounded her pride. I needed time to think how I could help her. My stomach growled, so I decided to grab lunch.

November in North Harbor, Michigan, can be schizophrenic to the uninitiated. One minute, it's warm and sunny. The next minute, a biting wind had rolled off Lake Michigan that rattled your teeth and made your skin quiver. Today was, thankfully, sunny and bright. The wind was crisp, so I walked more quickly and lingered less often as I made my way to North Harbor Café.

Even after the noon rush, the restaurant was crowded. I looked for a seat, and my eye caught the gaze of the proprietor, Frank Patterson, behind the bar. He smiled, and my stomach fluttered.

I hopped on an empty seat at the bar.

Frank finished mixing drinks and handed them to a waitress. Then he grabbed a pitcher of water from a small fridge, along with a few sliced lemons, which he placed in the pitcher. He grabbed a glass and placed them in front of me.

He leaned close. "I'm glad you came. I missed you."

The warmth of his breath brushed my face, and I inhaled his scent. He smelled of a strong herbal Irish soap, red wine, coffee, and bacon. He was surprised that a non-wine drinker like me could tell the difference between red and white wines. My late husband used to say I had a nose like a bloodhound, but I called it a gift. Coffee and bacon were two of my favorite things, and my pulse raced.

"You smell good."

Frank grinned. "Let me guess, coffee and bacon?"

I nodded.

He joked he drank so much coffee the aroma seeped through his skin. The bacon was either a figment of my imagination or grease from the kitchen attached to his shoes. Whatever the reason, it was extremely sexy.

Frank Patterson was in his forties. He cut his salt-and-pepper hair in a way that betrayed his military background. He had soft brown eyes and a lovely smile. "As much as I'd like to believe my manly charm brought you in today, I suspect it's my BLT."

I laughed. "What can I say? A man who can make a good BLT is irresistible."

"Whatever it takes to keep you coming back."

Heat rose up my neck. I took a sip of my lemon water to try to hide it.

"One BLT minus the T and a cup of clam chowder?"

I nodded. I loved how he remembered things like that.

"I'll be right back."

I tried to suppress a grin, but it wouldn't be suppressed, and I dribbled water down the front of my shirt. Our conversation was lame, but it'd been a long time since I'd flirted. Leon and I had been married for over twenty years when he died. It'd been a year, but I'd just now opened myself to romance.

Frank returned carrying a tray with a steaming-hot bowl of clam chowder, a BLT (no T) that was piled high with bacon, and a rose. He placed the food in front of me, got a tall beer glass from behind the bar and filled it with water, and placed the rose in it.

"Thank you."

"That looks delicious." A large man next to me glanced at my plate and then picked up his menu. "Is that clam chowder? I didn't see it on the menu?"

Head down, I crumbled crackers into my chowder.

"It isn't on the menu. It's something I keep in the back for my...*special* friends." He winked at me.

My neighbor took a whiff. "It looks and smells wonderful." He looked at me. "You're a lucky lady."

I smiled and shoved a spoonful of soup into my mouth.

Frank pretended not to notice the heat that came up my neck, but I could tell by the look in his eyes he had seen the redness. "There may be enough for one more bowl. Would you like to try it?"

He nodded eagerly. "If you have enough, that would be great. I love clam chowder."

Frank headed off to get another bowl of soup.

I didn't have time to practice flirting. The restaurant was busy, and I felt guilty taking up a seat. So I finished eating, waved good-bye, and left.

The rest of the afternoon at the bookstore was uneventful. Nana Jo got rid of the girls, and we worked in relative silence until closing. I'd hoped we could talk, but she stayed busy and unapproachable until I locked the front door. When we were done cleaning, she announced she had a date and hurried upstairs to change.

My assistant and tenant, Dawson Alexander, was out of town for an away football game. When Nana Jo left, I was alone in my upstairs loft, except for my two poodles, Snickers and Oreo. It was peaceful. Although I was alone, I didn't feel lonely. At some point, Frank had left a large container of chili in my refrigerator, which I heated up for dinner. There was also a platter with lemon cream cheese bars on my kitchen counter. Besides being a great quarterback for the MISU Tigers, Dawson was an amazing baker. His small studio apartment over my garage didn't have a large stove, so he often baked in my kitchen. I placed two of the lemon bars on a plate and poured a cup of Earl Grey tea. The two men in my life, Frank and Dawson, kept me well fed.

Frank cooked when he wanted to relax, and Dawson baked. I wrote. Opening a mystery bookstore was a dream my husband, Leon, and I had shared. We both loved mysteries, and a bookstore specializing in mysteries seemed ideal. However, my dreams extended beyond selling mysteries to writing them. I kept that dream hidden, out of fear and insecurity, from all but Leon, my sister, Jenna, and my grandmother. After Leon died, I filled the lonely nights by writing a British historic cozy mystery. When Nana Jo sent my manuscript to a literary agent in New York, the dream moved from a hazy wisp of smoke and fairy dust into a solid reality in the form of a contract for representation. I was both thrilled and terrified at the same time. Even though the thought of people I didn't know reading my book sent a cold chill down my spine. I sat down at my laptop with my lemon bars and tea and realized the thrill was greater than the terror. I started writing.

* * * *

Drawing room, Chartwell House, country estate of Winston Churchill —November 1938

Lady Elizabeth Marsh sat on the sofa in the comfortable, sunlit drawing room. Despite the sunshine streaming through the windows, there was a nip in the air. She was grateful for the warmth from the large fireplace and extended her legs to enjoy more of its heat.

"Elizabeth, dear, would you care for a cardigan?" Clementine Churchill rose from her seat.

"No. I'm fine, really. I've thawed out now."

Mrs. Churchill sat back down. "I don't know what Winston was thinking, dragging you out in the cold to show you his brick wall." She tsked.

"He was very proud of his masonry skills." Lady Daphne stroked the large yellow tabby, which jumped onto her lap the moment she sat down.

"You'll have cat hair all over your skirt. Tango, get down," Mrs. Churchill ordered.

Tango looked up at the sound of his name but apparently decided the order was an empty threat and ignored it.

"Stubborn cat. Let me take him." Mrs. Churchill rose.

"It's okay, Aunt Clemmie. I rather like him." Daphne smiled. "A little cat hair won't matter. Besides, he gives me courage."

Clementine Churchill was only a distant cousin to the Marshes but had always been "Aunt Clemmie" to Daphne and Penelope Marsh. She settled back onto her seat and looked fondly at her adopted niece. "You don't need courage. I'm sure Lady Alistair will love you as much as we do."

Lady Elizabeth pulled a ball of yarn from her knitting bag. "What's not to love? You're intelligent and beautiful, and you come from an excellent family."

"I wish I could feel sure. James seems so nervous about me meeting her that's it's got me frazzled."

"Your aunt's right. You come from an excellent bloodline and have an impeccable pedigree. She could hardly do better."

Daphne laughed. "You make me sound like a race horse. I hope she doesn't want to examine my teeth and medical history as potential breeding stock."

Daphne intercepted an odd look between Lady Elizabeth and Mrs. Churchill. "Oh, no, you're joking right?"

"I wouldn't put it past her. You know the monarchy still require new brides to submit to...tests," Mrs. Churchill said.

"You can't be serious. That's archaic." Daphne stared from one to the other. Her outrage had stayed her hand from stroking Tango, who made his displeasure known by standing up, turning around, and kneading his claws into her lap. "Ouch. Okay. Okay." Daphne resumed her stroking, and Tango resumed his position and allowed himself to be stroked.

"I agree the practice is outdated and completely unfair." Lady Elizabeth was, to her husband's dismay, a strong proponent of women's rights and equality. "I've heard Lady Alistair is a bit...old-fashioned and—"

"Pretentious," Mrs. Churchill supplied.

"Yes, but James is only a duke and rather far down on the list for ascension to the throne. I think we're safe in assuming Lady Alistair wouldn't demand anything of the kind," Lady Elizabeth said.

"I'll refuse. That's what," Daphne declared.

Lady Elizabeth knitted. "Of course, dear. You'd be well within your rights to do so."

The elder ladies sat quietly.

"But if I refuse, they'll say it's because I have something to hide. They'll say I've done something to be ashamed of."

Mrs. Churchill sipped her tea in silence.

"Well, I won't do it." Daphne sulked. "It's not fair."

"I agree, dear." Lady Elizabeth knitted.

"I do love him so." Daphne bit her lower lip. "But modern women must take a stand. I won't submit to any tests unless James is required to submit to the same humiliation."

Lady Elizabeth smiled and continued to knit. "Of course, dear. Whatever you think is best."

"When does her highness arrive?" Daphne asked.

Clementine Churchill suppressed a smile. "Lady Alistair Browning's train arrives later this afternoon."

"Who else are you expecting?" Lady Elizabeth asked.

Clementine Churchill poured more tea and returned the pot to the tray. "Leopold Amery."

"Leo is one of the nicest men I know." Lady Elizabeth smiled.

Mrs. Churchill nodded. "I suppose he's here to keep Winston in line." Lady Elizabeth frowned.

"Someone named Guy Burgess with the BBC arrived earlier. He's trying to convince Winston to commit to a talk on the Mediterranean. I suppose Leo is arriving to convince Winston *not* to talk about it." She took a sip of tea before continuing. "Lord William Forbes-Stemphill."

"Oh...my." Lady Elizabeth stared at Mrs. Churchill.

"Yes, I know, but he wrote and asked if he could come. He mentioned his mother, and I couldn't say no."

"Wasn't there something about him in the news?" Daphne asked.

Mrs. Churchill nodded. "Yes. He's a traitor."

"A traitor?" Daphne gasped.

"He leaked secrets to the Japanese back in the twenties." Lady Elizabeth sipped her tea.

"Why wasn't he arrested? He should have been hung," Daphne said.

Lady Elizabeth and Mrs. Churchill exchanged glances.

After a few seconds, Lady Elizabeth said, "He's a British peer. No one wanted a scandal that might reflect negatively on the royal family."

Lady Daphne digested this bit of information. "How did they catch him?"

Mrs. Churchill sighed. "Supposedly, he had quite a few gambling debts to some unsavory characters. He needed more money and tried to blackmail his contact."

Daphne stared. "You mean the money he received for betraying his country wasn't enough to pay off his gambling debts, so he tried to blackmail his cohort in crime? What unbelievable gall."

Lady Elizabeth shook her head. "Apparently, the cohort had a sliver of conscience and wanted out."

"He had to know if he gave in to blackmail, he'd have to pay forever. So, in exchange for clemency, he gave Stemphill up to the authorities."

Daphne shook her head in disbelief.

After a moment of silence, Mrs. Churchill continued, "Anthony Blunt."

"Anthony Blunt?" Lady Elizabeth stared at the fire. "Why do I know that name?"

"He's an art historian from Trinity College," Clementine added.

"Is he here to look at Winston's paintings?" Lady Elizabeth asked.

"I believe he's here to value something or other." She frowned. "And, I'm sorry to say, Randolph phoned to say he's coming and bringing a young woman he wants us to meet."

Lady Elizabeth squeezed her friend's hand. "I'm sure it'll be alright. Maybe the young lady will be a calming influence on Randolph."

"I doubt it. Some girl he met at a party with John Amery. She's bound to be unsuitable." She sighed. "I just hope he doesn't cause a scene. Winston's been depressed about the way things are going in Parliament. The last thing he needs is Randolph stirring things up."

Lady Elizabeth patted her friend's hand and continued knitting. "Is Diana coming? I'd love to see that adorable grandson of yours. He must be so big now?"

Mrs. Churchill smiled. "Julian's two and practically grown. Diana's expecting her second child soon. So they're staying close to the hospital in London."

"What about Sarah and Mary?" Lady Elizabeth asked tentatively.

Mrs. Churchill's smile faded. "Sarah's in America. The last I heard, she was working on a film with her husband. Mary's in Limpsfield at Manor House School."

"Sounds like you'll have a full house. Penelope and Victor should be down tomorrow."

"The more people, the harder it'll be for Winston to brood. He does have a tendency to brood." Mrs. Churchill turned to Lady Elizabeth. "I'm so thankful to have Thompkins. He'll be a tremendous help. Inches would have tried to muddle through with a broken ankle, but he needs rest. He likes Thompkins and trusts him."

"You're very welcome." Lady Elizabeth smiled.

"How *did* Inches manage to break his ankle?" Lady Daphne asked.

Mrs. Churchill's lips twitched. "Winston climbed atop the garden wall to get a better perspective for a painting. Inches and one of the gardeners was trying to help him down when he stumbled."

"Oh my," Lady Elizabeth said. "Was Winston injured?"

Mrs. Churchill shook her head. "Thankfully, no. I'm afraid Inches broke his fall."

Daphne cringed. "That had to be painful. Uncle Winnie is a considerable amount heavier than Inches."

Mrs. Churchill nodded. "I'm sure it was. Winston doesn't show it, but I know he felt badly, even though he scolded Inches for not moving out of the way quickly enough." She smiled. "Of course, he told the doctor to send us all of the bills."

Lady Elizabeth stared at her friend. Rarely would she consider love for one's husband a fault, but Clementine Churchill's love for her husband blinded her to almost all of his flaws. Winston was Elizabeth's cousin, and she was well acquainted with both his virtues and his flaws. He was intelligent, articulate, well read, and witty, with a large capacity for kindness, when he chose. He was also egotistical, self-centered, self-absorbed, given to excess with food and drink, a gambler, and a poor manager of funds. Elizabeth looked around the drawing room. The large room was awash with light. It was comfortable and cozy, with the large fireplace and a boldly patterned Mahal carpet. This room was part of the section he'd added to the house. Family gossip reported that Winston had spent a minor fortune purchasing and renovating it. Winston loved Chartwell House and the vast grounds, and Clementine loved Winston. The house she merely tolerated.

The peaceful setting was interrupted by the arrival of Winston, Lord William, and Rufus, the Churchill's brown miniature poodle.

Winston bound into the room huffing and puffing on a fat, smelly cigar. He left a trail of ashes in his wake. Rufus waited for his master to get settled into his chair and promptly jumped into his lap and lay down.

Mrs. Churchill looked adoringly at her husband, shook her head, and poured him a cup of tea.

"Thank you, dear."

Lord William followed and warmed himself near the fireplace. "You ladies should have joined us. Bracing walk across the property and down to the pond."

Lady Daphne laughed. "Thanks, but I'm perfectly content right here with a cat, a good book, and a warm fire."

Lord William walked over to his niece and looked at her choice of reading material. "*Burke's Peerage*? Not exactly light reading." Lord William frowned at the large tome, the definitive guide to the genealogy of the titled families of the British Isles.

Lady Daphne blushed. "I thought I should brush up on James's family history before I meet Lady Alistair."

Lord William smiled indulgently at his niece. "Good idea. Good idea. Never hurts to learn about the family skeletons."

Daphne's blush deepened. "Maybe I'll look up the other guests while I'm at it. It'll give me something to talk about with them."

Lady Elizabeth knitted. She turned to her cousin. "How is the great opus coming along?"

Winston sipped his tea. "Slowly."

"Whatever possessed you to write the history of the English-speaking people, Uncle Winnie? It sounds like a daunting task to me."

Winston stared out the window. "I was possessed by the need to complete the swimming pool and create an orfe pond."

Lord William puffed on his pipe. "But to write the history of the English-speaking people...it'll take a hundred men. The British Empire is...vast. Where does one even start writing?"

"Where does one end?" Lady Daphne asked.

Winston petted Rufus and puffed on his cigar. "I started at the beginning. I'll end when I no longer have anything to say."

The door to the drawing room was opened by the Marsh family's stiff and proper butler, Thompkins. "Lady Alistair Browning."

Lady Alistair Browning wasn't expected until later in the afternoon, so her sudden arrival more than three hours early caused a slight amount of confusion amongst the ladies. Surprise crossed the face of Mrs. Churchill, while Daphne turned a shade paler. Lady Elizabeth hurried to put away her knitting and dropped a ball of yarn. The yarn rolled across the floor, catching the attention of Tango, who had been reposed on Lady Daphne's lap. Before Lady Elizabeth could retrieve the yarn, Lady Alistair Browning entered.

Helen Browning was a tall, slender woman with piercing blue eyes and unnaturally blond hair, which she wore in a conglomeration of styles from the last two decades, including finger waves, pin curls, and coils. She wore a chocolate brown suit with a fur collar, matching fur muff, and cloche hat. The hat was festooned with large ostrich feathers that fluttered whenever she moved her head. In her arms, she held a small Chihuahua.

Lady Daphne lifted Tango from her lap, stood, and moved forward to greet Lady Alistair. As she moved forward, Tango caught sight of the Chihuahua.

Rufus growled. Tango arched his back, hissed, and lunged forward. The Chihuahua yapped. Daphne reached for Tango but tripped over the ball of yarn and fell onto the table, knocking the teapot and tray off the table. The teapot flew up into the air, spraying hot tea onto Lady Alistair.

Despite his age and stiffness, Thompkins grabbed Tango out of the air, seconds before the cat landed on the yapping dog.

Clementine Churchill stood openmouthed and frozen.

Lady Elizabeth and Lord William helped Daphne up from the ground. Thompkins retreated with the screeching cat, and Lady Alistair shrieked.

Daphne was red-faced and on the verge of tears.

Only Winston seemed at ease. He puffed his cigar, stood, and bowed curtly to Lady Alistair. "Now that was a bloody fine entrance, madam."

Chapter 3

Weekends were when I missed my nephews, Christopher and Zaq, and my assistant, Dawson, the most. The twins were juniors at Jesus and Mary University—or JAMU, as the folks around River Bend called it. Even though neither of my nephews shared my love of mysteries, the bookstore provided the freedom to try out their natural talents and education in different ways. Christopher was a business major and enjoyed incorporating marketing and sales techniques from his classes in the bookstore. Zaq was my technology wizard and kept my point of sale system and computers humming. They were going to keep the store running while I went to New York with Nana Jo during Thanksgiving break. I was both nervous and excited at the prospect. However, as Nana Jo said, "How much damage could they wreak in a week?"

Dawson Alexander was my former student from North Harbor High School; he had gotten a football scholarship to Michigan Southwestern University. MISU was a small local school, and Dawson was a sophomore and the star quarterback. He'd come to live with me six months ago and discovered a talent for baking. Between the three of them, the store would be fine. Frank promised to check in too.

MISU had an away game, so I had the radio tuned into the action. Hot apple cider and football-shaped sugar cookies decorated with MISU's colors were the treats Dawson left for bookstore patrons, and they were vanishing quickly. We didn't have our restaurant license yet, so we put the baked items out along with a jar for donations. His baking was gaining him quite the reputation, especially after the local news interviewed him a few weeks ago. The interview was intended to show him as a local kid trying to rise above his poor beginnings and abusive father, when Dawson was arrested for killing his ex-girlfriend. Thankfully, we were able to discover the real killer and prove Dawson's innocence. By the time the interview aired, he was no longer fighting for his life. The extra publicity had been good for the bookstore too.

A steady stream of customers kept me busy, and closing time arrived before I knew it. After work, Nana Jo and I were going to the retirement village to pick up the girls for a night on the town. I'd convinced Nana Jo to go into the auditorium later and talk to the Tony Award–winning producer, Horace Evans. If for no other reason, she still had the costume from last year and could return it. She'd had it dry-cleaned and never bothered to return it, since everyone assumed she'd be playing the role again this year.

The drive from my building in downtown North Harbor to Nana Jo's South Harbor retirement village went fairly quick. Nana Jo owned a villa in Shady Acres Retirement Village. It was a private, gated community for active seniors with a variety of housing options. There were detached single-family homes the residents called villas, town houses, condos, and apartments.

Each resident had a card that opened the gates and unlocked the main doors. I pulled up to the main entrance and parked. Dry-cleaning bag in hand, we entered the lobby. The security guard at the front desk looked up when we entered. He recognized Nana Jo, waved, and continued watching a football game.

We passed a number of people we knew, but Nana Jo kept walking. The first floor of the building looked like any other apartment complex. There was a comfortable lounge area with sofas, flat-screen televisions, and a massive fireplace. On one side was a workout facility. There was a pool and a large auditorium, which was where we headed.

Nana Jo stood outside the auditorium door, took a deep breath, and then opened it and marched in. The room was a large open area that could be reconfigured for whatever activity the residents wanted. Today there were folding chairs near the rear. In the front of the room, a group practiced leg kicks and choreography on a platform. A man played the main number on a piano. One woman stood at the microphone wearing a tight leotard, which showcased every bulge and ripple, of which there were many. She had the largest chest I'd ever seen, and her hair looked orange. I hoped it was a result of the spotlights directed at her. She had a large bow atop her head and was belting out a nasally rendition of the main song.

I halted. "Oh my."

Nana Jo stopped and stared. "*That* is my replacement."

"Oh my." I realized, after a few moments, that my mouth was open, and I closed it.

Saying Maria Romanov couldn't sing was akin to saying Lake Michigan was a large body of water. It was obvious and didn't begin to scratch the surface. Maria Romanov was a horrible singer. Not only couldn't she hold a tune, she didn't appear to have any rhythm. She was chunky and out of shape and moved as if she had two left feet.

"Wow." I looked at my grandmother.

"She's got a voice that would curdle milk."

The producer, Horace Evans, was seated in the first row. He hopped up and stopped the music. He sounded as though he was gritting his teeth. "Maria, I believe you've changed keys again." He walked over to the piano. "Can you please give us the chord again, Freddie?"

When Horace went to the piano, I saw the pianist was Nana Jo's boyfriend, Freddie. They'd been dating for close to a year and seemed pretty committed.

"I didn't know Freddie played the piano?"

Nana Jo nodded. "He rarely plays now, but our old pianist broke a hip skydiving, so Freddie agreed to help out."

Freddie obliged by playing the chord again.

Maria turned red, flung the sheet music down on the floor, and stamped her feet. "How can you expect me to stay on key when I'm being blinded by that light?"

I failed to see how the light affected her vocal chords, but with one throat-slashing motion, Horace gave a signal that killed the spotlight. "It is a dress rehearsal, so you will need to get accustomed to the lights before the performance."

When the spotlight was turned off, I realized the unnatural orange color of her hair was the result of hair dye and not the lights. I leaned over to Nana Jo. "Are my eyes playing tricks, or is her hair tangerine orange?"

Nana Jo nodded. "Looks like she's got a pumpkin on her head, doesn't it?"

"I'm accustomed to performing on larger stages with the latest lighting," Maria boasted with an accent that sounded like a cross between Russian, French, and the Bronx. "I have performed on the grandest stages in the world and with some of the greatest musicians and dancers. This"—she swept her arm to encompass the entire stage—"is beneath me."

"If you'd prefer not to perform—" Horace said with a certain amount of eagerness.

"No! A star must adapt. I would never disappoint my audience." She smiled. "Besides, the show must go on, despite the...obstacles." She gave a condescending look to Freddie. "As my Eddie used to say, you cannot deprive the world of your gift."

I could feel the steam emanating from Nana Jo. She huffed and pursed her lips.

I frowned. "Who's Eddie?"

"Supposedly Edward the Eighth."

"Edward the Eighth? King Edward the Eighth who married Wallis Simpson and abdicated the throne of England? That Edward the Eighth?"

Nana Jo nodded.

"But no one called him Eddie...ever." I'd just finished writing a book that featured Wallis Simpson. I had tons of books on the abdicated king and his American wife. "His family and friends called him David."

She nodded. "Yep. The dumb twit has no idea." She fumed.

"Why don't we take a short break?" Horace said.

Nana Jo's eyes narrowed, and she marched to the front of the room. When she got to the stage, she flung the costume at Horace and walked up to Maria. "Now listen here, you no-talent, two-bit hack. If you ever insult my friend again, I'll take that microphone and wrap it around your neck."

Freddie hopped up from the piano and hurried to Nana Jo's side. He placed a hand on her arm to calm her, but she shook it off.

Maria's smile looked more like a grimace. "You are jealous. Did you come to see a *real* actress perform?"

Nana Jo snorted. "When you find one, let me know."

The argument got louder, and the ladies attracted a crowd. Not only were the performers watching, but several of the employees, including the property manager, Denise Bennett, entered the auditorium to watch.

Maria bristled. "I see you've brought my costume. I shall, of course, have to have it altered. You are so tall and masculine, it will not fit." She straightened her back and thrust out her huge chest.

"Right. You'll have to add fabric to cover those watermelons you've got strapped around your neck."

"Why, you...you...brute. How dare you?" She turned away from Nana Jo, took two steps, and then stumbled. She would have fallen if Freddie had not instinctively reached out to steady her. When he did, Maria leaned into him and clutched him as if he were a life preserver.

"I have a very delicate disposition. I'm not accustomed to being treated in this way."

Freddie was holding up Maria while Nana Jo scowled and steamed. He looked panicked.

Maria heaved a heavy sigh and flung her arms around his neck. "You are so kind." She stared lovingly at Freddie. "If you will help me back to my room, please, I must take my medicine."

Her face was mere inches from Freddie's.

"Perhaps you'd prefer to sit down. I can go and retrieve your medicine." Freddie attempted to steer her to a nearby chair, but Maria refused.

"No. No. I moved into a new apartment. Everything is in turmoil. You would not find it. I alone can find the medicine. I knew you were a gentleman." She stared into his face. "You have kind eyes. I know you will not fail to help me."

Freddie turned to Nana Jo.

If she weren't so angry, she would have seen the anguish in his eyes, but Nana Jo was furious. "Freddie, if you go off with that hussy, then you can just stay with her, for all I care."

His eyes pleaded, "Jo, you don't mean that. Look, I'll just help Miss Romanov to her room, and I'll be right back. I promise."

Maria gasped and clutched at her chest. "Oh, please, I am unwell."

Freddie helped Maria out of the room. He looked back at the stone-cold wall of Nana Jo's face one last time as they went through the doorway.

"If I had my gun, I'd deflate those weather balloons and turn Freddie from a rooster to a hen in one shot." Nana Jo turned on her heels and marched out.